THE END OF
THE
NINETEENTH CENTURY

THE END OF
THE
NINETEENTH CENTURY
(1857–2010)

A NOVEL

BY

ERIC LARSEN

THE OLIVER ARTS & OPEN PRESS

Larsen, Eric, 1941-
The End of the 19th Century

ISBN: 978-0-9829878-4-1
Library of Congress Control Number: 2011944190

The Oliver Arts & Open Press
2578 Broadway, Suite #102
New York, NY 10025
http://www.oliveropenpress.com

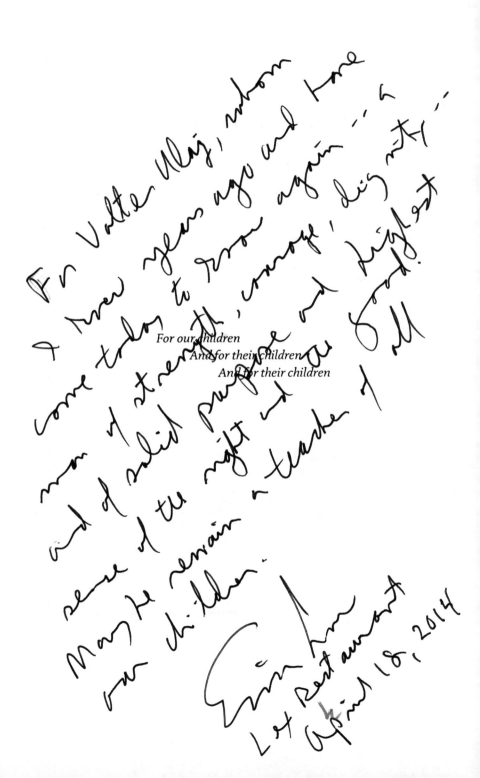

For our children
And for their children
And for their children

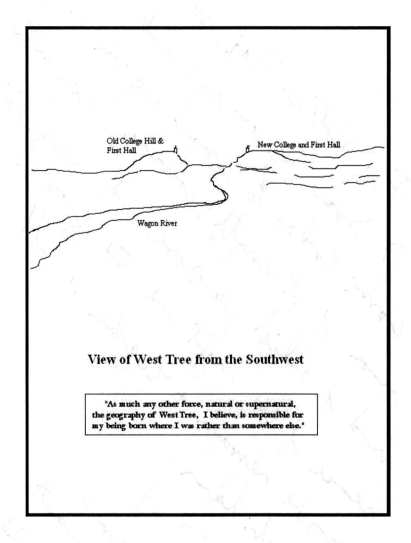

Old College Hill &
First Hall

New College and First Hall

Wagon River

View of West Tree from the Southwest

"As much any other force, natural or supernatural,
the geography of West Tree, I believe, is responsible for
my being born where I was rather than somewhere else."

"The absoluteness of those loves can never be recaptured: no geometry of the landscape, no haze in the air, will live in us as intensely as the landscapes that we saw as the first, and to which we gave ourselves wholly, without reservations."
— Eva Hoffman, *Lost in Translation*

"The largest presence within me is the welling up of absence, of what I have lost."
— Eva Hoffman, *Lost in Translation*

"... and [my father] was determined that what was in his head should be real for me, and so I entered a story that had essentially ended."
— George W. S. Trow, *My Pilgrim's Progress*

"... I have seen both the social systems I grew up under dissolve. The Roosevelt social system and the Eisenhower social system are both gone. It makes me sad because I don't understand my country anymore."
— George W. S. Trow, *My Pilgrim's Progress*

The future is the past.
— Malcolm Reiner

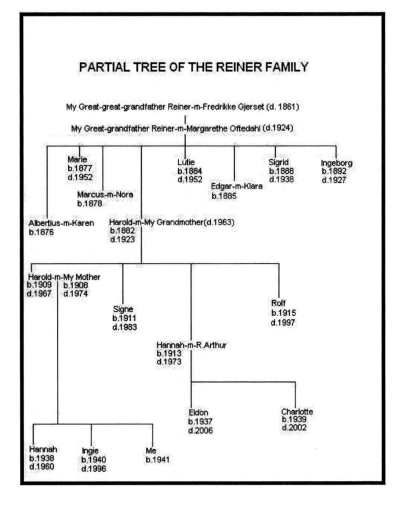

PARTIAL TREE OF THE REINER FAMILY

My Great-great-grandfather Reiner-m-Fredrikke Gjerset (d. 1861)

My Great-grandfather Reiner-m-Margarethe Oftedahl (d.1924)

Marie
b.1877
d.1952

Lutie
b.1884
d.1952

Sigrid
b.1888
d.1938

Ingeborg
b.1892
d.1927

Edgar-m-Klara
b.1885

Marcus-m-Nora
b.1878

Albertius-m-Karen
b.1876

Harold-m-My Grandmother(d.1963)
b.1882
d.1923

Harold-m-My Mother
b.1909 | b.1908
d.1967 | d.1974

Signe
b.1911
d.1983

Rolf
b.1915
d.1997

Hannah-m-R.Arthur
b.1913
d.1973

Eldon
b.1937
d.2006

Charlotte
b.1939
d.2002

Hannah
b.1938
d.1960

Ingie
b.1940
d.1996

Me
b.1941

CONTENTS

PICTURES

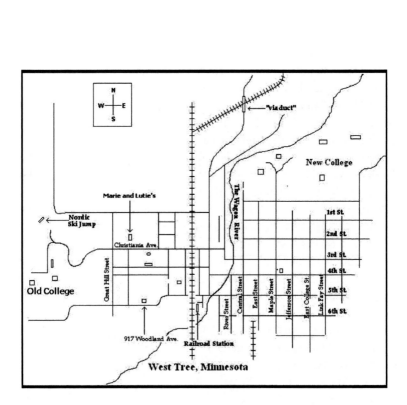

West Tree, Minnesota

SECTION I

MY EARLY LIFE BEGINS

CHAPTER 1

(1857-1949)
THE END OF THE 19TH CENTURY:
I LEARN THAT I AM TO BE A STUDENT
OF THE MYSTERIES
OF SPACE AND TIME

1

In the short part of their lives that overlapped with my own, my great-aunts Marie and Lutie had a far greater influence on me than they could possibly have known. Even I, at the time, was largely unaware of it. I was certainly unaware of its permanence or depth.

•

Now, as I think back over the lives of my vanished great-aunts, time itself seems to change in a strange and curious way. The very concept of it grows paradoxic and perverse. Time is unchangeable, eternal, and immutable. It exists forever. It never changes in the least way. Yet those whose lives are captured inside it vanish entirely. They become wholly, absolutely, utterly gone.

I don't understand this. I begin to think, now, the more I look back and consider the past, that I never will.

2

Marie Reiner, my great-aunt, was the second of eight siblings and the first of that branch of the family, on my father's side, to move to West Tree. She arrived in 1910, at age thirty-three, to take up a teaching post in history at Old College. Four years after that, she was joined by her sister Lutie, also un-married. Lutie, by then, was thirty, being seven years younger than Marie.

•

For me, there is a thrill of disbelief and strangeness at the thought of Marie and Lutie having ever been in their thirties, let alone younger: say, eighteen and twenty-five, or—inconceivable—girls of twelve and nineteen.

I never knew my great-aunts until they were quite near the end of their own lives. Even in my first memory of them—one summer afternoon in 1944—they seemed old. They died eight years later, when I was nearing my twelfth birthday. It seemed to me, in that eight or nine year period, that they hadn't ever changed.

•

When she came to West Tree on a summer day in 1910, Marie traveled by train. This is what comes to my mind when I imagine her arrival:

She gets down from the carriage and, a step or two away from it, pauses before moving farther. She stands straight, but her posture isn't stiff. She holds her head up, chin raised slightly, but about her there isn't any air of haughtiness or disdain. It's more as if, like any animal, she were trying to reach upward in order to see slightly farther. Her hands are gloved, one clasped by the other. A dark cloth bag hangs from the crook of her left elbow. As she stands there, she looks forward and then backward along the length of the train. The day is warm, without wind, and the midday air is filled with sunshine. Marie wears a wide-brimmed hat that keeps her face, with its tall forehead and long jaw, out of the direct light. Her hat is fitted with ties of pleated cloth that come down the two sides. These have been brought together under Marie's chin and tied loosely. The hem of her dress falls down to within an inch or two of the red brick platform she stands on.

•

(A generous handful of other passengers have also gotten off the train, and by this time eight or ten new ones have stepped up into the cars. A short distance down the platform, suitcases and bags are being handed out of the train. The man receiving the bags piles them on a flat wagon with no sides but with upright wooden ends. On a cobblestoned area near Marie, to one side of the station, a horse and buggy stands waiting for passengers. Its driver leans against one of the spoked wheels, nonchalantly cleaning his teeth with a splinter of wood, as if lunch might have taken place shortly before.

•

(In 1953—when she still lived in West Tree although in a world wholly unlike the one of 1910—Marie died after a brief illness. She was seventy-six years old at the time of her death. Only seven months later, Lutie followed her, at the age of sixty-nine.))

3

The house that Marie and Lutie lived in, on upper Christiania Avenue near the base of Old College Hill, was set back from the street slightly farther than the houses on either side of it. I don't know why this was so. Perhaps, when it was built in 1921, its standing place was determined in part by the unusual depth of the property. From the back side of the house, the yard sloped down for eight or ten feet and then went on the level for what always seemed to me a very great distance, perhaps twenty or so yards. Throughout this orderly back yard, in patches, rows, and small plots, Marie and Lutie, during all the years (except for the first and last) that they lived in the house, kept a garden of flowers, vegetables, herbs, berries, trees, and shrubs.

•

Although modern for its time and place, the house was modest and small. It was built in the bungalow style, a story and a half, finished out in gray stucco with brown wood trim. A screened porch was wrapped around its east side and part way across the front. The roof beam ran north and south, so gables appeared at the front and rear, and the eaves, coming down at a relatively shallow pitch, ended in wide overhangs on the sides. The shingling was also curled slightly over the edge in front and back, hinting faintly at a thatched roof, or a mossy one, or a cap pulled down low. This effect, along with the large expanse of roof in relation to the small size of the whole building, gave a suggestion of coziness and charm, as if the house had been designed not only with practical considerations in mind, but also to give a suggestion, say, of a fairy tale house, a quiet and secluded retreat in some far away valley, forest, or meadow.

The Hansel and Gretel snugness of the house, however, reflected only one of its dominant aspects. Being modern for its day, as I said, its design was consciously simple. On the outside, for example, except for the slight curl of the roof in front and back, it was free of excess trim, and the woodwork on the inside, around the windows and doors and along baseboards and moldings, was neither fluted nor grooved, but all made of plain, flat, pioneer-style boards, though darkly varnished. The floors also—where many times I played Authors or pick-up-sticks or Chinese checkers with my sisters—were made of the same long flat boards rather than parquet.

In spite of its simplicity, though, the house didn't give an impression of being spartan or plain. Instead, even though it was uncluttered enough so as almost to border on the austere, it gave a stronger impression merely of being orderly and compact. On two walls of the living room were bookcases with glass fronts, and on the shorter wall at the north end, built around the fireplace, stood more bookshelves. Through an arched door to the right, you passed into the dining room. In its east wall, directly in front of you, a set of three windows opened onto the screened side porch. These extended down a foot or so from the floor, and I always thought they had a tall and elegant look. For a long time, I thought of the tantalizing pleasure of stepping out through the windows to go outside.

•

(Lutie was smaller-boned than Marie, and one or two inches shorter. Both in behavior and temperament, she always seemed the more retiring and dependent of the sisters. When visitors came to the front door, it was Marie who opened it to them. Lutie would stand just behind, hovering expectantly.

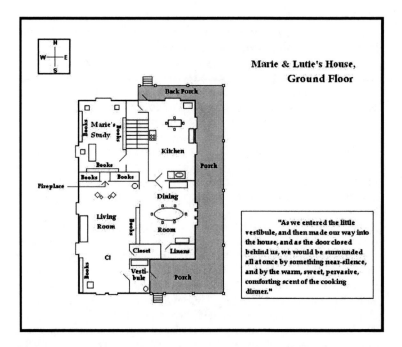

Marie & Lutie's House,
Ground Floor

"As we entered the little vestibule, and then made our way into the house, and as the door closed behind us, we would be surrounded all at once by something near-silence, and by the warm, sweet, pervasive, comforting scent of the cooking dinner."

With tradesmen, merchants, or local authorities, Marie would speak first, then turn to Lutie only afterward to verify whether she had omitted anything of importance. The differences in temperament between the sisters were indicated also by the arrangement of their household duties. Both shared, as a rule, in the garden work and in the routine house-cleaning, although Lutie's role in each of these dominated in subtle ways over Marie's. It was understood clearly that Lutie was the cook and thus the one mainly responsible for keeping track of groceries and provisions. Marie, on the other hand, had her study in the little room in the northwest corner of the ground floor. There were her desk and lamp, writing materials, and a great many of her books. Lutie's place was in the kitchen, across the narrow back hall from Marie's study. Of those two rooms, the kitchen was the larger and more filled with light, since it had three windows and also the back door, which stood open in warm weather and in winter, though closed, let in light through its large square pane.

•

In a number of ways, the back of the house seemed to me the most exotic part. It was more plain, but it had a quality of the undisturbed, private, and hidden.

The back door and window looked out through a small porch to the lawn and gardens. In Marie's study, the same was true: one of the two windows there also looked north, though not through the back porch, since that structure extended only halfway across the width of the house.

In the kitchen, just a step or two away from Marie's study, the light and air were entirely different, whatever the season. Wainscoting the color of cream reached up the walls, and above it was pale blue wallpaper with narrow vertical rows of small yellow flowers. Above a counter on the east wall, between the twin windows, cabinets rose to the ceiling. Opposite them was the range. The sink, against the south wall, rested on iron legs running down onto the bare linoleum. There was no cabinetry under the sink, so that drain-pipes were visible under the two sink-bellies. On the wall above the sink, a trio of narrower pipes rose to the ceiling. There, they bent at a right angle and continued to the inside corner of the kitchen, above the dining room door, where they went up through the ceiling and disappeared from sight.

In the middle of the kitchen stood the plain wooden table where, except when they had guests, Marie and Lutie ate their meals.

•

(At the north end of the living room, in front of the fireplace, stood Marie and Lutie's two armchairs, each with its own side table and lamp. The chairs were upholstered but they were neither soft nor deep. They were placed next to one another, angled slightly inward toward the fireplace. In them, in the evenings, after dinner, facing the fire, Marie and Lutie would sit.

The front of the house was the Christiania Avenue side, so that if a person were to have looked in through the front windows at just the right time of evening, they would have seen the two lamps, the two tables, and the backs of the two chairs, with Marie's gray head visible above the left one, Lutie's above the right. In front of my great-aunts would have been the fireplace, its light, perhaps, reflected faintly in the glass fronts of the bookcases on either side.))

4

My great-aunts were born and raised in the town of Archer, Nebraska, twenty miles or so west of the Missouri River, not far from the point where Iowa, Nebraska, and South Dakota come together. Archer was the town their father had chosen, eight years after his immigration from Norway, to settle in for good. He reached Archer in 1860, not even a year before the death of his first wife.

When my great-grandfather came to the United States, he was twenty-two years old, a recent university graduate, and an ordained Lutheran minister. He landed in New York, and from there made his way to Wisconsin with the intention of working in the settlements scattered through the central, wooded areas of that state. Once there, he met and married Fredrikke Gjerset, and for the next five years, although their marriage remained childless, Fredrikke accompanied my great-grandfather on his itinerant ministry.

After those five years, partly out of concern for his wife's health, and partly in response to other communities that were advertising for pastors, my great-grandfather moved south to more open country. He stopped for varying lengths of time in La Crosse, Cresco, Fort Dodge, and Sioux City before coming to Archer in the autumn of 1860. Later during their first year there, in the spring, Fredrikke died of tuberculosis, at the age of twenty-five.

On his travels throughout that area of the middle west, my great-grandfather had become convinced that a preparatory school, and after that a college, should be established for the benefit of students in the new country who could gain their educations and then, if they chose, enter the Lutheran ministry, as he himself had done when he was still in Norway. In the months following his wife's death, he determined that he would undertake this task himself and devote his life to it if necessary. Late in 1861, as a result, Archer Preparatory Academy came into existence in the downstairs front room of a house that stood a block east of the main street. Three years later, Archer College was established, graduating its first senior class—of four students—in 1867. In 1872, the college moved to a new building made of brown Missouri granite, two stories high, with a tower and flagpole, on a hill half a mile south of downtown Archer.

By the time the college moved, my great-grandfather was forty-one years old and had not yet remarried. Then in 1874, on a visit back to Norway, he met Margarethe Oftedahl, my future great-grandmother, then twenty-one. After a two-month courtship, the two were married and made plans to travel back to Nebraska immediately. There, in Archer, their first child, Albertius, was born, destined to be known as my great-uncle Albert. Their second child, Marie, was born in 1877. Over the years, there were six others, three girls and three boys. The last, Ingeborg, was born in 1892.

•

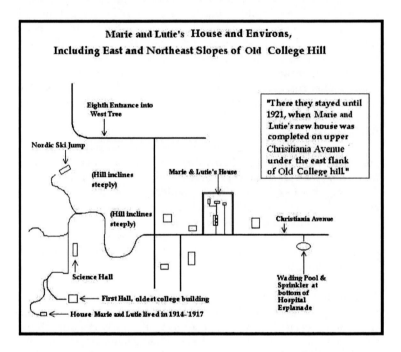

Marie and Lutie's House and Environs,
Including East and Northeast Slopes of Old College Hill

Eighth Entrance into
West Tree

Nordic Ski Jump

(Hill inclines
steeply)

Marie & Lutie's House

"There they stayed until
1921, when Marie and
Lutie's new house was
completed on upper
Chrisitiania Avenue
under the east flank
of Old College hill."

(Hill inclines
steeply)

Christiania Avenue

Science Hall

First Hall, oldest college building

House Marie and Lutie lived in 1914-1917

Wading Pool &
Sprinkler at
bottom of
Hospital
Esplanade

(By the time his last child was born, my great-grandfather was sixty-one years old. Numbers and dates of this kind create a feeling of awe in me. At the turn of the century, in 1900, when there weren't any automobiles yet, or airplanes or movies, my great-grandfather was already sixty-nine years old. When he died, sixteen years later, in 1915, in the first year of The Great War, his widow, my great-grandmother, was sixty-four. Their oldest child, Albertius, was forty years old. Their youngest was twenty-three. As for me, I was still minus twenty-six. By the time I was finally born, in 1941, only five of the original eight siblings remained, two of the girls and one of the boys (my paternal grandfather) having died.

•

When her father passed away, in 1915, Marie was thirty-eight and had lived in West Tree for half a decade. Lutie had been with her there

7

for almost a year.

At that time, they lived at the top of Old College hill, on the college campus, in rooms on the second floor of a house that was set aside for single women on the faculty and staff who chose to keep lodgings there.

That house was torn down in 1936, so I never saw it, although I've seen photos of it and know where it stood. When I bring it up now in my imagination, I think of my great-aunts and make a special effort to conceive of what it would be like to see them there. Most often, as it happens, I imagine them quite early in the morning, as they emerge from the front door of the house, go down its wooden steps, then turn together in the direction of the main campus.

The year I see them in is always 1916, and so the hems of their dresses are higher than Marie's was when she arrived in West Tree. The hems, now, come a third of the way or so up to my great-aunts' knees. But, of course, Marie and Lutie wear opaque stockings to prevent any hint of skin from being seen.

Without exception, at this time, my great-aunts wear hats when they are outdoors and in public. In my imaginary glimpse, I follow them—Marie first, then Lutie—as they part from one another and diverge onto different sidewalks, go into different buildings, then up different stairs and into different rooms, where each removes her coat, jacket, sweater, and also, of course, hat. This is the way I discover, breath-takingly, that Marie's hair is so dark a brown as to be almost black, and that Lutie's, even more astonishingly, is enough lighter than her sister's to be almost the color of straw.

•

Both are tall (although Marie is taller), and both are strong-boned (Marie the more so). With their high foreheads, long noses, strong teeth, and powerful jaws (though admittedly faintly receding chins), their appearance is more likely to be considered handsome than pretty or beautiful. They hold themselves with their necks and backs straight, though not stiffly. And although they conduct themselves with a degree of formality that would seem extreme now, they are both, notwithstanding the real seriousness of the work each does at the college, unvaryingly considerate, kind, good-natured, and helpful. Neither of them is rigid, proud, or aloof, on the one hand, nor coyly demeaning of themselves on the other. They are serious, industrious, and formal as occasion demands, yet at the same time they react readily with warmth to small personal acts of friendliness or helpfulness, and they respond in kind. They not only appreciate but enjoy laughter, as they would until the end of their lives.

In spite of their numerous appealing, captivating, and admirable traits, however, there is nothing about my great-aunts, in appearance, demeanor, habit, temperament, or clothing, that can change the near-absolute certainty of the fact that, at the advanced ages of thirty-one and thirty-eight, neither of them will ever marry.

•

By the time I knew them, their hair was gray, and they wore it, each like the other, in a style from the 1920's: short, curled forward beside the ears, and clipped quite close halfway up the neck. They no longer wore hats but went bareheaded in public. By the time of my first memories, they had already changed in physical posture. They no longer stood perfectly upright but always bent forward slightly from the waist. I always thought that this sign of age gave them a faintly bird-like appearance, especially when they were walking outdoors. If they were going any distance, they walked arm in arm, and their slightly forward-stance as they moved suggested a quality of eagerness and hurry. That suggestion—it took the form also of a fidgety nervousness—was more present, however, in Lutie than in Marie. Lutie was slighter than Marie, and her narrower body became the more angular of the two as she aged. Her nose, also, was somewhat longer, sharper, and more pronounced than her older sister's.

•

(My great-aunts, for me, were history. They had lived through time; therefore they were the past.

•

I admit that at times I was somewhat frightened by them. I sometimes felt ill-at-ease and self-conscious, intimidated by their oldness and by the many ways in which they seemed unfamiliar, strange, exotic, and foreign.

It would be untrue if I were to say that I felt then everything that I feel about them now.

•

It must have been a kind of intuition, a passive or semi-conscious working of memory, that caused me to sense much more about my great-aunts than I realized at the time. However true that may be, I also know that during a number of brief, intensely evocative moments (like the summer afternoon when I went upstairs to use the bathroom) I all at once absorbed boundless amounts of information, some of it directly—through color, sound, and scent—and some through a more oblique, shadowy, half-understood association, sense, or feeling.

I believe now that much of what I learned from my great-aunts was the cause, in good part, of my intellectual life finding its first awakening, and of that life's growing then to take the particular shape, quality, and dimension that it did.))

5

In the last quarter or so of the nineteenth century, Nebraska was still part of the frontier, and the lives of my great-aunts, as a result, were to a considerable extent, primitive, rigorous, and plain.

At the same time, there were beneficial and compensatory influences in their lives. Their father was educated, eminent, and widely respected. Through his influence, and also through that of their mother, their home life was busy, resourceful, industrious, and orderly. The household was observant in religion, yet at the same time the atmosphere in it was free of the narrowness, rigidity, and zeal that would later plague other branches—and members—of the family. The influence that may have been most important of all on my great-aunts was the fact that they and their siblings were raised in an atmosphere that strongly and undeviatingly encouraged learning and that extolled the value of education, not only for boys, but for the girls as well.

As it turned out, seven of the eight children finished their studies at Archer College before they left home, taking bachelors' degrees with them. All four of the sons went even farther in their educations. Two of them—Albertius first, then Harold, who was to be my paternal grandfather—followed their father's example in becoming ministers. Marcus and Edgar, the younger brothers, earned doctors' degrees and became professors, Marcus in medieval language and literature, Edgar in ancient history.

Of the girls, Marie was the one who went farthest academically and the one who served as trail-blazer in other ways as well. Though the second-born, she finished college at age seventeen—in 1895—even before her older brother had finished his. The next autumn, she became the first among all her siblings to enroll in a university for an advanced degree.

She went to Columbia, Missouri, to become a graduate student in history at the state university. This was in September 1895.

I have never been to Columbia and I have never seen the university there. In my mind, though, I have an image of Marie that has never changed.

In the image, she is reading at a wooden table. The table is in a narrow room with a single tall window. Marie wears a long dress with a full skirt and high collar. Her back is straight and she sits upright as she reads. Her head is bent slightly forward, and she holds the book so that its lower edge rests on the surface of the table. Her voluminous hair, so dark as to be almost black, is twisted loosely into a bun and pinned low at the back of her neck.

•

(When Marie was studying at the University of Missouri—in 1896 or 1897—Lutie was still back in Archer, a schoolgirl of twelve or thirteen.

Not for seventeen more years, in 1914, when she was thirty and Marie thirty-seven, would Lutie travel to Minnesota to join her sister.

When Lutie came to West Tree, it was to take a position as assistant librarian at Old College. Years later, in the mid-1930's, she herself became chief librarian. Before that, however, she went across the river to New College, on the opposite side of West Tree, as chief assistant librarian for a period of four or five years.

The fifth child and third daughter, Lutie, in her early adult years, went east to Philadelphia to take a year's course in cooking and nutrition. Only after she came back to Archer did she begin library work, and for some time she stayed in Archer, at home, working in the college library. By then, Marie had completed her doctor's degree, and for the next seven or eight years, through 1909, she taught as an assistant professor at the University of Nebraska in Lincoln. In 1910, she came to Old College as associate professor. Ten years later, in 1919, after she had written two books, she was made full professor.

.

(When my great-grandfather died—in Nebraska, in his sleep, in 1915, at age eighty-four—there was no one left in the house except his widow and his youngest daughter, Ingeborg, who was then twenty-three. Later that year, as planned, Ingeborg married and moved with her new husband, a doctor, to Kansas City. For the next fifteen or sixteen months, my great-grandmother stayed in the family house alone. Visitors came, of course, from among her numerous friends, but her children had all moved away from Archer, and, since she was the only one in her own family to have come from Norway, there were no other close relatives nearby. Her sons had all married and were living elsewhere, and now so was Ingeborg. The third daughter, Sigrid, was in China. In this way it came about that my great-grandmother, at age sixty-six, after settling the last of her affairs in Archer and selling the old house, came to Minnesota to live with Marie and Lutie.

By this time it was 1917. Marie, Lutie, and their mother moved into the upstairs of a bare-looking frame house on the west side of town a block or so uphill from the train station. They stayed there until 1921, when Marie and Lutie's new house was completed on upper Christiania Avenue, tucked under the flank of Old College hill. The three women moved into the new house in October, all of them to stay, as it happened, until the end of their lives. Marie and Lutie slept in the bedroom upstairs, while my great-grandmother took the little room in the northwest corner of the ground floor that was later to be Marie's study. After a year or so, my great-grandmother's health unexpectedly began to fail. Beginning late in the following spring, she was confined to bed, and, five days before Christmas 1924, having been nursed assiduously by her two daughters for the preceding eight months, she died.

•

(Twenty-five years later, one day in the summer of 1949, after standing for a moment in the doorway of that room, I stepped inside. I remember the stillness and the silence. And I remember the way the west window, behind Marie's desk, was covered with vines that filtered and darkened the light as it came inside, converting it into a deep shadowy green.)))

6

⌈Every detail; every scent and image; every nook, particle, and fragment; every vestige of my great-aunts' house seems to me now replete with the atmosphere, quality, flavor, scent, and meaning of their lives.⌋

•

My family made a visit to Marie and Lutie twice a year, in an unchanging ritual. We went once on the 23rd of December and again in the summer, near the middle or end of August.

In my memory, the tradition of these visits seems to have gone on for a very long time, but it can't really have lasted many years. My earliest memory of Marie and Lutie doesn't date from before 1945 or possibly 1946. And our visits couldn't have continued past 1952, since Marie died in March of the next year, then Lutie in November.

•

(During the August visit when I went to use the bathroom upstairs, my family weren't the only guests. My great-uncles Edgar and Marcus were also visiting, along with their wives Klara and Nora. And there were my paternal grandmother Elizabeth and my aunt Signe as well.

After thinking about it carefully, I would place this visit in August of 1949, neither earlier nor later.)

•

The door into the kitchen was hung in such a way that it would open either inward or outward, swinging by itself back into a closed position after anyone passed through it. On the dining room side, the door was covered with a dark varnish. On the other side, it was painted the same color of thick cream as the kitchen wainscoting.

This door aroused an intense curiosity in me, and I remember it with clarity. It had, I remember, a round window a quarter of the way from the top.

•

During our visits at Christmastime, as the rest of us took our places at the table, Marie would go back and forth through the swinging door, bringing in covered dishes from the kitchen. Only after all the other preparations were complete, and just as Marie carried in the platter of baked ham, would Lutie herself follow. She would pause a moment, pursing her lips tightly with a suppressed pleasure, her hands clasped together in front of her apron bib. Then she would step forward and take her own place at the table.

•

Lutie's Christmastime dinners took place late in the afternoon, near five o'clock or slightly after, when the early nightfall of the solstice had already turned the windows dark. Year after year, the menu was the same: baked ham with raisin sauce, glazed sweet potatoes, split peas, olives, home-made pickles, tomato aspic salad, warm biscuits. For dessert, there would be Lutie's home-made peppermint ice cream along with sugar cookies, pfeffernüsse, and krumkake. For the adults, coffee was served in thin china cups and saucers.

Entirely different, the summertime dinners were served earlier in the day, at one-thirty or two in the afternoon. For these meals, there were varieties of salads and cold cuts, tomatoes and cucumbers, soft white rolls, and, for dessert, homemade vanilla ice cream smothered under fresh berries.

In the summer, a vase of cut flowers would stand at the center of the table, with two or three others, like reflections, on the sideboard. The dining room windows would be opened wide, and their thin curtains would billow out now and then with passing breezes.

(At Christmas, the contrast was great: the house felt smaller, more sheltered, compact, and warm. The windows, of course, would be tightly closed. The fireplace would be crackling. Candles would glow on the mantelpiece amid sprays of pine and holly. On the dining room table would be two candles, and another pair on the sideboard, their light shining in the mirror behind them.

•

(The pattern never changed. We would arrive at Marie and Lutie's in the last hour of thin winter daylight, and we would go home—after dinner, after the drinking of coffee at the table, after the exchange of presents in front of the fireplace—under the enormous, high, freezing, star-strewn winter sky.

•

At four-fifteen or four-thirty each December 23rd, my father would pull up to the curb at Marie and Lutie's house. We would all get out of the car and go up the walkway—my parents, my two sisters, myself— and then up the four steps to the porch. Still behind us on the walkway, my father would take a last draw on his cigarette while my mother— in later years, it would be Hannah—knocked at the door. After a delay during which the world seemed to fall utterly silent, there would be footsteps from inside, then also voices, drawing nearer. When the door opened, there would be Marie—tall, leaning toward us slightly, at once nervous and eager in her greetings, smiling widely. Behind her, like an after-image, smiling in the same pleased and nervous way, a kitchen towel over her arm, would be Lutie.

As we stepped into the house, we would be surrounded immediately by the warm, sweet, and comforting smells of cinnamon and cloves, baking ham, and fresh bread still hot from the oven.

•

(I didn't know it then, but I understand it now: during my visits to Marie and Lutie's house I stepped inside history; and, when the visit came to an end, I stepped out of it again.

•

Because their lives had been born and shaped in a previous century, I later came to think of my great-aunts as having been nurtured and sustained by time itself. It seemed to me that Marie and Lutie, in the manner of birds, arranged the past around them in attentive, painstaking weavings. They carried the past with them from an earlier place, much as lungs might carry air from one room to another. I would think of them later as having emerged from the past in the same way that bathers might emerge from the sea, bringing with them vestiges of sand that would find their way to bedroom floors or upstairs hallways, to be discovered later, by others, who would wonder how these traces of the sea could have gotten there, such a great distance from the shore, and marvel at their existence.

•

Until it was time for dinner, we would wait in the living room, on the hard cushions of the Mission Oak chairs and settees that my great-grandmother had brought with her from the house in Nebraska. Firelight glinted on the glass fronts of the bookcases, the shelves inside filled with volumes mysterious to me, many in languages I couldn't recognize. On the east and west walls of the living room, facing one another, hung two tapestries of dark bold colors in geometric designs. These had been woven in Norway in the middle of the nineteenth century by an elder sister of my great-grandmother, who in turn brought them to Archer when she came there as a bride. Later, my mother, in our farmhouse outside of West Tree, would use one of them as a table cover. It now hangs on a wall of my apartment in New York City.

•

My sisters and I were offered fruit juice to drink. The adults had sherry in tiny crystal glasses, brought in by Marie on a tray. My mother took the first. My father, with the odd, thin, twisted smile that took over his mouth when he was self-conscious or constrained by divided feelings, lifted up the second. Lutie came from the kitchen for hers. Marie's was last. She raised it discreetly in a toast, and all four of them sipped. After talking with my mother for a few minutes (while Marie talked with my father), Lutie excused herself, went out of the living room, crossed a corner of the dining room, and disappeared through the swinging door into the kitchen.

•

Marie and Lutie never had a Christmas tree. Instead, nestled in pine boughs on a telephone table near the door to the dining room, was a model of the stable in Bethlehem. It was there every year, and it was always the same.

The little building was realistically detailed, its roof thatched with real straw and, under the thatch, rafters and walls that were made of real wood. The front side was left open so you could look inside. Gathered closely around the cradle, in the customary manner, were the three magi, while behind them stood figures of village people and shepherds. There were sheep, cattle, and oxen. A tiny electric bulb, tucked out of sight under the front edge of the ridgepole, sent a faint light down onto Mary, Joseph, and Jesus.

•

The dining table was covered by a snowy white cloth. At its center stood twin candlesticks, their bases hidden under arrangements of holly. The dishes we ate from were ridged and bumpy with designs along their edges and adorned with patterns of blue flowers intertwined among tendrils and pale green leaves. Instead of salt shakers, Lutie set out tiny glass dishes that were filled with low mounds of salt. Projecting from each little heap of salt was a miniature, yellowed, cracked ivory spoon hardly an inch long that, as Lutie was fond of reminding us, had been brought from Nebraska, and from Wisconsin before that, and from Norway before that, and from India before that, where they had been carved from the tusks of elephants.

7

(Marie and Lutie's house, it seems to me now, was order and continuity, cleanliness and quietness.

I remember exactly the appearance of the kitchen, to the right off the tiny back hall, and, to the left, the look of Marie's study. Yet I don't remember passing the door of either of them that summer afternoon as I placed a foot on the stairs on my way up to the bathroom. Nor do I remember climbing the stairs themselves, or making the hairpin turn at the landing.

I remember leaving my place at the table, conscious of trying to remain unnoticed as I did so. I pushed my chair back carefully, moving it as little as necessary in order to squeeze out between my great-uncle Marcus on the right and my aunt Signe on the left. Then after that—it seems in memory—I was upstairs.

This was in August, in broad daylight, in the middle of the afternoon, after the end of one of the summertime meals.

•

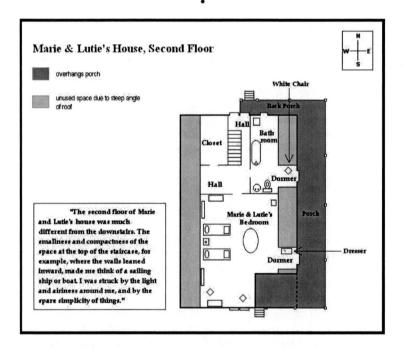

Marie & Lutie's House, Second Floor

overhangs porch

unused space due to steep angle of roof

White Chair

Back Porch

Hall

Closet

Bath room

Hall

Dormer

"The second floor of Marie and Lutie's house was much different from the downstairs. The smallness and compactness of the space at the top of the staircase, for example, where the walls leaned inward, made me think of a sailing ship or boat. I was struck by the light and airiness around me, and by the spare simplicity of things."

Marie & Lutie's Bedroom

Porch

Dresser

Dormer

The second floor of Marie and Lutie's house was much different from the first. The smallness and compactness of the house at the top of the stairs, where the walls leaned inward over my head, made me think of a sailing boat. At the same time, I was struck by the light and airiness around me, and by the spare simplicity of things.

Unlike the dark floors downstairs, the floors here were blond and smoothly waxed, unadorned even by scatter rugs. Daylight flowed in from a pair of windows behind me, facing the garden and yard. Meanwhile, directly in front of me was Marie and Lutie's bedroom. The door stood open. I could see through the room to the two windows in its south wall, matching the pair behind me.

Immediately to my left, in the meantime, was the open bathroom door.

I turned in that direction, went into the bathroom, closed the door behind me, and locked it.

8

At this period in my life, so far as I remember, I had no particular interest in the future. Not much later, however, at age eleven or twelve, perhaps thirteen, I was to go through an illness-like period of morbidity, when I would be wrung by a fear of dying. I suppose this state of mind implied an interest in the future, though perhaps in no way different from any animal's base, instinctive wish for survival.

On the other hand, I can't remember a time in my life when the past wasn't of intense interest. I can't remember a time beyond earliest childhood, that is, when I lacked a strong awareness of what had already passed, a feeling of being surrounded by it, along with an alluring sense of how desirable it would be to fall softly back again into its timeless, patient, unmoving pool.

•

How much I may have forgotten from my visit upstairs in Marie and Lutie's house, I can't possibly know. But I'm certain, even after the six decades that have passed, that what I do remember, I remember with perfect clarity.

The month was August, the day Saturday, the hour doubtless sometime past three. The sky was clear, the temperature moderate, the air soft, moving with nothing more than an occasional passing breath.

The day and the moment were still, hushed, calm, perfect.

•

The bathroom was tucked neatly under the slope of the roof. A dormer window let in air and light from the east, and a smaller, square, window swung out on hinges high up in the north wall. Against the wall to the left of the door when you came in was a claw-footed tub. The ceiling, following the pitch of the roof, fell from its highest point over the tub down to within a foot or so of the floor on the east side of the room, excepting where the dormer window was cut out. In the window area, there was a space large enough to stand up in, like a miniature secondary room. In this space stood a white chair with a towel over its back.

The toilet was against the south wall, where I sat with my pants bunched at the ankles and my feet not quite reaching the floor. Immediately to my left was the sink, with its two faucets of white ceramic as thick as sausages, while the basin itself rested on a wide pedestal of the same material. The entire floor of the room was covered with white tiles the size of half dollars, except hexagonal. They were laid down, too, in a pattern of hexagons, each the size of a hand, with a single black tile at its center.

•

This little room, filled with soft air and afternoon light, seemed to me then—as it does now, even in its absence—remarkable, historic, and perfect. Modest and humble, it was, in its unpretentious way, a masterpiece of style. It was utilitarian and plain, yet also perfectly measured in its balance of ornament and amenity, in its harmony of form and space, and, perhaps above all, in the carefully realized placement of each part within the whole. How charmed, graceful, and well proportioned, for example, seemed to me the dormer window to my right, and the swiftly dropping line of the ceiling where it met the vertical plane of the dormer wall. Following clockwise around the room were the sink, door, tub, and small high window. My eye, having made that journey, came once again to the point where sloping roof met vertical plane of dormer wall, then it came around that corner into the open space itself where the chair stood, comfortingly unmoving, its bent-wood legs splayed slightly outward, the towel folded neatly over its back. Near the chair was the window itself: open wide, curtained with white lace, the sill not even six inches from the floor.

•

1) I stayed in the bathroom, I suppose, for twenty minutes or so, possibly more. For me, that wasn't long. Even then, anxiety and uncertainty sent me to the bathroom often and caused me to remain there for extended periods. The length of this particular visit, consequently, was unlikely to draw attention, at least from my parents or sisters, who were familiar with my odd patterns of behavior.

In truth, due to my having slipped away—so I believed—without being noticed, I imagine now that during my time upstairs I was in the thoughts of no one at all: not of those just a few feet away, under the floor below my feet, nor of any others who might have been far away indeed, beyond the horizon, in Africa, the Philippines, China, or any distant reach of the planet.

The nearest to me included not only those still at the table, but any who might have gone into the living room—my sisters Hannah and Ingie, for example, who by this time had likely excused themselves and were sitting on one of the scatter rugs in the living room (Ingie Indian fashion, Hannah, more demurely, with her legs to the side, one arm supporting her weight), playing pick-up sticks, Chinese checkers, or Authors. And the nearest also included those who might have gone into other rooms—Lutie, for example, who, with my mother and my aunt Signe, may have gotten up to carry cups and dessert plates through the swinging door to leave them on the ribbed drainboard of the sink, where, very easily, it seemed to me that I could not only imagine but also actually see them.

2) As I said, I have no memory of passing through the back hall or

coming up the stairs. I have no memory, either, of getting up from the toilet, leaving the bathroom, or going back downstairs. This second blank space in memory sometimes has the strange effect of causing me to imagine that I am in fact still there, still upstairs, on the toilet, beside the dormer window, as if, after sixty years, I had never left that spot, not even though the house itself and everything around it are now gone.

3) The origin of the bathroom seemed a miracle and mystery to me after my experience in it, and it seems only the more so now. This is true especially when I think back to the room's distinctiveness in harmony, balance, and proportion, and back to the resultant and commensurate pleasures brought into being by those qualities. How could such a room, in the first place, ever have come into existence? How could it have been conceived, then subsequently brought about physically? How, above all, could the great number of necessary, varied, timely, and complex impulses, motives, and actions toward that end have been brought into so perfect a convergence, as they obviously had been, to bring such a room into existence at just such a time, in the autumn of 1921, that distant, single, particular year whose very sound is now both hopelessly antique and dizzyingly modern?

4) (Two pipes came up through the floor and disappeared under the curled rim of the tub, presumably connecting there with the tub's thick white ceramic faucets. Downstairs, on the wall behind the kitchen sink, there had been three pipes. Where, now, was the third one, and what had its purpose been?)

5) I was never again to visit the upstairs of Marie and Lutie's house, a fact that may help explain the occasion's having proved as memorable as it did. Of the things that happened afterward, I don't know how many were direct results of my visit. But I do know, with an unqualified certainty, this much: that on my visit upstairs I received the first sustained and lucid premonition, however I may or may not have understood it at the time, that, through no choice of my own, I was one of those destined to scrutinize and ponder, for the remainder of my life, the mysteries of space and time.

•

In that now-unexistent little room, that is, where I had never been before and was never to be again, I felt, for a handful of minutes, and simultaneously, these things: 1) that I was suspended inside time itself as if in an enormous, warm, embracing sea; and 2) that I was situated perfectly, for those same few moments, at the very center of all things.

•

(As had happened once before in my life, my consciousness grew first in a vertical direction, bringing with it a heightened awareness of what was below me. It then changed direction and expanded horizontally, in the manner of waves moving outward on a pond. It brought with it, in this second way, a heightened consciousness of things around me and at varying distances away.

•

The immediate effect of the vertical form of development was to make me aware of the rooms below with such a degree of vividness that I actually saw them, although not always in complete form. For a moment, for example, I saw Lutie's hands (sleeves pushed to her elbows) as she held a china plate under running water. For another moment, I saw not Lutie's hands but Marie's as she placed a new stack of dishes on the drainboard (her sleeves were cuffed neatly at the wrists). I saw the kitchen door swinging, then slowing to a stop. In the living room, I saw Hannah and Ingie playing pick-up sticks on an oval braided scatter rug. Both of them were now leaning sideways, their weight on one elbow.

Mainly, however, I saw things directly below, in the dining room. I saw Marie and Lutie returning to the table; a fresh pot of coffee being poured into cups; the curtains at the windows blowing briefly inward, like pale hands reaching toward the table, then emptying out again and falling limp.

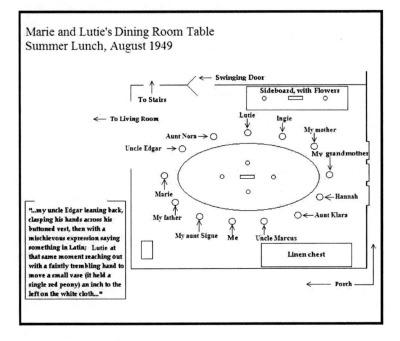

Marie and Lutie's Dining Room Table
Summer Lunch, August 1949

My grandmother, in her wheelchair, sat at the far end of the table, with her back to the windows. At her left was Hannah's place, empty now since she had gone into the living room with Ingie. To the left of Hannah's chair sat my aunt Klara, the wife of my great-uncle Edgar. To Klara's left was Marcus, followed by my own chair (it was one of the three yellow straight chairs that had been brought in from the kitchen). On what had been my own left was my aunt Signe, and next to her my father. Then came Marie herself, directly across the table from my grandmother, her back toward the arched doorway into the living room. To Marie's left was my great-uncle Edgar; then my aunt Nora; after her, Lutie (who sat nearest the kitchen door); then Ingie's empty chair; and at last my mother, in her usual place at my grandmother's right.

Seeing the table from above in this way provided an unusual perspective, so that I saw people's arms extend outward as they picked up their coffee cups and then drew them toward their lips. My father, with a cigarette between his first two fingers (his only cigarette since the one he stubbed out on the sidewalk), moved his hand also from an ashtray to his lips. Now and then (he sat forward on his chair, his elbows resting on the tablecloth), he turned his head toward the ceiling in order to exhale smoke away from the others at the table. (When he did this, it was almost as if he were secretly glancing up at me.)

The oddity of these movements, along with other arresting details—my mother's large blue earrings, for example, and her yellow summer dress; the billowing of the curtains; my aunt Signe and my grandmother relaying something to one another across the table, moving their lips but using no words; my uncle Edgar leaning back, clasping his hands across his buttoned vest, then with a mischievous expression saying something in Latin; Lutie at that same moment reaching out with a faintly trembling hand to move a small vase (it held a single red peony) an inch to the left on the white cloth—all of these details, along with the general impression of the room and the scene, seized my attention powerfully and yet proved able to hold it for only a short time, the reason being that the horizontal growth of my consciousness arose unexpectedly at almost the same moment and began at once to intensify rapidly.

The sudden and powerful sideways expansion of my consciousness, as I've suggested, was to provide the true climax of my trip to the bathroom. I now believe, in fact, even though such an experience had occurred once before in my life, that this one constituted the earliest altogether synthesizing moment in my embryonic intellectual life, the first moment of its kind that gave me—as it was taking place instead of later—an awareness, faint as it may have been, of the magnitude and significance of what was happening to me.

There should be little surprise, therefore, that I found myself gripped more firmly by this new consciousness than I had been by my vertical one. And there should be little that seems unusual in the three-step movement of the powerful energy that was involved. First, somewhat like an anchor being weighed, this energy drew my attention upward from the rooms below. Then it consolidated and compressed itself, for a brief time, entirely within myself. And finally, making its exit from me, it moved outward in all directions in its widening circumferent journey.

It is agreed universally that nothing can be set into motion except through a stimulus separate from itself. Therefore, I have studied assiduously, searching back carefully into these memories in an effort to find the one energizing power that most probably triggered this episode of consciousness. And that catalyst, I'm now all but certain, was the glimpse I'd had, as I came to the top of the stairs, of Marie and Lutie's bedroom.

Directly in front of me, as I said, before I entered the bathroom, stood the open door to my great-aunts' room. And, clearly, the memory of what I saw through that door remained with me as I sat gazing up at the wallpaper on the underside of the slanted bathroom ceiling; at the open window to my right; and at the white chair standing nearby, with the towel folded over its back.

Before I went into the bathroom, it had never occurred to me in even the most faintly conceivable way that any part of Marie and Lutie's lives might have had to do with sleep. Before I reached the top of the stairs and saw the bedroom door, I had never once given thought to my great-aunts' experience of nighttime or to the phenomenon of their sleeping through it. Never had I thought of them as growing tired in such a way as to call for sleep—or even as being, for that matter, associated in any way whatsoever with the homely, commonplace, intimate act of sleeping itself, with preparations for it, the appurtenances of it, participation in it, or risings from it.

Now, however, my glimpse into their bedroom had changed everything and had already begun to create a consciousness that was destined to influence, alter, and change the very path of the life that stretched out before me.

What I'd seen through the door, in short, had had for me a vividness sufficiently intense that, even when was I no longer looking at it directly, it stayed in my consciousness with the clarity not only of something remembered but of something physically still there. The intensity of the impression, in other words, gave me a consciousness, as I sat on the toilet, not only of the memory but of the yet-concrete presence of my great-aunts' room. And this degree of tangible physicality—the actuality, as it were, of the room's existence inside myself, and therefore of my self's existence inside the room—made tangible and real to me for the very first time in my life the following uncertainties:

1) the uncertainty of knowing where I was;
2) the corollary and attendant uncertainty of knowing where I was not;
3) the difficulty of knowing the difference between the two;
4) the difficulty of understanding why such a difference existed at all.

9

(With the result that my sensitivity to the world around me, and to the relationship among its parts, changed suddenly, was enhanced, and grew.

•

A transformation of such a kind as this couldn't, of course, have been brought into existence by chance alone, and yet I can't help acknowledging the part that chance must have played. Unquestionably, such a transformation depended, first, on the simultaneous existence of three forces, each holding a personal significance to me; second, on the coincidence of each of the three forces, in and of itself, being situated in a certain, strategic way; and, finally, on the coincidence of each being situated also in a particular and strategic way in relation to the other two.

The initial locations of these forces, as I've suggested, were:

1) The dining room
2) The bathroom
3) The bedroom

And, as I came to understand them later, the significance of each of the locations was as follows:

1) The significance of the dining room (through my vertical consciousness) lay in its containing (in the persons of those gathered there and in the ceremoniousness of what they did) evidence of the depth, longevity, and continuity of my family's biological origins as well as of their roots in a variety of historical and cultural traditions extending back to the early middle years of the nineteenth century, earlier than which the traces and lineages of their existence faded, grew dim, and disappeared from my view.

2) The significance of the bathroom (which I was conscious of neither vertically nor horizontally, but as a place unified, compact, secure, holistic, and both physically and aesthetically comforting) lay, first, in its evident perfections of light, air, design, and proportion; second, in its being a marvelously achieved and exactly preserved manifestation

of the touch, feel, texture, and thought of the year 1921; and, last, in its being a transformative meeting place of the energies approaching me from the other two directions: from the dining room below, and from my great-aunts' bedroom upstairs, through the wall behind me and slightly to the right.

3) The significance of the bedroom (which I became conscious of as being actually inside myself, and myself inside it) lay in its providing me with an awareness for the first time in my life of the intimacy of sleep; of the many customs and habits associated with it; and therefore and simultaneously an awareness also of the formality, omnipresence, and inevitability of death.

•

(The open bedroom door allowed me, as I mentioned, to see through to the twin windows in the far wall, looking out over Christiania Avenue. In accordance with the lowness and pitch of the roof, the bedroom walls sloped inward, leaving a narrow strip of flat ceiling only at the top center, a configuration that accentuated the compactness of the room and made me think of a Roman tent, a nineteenth-century house, or a ship's cabin. The room was spare and absolutely tidy, without, for example, even a piece of clothing or pair of shoes visible to the eye. The wooden floor was bare except for a small scatter rug at the foot of the beds. The curtains—at far left and far right, the center post remaining bare—were gathered and held open, like stage curtains.

Marie and Lutie's two beds projected into the room from the right-hand wall. High and appearing slightly mounded across their tops, they were covered with quilted spreads that hung over the sides down to a hand's-breadth from the floor. At the foot of each bed lay a folded blanket, and at the head of each was a very large white pillow. The beds were placed two or three feet apart, not more. Between them stood a small table with a shaded lamp.)

10

I was, that is, pushed upward by the forces of the dining room; held stationary by the harmonizing energies and intellectual coherence of the bathroom; then driven outward by the intimacy and searing absoluteness of the bedroom.

This sequence of events was memorable, powerful, and complex. From it I gained not only my earliest mature awareness of the existence of space and time, but my first consciousness of the necessary relationship between those two forces on the one hand and death on the other.

11

Before my visit upstairs, and before looking through the door, I had never thought of my great-aunts without clothing. I had never so much as thought of them, for that matter, as wearing nightgowns, or as crawling in between sheets, or as settling their heads into white pillows, or as extending an arm to turn out the light. I understood now, however, that in this small room they had done all that and more: over and over, they had taken off their clothing, put on nightgowns, gotten under their covers, and slept through the night, doing all this in a long and unbroken chain of nights and days that reached back all the way to the remote, barely imaginable, aesthetically perfect year of 1921. In that year itself, they had slept in this room. In 1924, as their mother progressed gradually toward death downstairs, they had slept here. They had slept here also in 1927, and in 1931, and in 1938, and in 1944. And they slept here even now, in their two beds, in the order and plainness and intimacy of their small room, as each night drew them, too, one step closer to the time when each would die, Marie first, then Lutie.

•

Because I didn't go into the room, I missed seeing, exactly parallel with the bathroom's, its own dormer window facing east. Against the wall inside that dormer, in a position equivalent to the white chair's in the bathroom, was a cherry wood dresser. On its surface lay a crocheted white cloth. Over the cloth was a cover of beveled glass. On the glass rested two hairbrushes, and beside each a large comb made of horn.

I never saw this dresser, or the brushes and combs, when they were still in the room. I saw them only years later, in my aunt Hannah's house in Baltimore, where my grandmother Elizabeth, having left West Tree, had by then also gone to live. That was the only time I saw them. I never heard of them again. I have no idea where they may have gone.))

12

My visit upstairs, as I said, took place on a perfect August day: the sky cloudless, the light clear, the air scented with a summertime sweetness and warmth. In the bathroom, the thin white curtain at the window lifted slightly, held for a second or two, then settled back.

13

Though I was sitting in the bathroom, the force that propelled my consciousness horizontally was generated from the vicinity of Marie and Lutie's beds. I am inclined to think of it as having originated near the pillows, gathering in the air a few inches above them. It may, however, have come from a broader area, located generally over the surfaces of the beds.

•

The bedroom was unmoving and silent.

•

There must have been, I suppose, the cries of cicadas from the tree-tops around the house and high above the roof, or the sound, say, of someone mowing a lawn nearby. Voices must have risen now and then from the table downstairs. Or the sound of crockery or silverware from the kitchen must have floated in through the bathroom window. But none of these has stayed in my memory. Along with all other sounds from that afternoon, they have vanished entirely.))

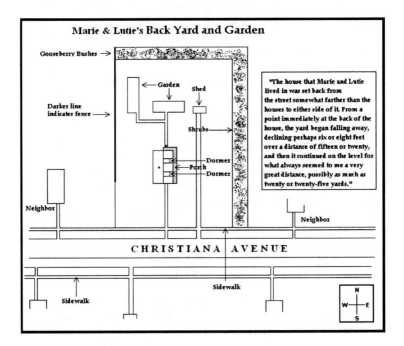

At a fairly gentle pitch, the yard sloped downward from the back door for a vertical distance of ten feet or so, then after that ran level. Along the left boundary of the yard stood a slatted fence with a narrow garden running along it. In the garden grew hollyhocks, sunflowers, zinnias, asters, all amid a profusion of various types of climbing plants, these in many places covering the fence. In another separate patch of tilled ground were vegetables—green beans, peas, tomatoes, cucumbers, lettuce, radishes—while yet a third patch contained tall blossoming plants of great number and variety. At the bottom, the yard was terminated by a thick hedge of gooseberry bushes, while along the east edge were currant and raspberry bushes, strawberry beds, and plum trees.

About a third of the way from the house toward the bottom of the lawn was a small unpainted wooden shed. It had a double door and three square windows of four panes each.

Once, in the back yard alone, I stepped into the shed and found that it was a museum of time. Old lawn supplies and gardening tools rested on shelves or leaned against walls, testifying to the unbroken chronology of my great-aunts' lives on Christiania Avenue. I considered the antiquity of the things around me, and imagined the dates of their acquisition. From May 1922, for example, during my great-aunts' first spring in their new house, there was a push-style lawnmower with cleated iron wheels and a wooden handle. From that same year, though later in the season, there were a three-tined garden fork and a square hoe, while a much smaller hoe, with triangular blade, dated from the following year. A hand-held trowel dated also from 1923; a small pointed spade came from 1925; a pair of hand-held snippers were from 1931; a lawn-sprinkler had arrived in 1937; and a twig-cutter mounted on a long bamboo pole came to the garden as late as 1940, a year before I was born.

Every one of these objects (at this moment, the curtain at one of the upstairs dormer windows stirred slightly, pressed outward against the screen, then fell back and was still) had been touched by Marie and Lutie's hands: had been with them, say, in the cool of summer mornings when the lawn and garden were wet with dew; or in the heat of afternoons when the air fell motionless and cicadas sent up lazy fountains of sound from the tops of trees; or in the later part of the day, when shadows gathered on the east side of the slatted fence and on the east side of the shed, and when Marie would at last emerge from her study, come out the back door, and walk down into the yard for the hour or so that remained before supper.

•

There were the faint traces of a driveway, scarcely indented wheel tracks now grown over with grass, leading from the street to the back yard along the east side of the house and up to the closed doors of the shed. Perhaps the builders of the house had used the little building for storing supplies, or perhaps at a later time someone had rented it and used it as a garage. Marie and Lutie, never having owned a car, and never having learned to drive, most of the time walked wherever they went.

14

1) I see Marie and Lutie in the garden. Each of them wears a long dress, and each has on a hat with very wide brim. I can't see their faces. This is not only because of the hats, or because my great-aunts are leaning forward at their work, but also because the angle of my view, from where I look down through the small square window in the upstairs bathroom, keeps their faces hidden from me.

2) The back yard is empty. No one is in it. The sun is shining. I have no idea what year it is.

15

At the time of my first experiences of horizontal consciousness, I knew much less than I do now, obviously. Naturally, too, the way I might express thoughts in adulthood differs from the way I might have expressed them then. And yet even so, the outline, structure, and shape of what I remember are entirely unchanged, in the same way as a cup is unchanged whether it is filled with water or with wine.

16

1) On the northeast shoulder of Old College hill, removed some distance from the college buildings, stands the Nordic ski jump. The season is winter. The trees are bare, the ground white. My father stands on the platform high up at the top of the jump. He looks small at so enormous a height. He is bent forward and has his poles planted beside his skis. He pushes off. Gravity pulls him down and he also pushes vigorously with his poles, accelerating into the swooping curve of the descent, until, at the last moment, he tucks down even closer to his skis than before and sails off the lip of the jump. He flies effortlessly for what appears to be an enormous distance and a very long time, suspended in the air.
My father jumps a great number of times between 1926 and 1932, from the time when he was a junior in high school until the last winter before he and my mother were married.

2) Space becomes interfused with time. On the top of Old College Hill, buildings are clustered loosely, some of them obscured by trees. Marie and Lutie, wearing long dresses with tight jackets, appear in one of the doorways and step down onto the sidewalk. Then they vanish suddenly.

3) In the other direction, to the east, across the river, on the far side of town, on a hill of its own, stands New College. Its own oldest building, standing on the brow of its own hill, faces westward, gazing back imperturbably toward Old College.))

17

As I think back now to my visit, it's as though thin, ductile, translucent, almost invisible strands, like tendrils of the silkworm or spider, are flung spontaneously outward from where I sit, flying out to their destinations in varying directions around me. One strand has already been flung to the top of Old College hill, another to the Nordic ski jump, a third across the river to New College.

Other tendrils follow, each cast outward in a high arc like a fisherman's line, but to a new distance and in a new direction:

a) a tendril goes south-southeastward, to a point only three blocks away, the West Tree Public Hospital, where I was born;

b) another is flung across town, to 301 East Fourth Street, where my family lived for the first six years of my life;

c) a tendril goes to the Emerson School, to the steps of the north entrance, where I lost control of my bowels after school one day in 1948, when I was in second grade;

d) a tendril is flung three or four blocks to the south-southeast, to my grandmother's house at 917 Woodland Avenue, where on a Saturday morning two or three years from now, partly as a result of the smell that arises from the clothing of Dr. F. K. Kampfer, professor of physics and German at Old College, I will recognize for the first time that the past exists but that it isn't there;

e) and a tendril is flung a mile and three-quarters north-northeast, to the farm where my family moved from East Fourth Street and where, early one morning a year or so in the future from my visit to Marie and Lutie's bathroom, I will stumble upon my father sitting naked in a chair on the front lawn, with the result that I will be brought to face once again the inescapable fact that my destiny is to be that of a student of the mysteries of space and time, regardless of the unhappiness and sorrow that such a calling will, I know perfectly well, bring upon me unremittingly for the remainder of my life.

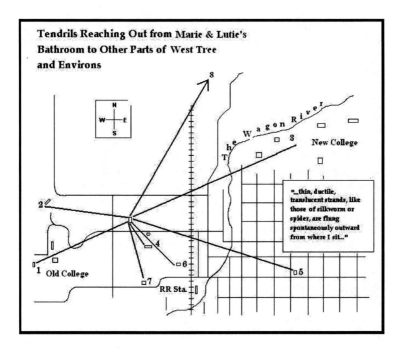

Tendrils Reaching Out from Marie & Lutie's
Bathroom to Other Parts of West Tree
and Environs

1)The House at Old College Where Marie & Lutie Once Lived
2)The Nordic Ski Jump
3)New College
4)The West Tree Hospital
5)Our House on Fourth Street
6)The Emerson School
7)My Grandmother's House
8)The Farm We Moved To

CHAPTER 2

MY LIFE BEGINS
(1847–1945)

1

I was born in late autumn, coming into the world on Sunday, November 30th, 1941, in the West Tree Public Hospital. The hospital was new, having been completed only two years before.

Having been born a minute or two before noon, I was almost exactly a week old when the Japanese launched their surprise attack on Pearl Harbor. My mother and I were discharged from the hospital late that Sunday morning, with the result that I was being carried through the doorway of my family's house on East Fourth Street at just about the moment bombs began falling on Pearl Harbor.

There is a photo of the five of us gathered in front of the house on this occasion. My parents are standing side by side, smiling with what pass for customary expressions of happiness and pride. My two sisters, meanwhile, have quite a different look about them. Each is pressed up shyly against the outside of a parent's leg as if they're thinking about slipping out of sight. In an odd sort of visual cacophony, no member of the family is the same size as another. My father, at six-four, towers over the scene as usual. The top of my mother's head reaches exactly to the bottom of his right earlobe. Hannah, not quite five years old, stands as high as my mother's waist, while Ingie's head comes even with my father's left knee. As for me, wrapped in a blanket and held in my mother's arms, I make up a bundle approximately the size of a loaf of bread.

The aim of this photo, presumably, was to capture the moment of my homecoming and therefore to commemorate the beginning of my life. But I think that it marks a turning point as much as it does a start. The truth about photographs, after all, is that, like plants, they have both roots and branches, although, instead of going down into the earth and up into the air, theirs go forward into the future and backward into the past. My homecoming photo is no different, hinting at the happiness and the sorrows extending off in each direction.

This thought comes to me partly—by no means only—because of the clothes that people are wearing in the photo. My mother, for example, has on a hat in the style of the 1920's. It is a kind of cloche, drawn down low onto the forehead so that my mother's eyes, which are dark, seem to peer out from among the shadows. My father also has on a hat, and he wears it with a similar hint of insouciance, the brim curved down dramatically on one side and ever so slightly up on the other. Then there are the coats everyone wears. My father's is a belted, heavy, voluminous affair with a turned-up collar, its thick fabric falling almost like drapery to a point well below the knees. My mother's coat is even longer. It goes down to her ankles and has a collar of dark fur that she wears turned up around her neck.

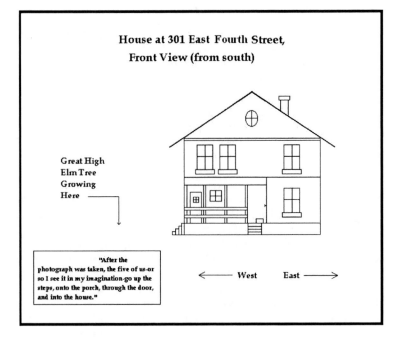

House at 301 East Fourth Street,
Front View (from south)

Great High
Elm Tree
Growing
Here

"After the photograph was taken, the five of us-or so I see it in my imagination-go up the steps, onto the porch, through the door, and into the house."

←———— West   East ————→

These hints of dash and flamboyance don't extend to my sisters. Their faces, by contrast with my parents', are guarded and suspicious. The way they stand, each leaning inward against an adult leg, makes them look rural, unworldly, and shy. Their coats, too, are unlike my parents'. Children grow fast and soon stretch the seams of their clothing, but even so, my sisters' coats have a look of the pawnshop about them. The flared shape and the hems that stop halfway above the knees make my sisters look like Christmas bells, and the strain of the fabric across the fronts where the buttons are pulled too tight has an inescapable look of the poor about it.

The photo, as far as the technical truth is concerned, dates from midday on December 7th, 1941. Following the broader truth about photographs, however, I estimate it to extend a decade or so to either side of that date, and perhaps farther. In any case, this would take it back at least, say, to 1931, which is two years before my parents' marriage and a time when I can easily imagine them buying the coats they wear. By the same token, the photo would reach forward to 1950 or 1951, a period that, having lived through it, I can speak of on the basis of direct experience. By 1950, my family would no longer live in West Tree, but in our farmhouse in the country. In that future period, the family would not have as much money as it did in 1941, this being in good measure due to my father's habit, as he steered less and less confidently through his middle life, of taking up one thing after another and continuing at none. Those years were to mark a period of unusual behavior in me as well, being the time when I began the practice of going into hiding during periods of anxiety, uncertainty, or doubt—periods of a kind that in that segment of my life were to be plentiful.

•

After the photograph was taken, the five of us went up the steps, onto the porch, through the door, and into the house.

2

My earliest memory took place in 1944, in August, in the afternoon, in the upstairs front corner bedroom of our house on East Fourth Street.

I'm certain that the month was August. This is because of the light, and the texture and timbre of sounds, and the particular quality of warmth in the air.

Most likely I had been sleeping, since, as the memory opened, I found myself lying on my bed. In the window that faced Fourth Street, the shade was drawn down all the way to the sill. Both windows were open. But at the second, the one that faced east and onto the side yard, the shade was pulled only halfway. I could tell, from the sound of voices that came in through that window, that my mother and sisters were there, in the side yard, up close to the house, talking among themselves.

•

By some trick of reflection, a pattern of light appeared on the ceiling of the room, as if sunshine were coming upward through leaves. Every now and then this arrangement of shadow and light stirred gently. I lay watching it for some time. As I did, I was conscious of the sound of the voices from below, and of the warmth and stillness that seemed to stretch out into the world everywhere around me for an indefinable and immeasurable distance.

•

Then, as abruptly as it began, the memory ended, and I fell back into nothingness and oblivion.

3

By the time I began looking out into life through the small and briefly opened windows of consciousness, the war had already caused a rearrangement in my family. It had done this by removing my father from home and placing him on a ship somewhere in the unknown reaches of the south Pacific.

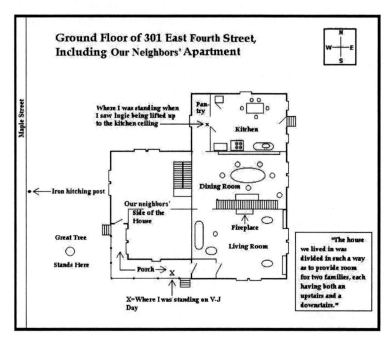

My father's departure constituted a change that was to have a measurable influence on my perception of myself later in life. His absence from home was obviously not the reason that I grew up to be a short, or relatively short, person. But I have no doubt that his being away from home at that time served in some degree to increase the self-consciousness I would later feel in regard to my size.

When he went away, in February of 1943, I was too young to retain any memory of him, so that my father's departure from home was a departure from my consciousness as well. On his return in the autumn of 1945, not only was he therefore a total stranger to me but he was an extremely large one as well. Tallness being a common trait on his side of the family, his own tallness would have been less intimidating to me, I'm sure, if I had had the experience, as would have been the case in normal times, of growing up with it on a daily basis. But instead I was presented with it, at the age of almost four, without preparation of any kind, all at once, and in its entirety.

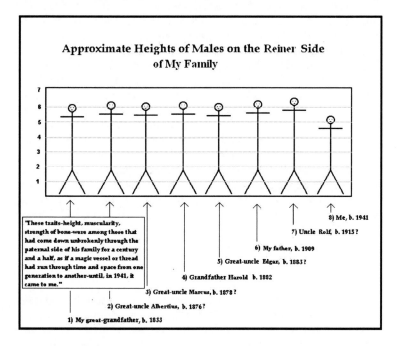

Approximate Heights of Males on the Reiner Side of My Family

"These traits—height, muscularity, strength of bone—were among those that had come down unbrokenly through the paternal side of his family for a century and a half, as if a magic vessel or thread had run through time and space from one generation to another—until, in 1941, it came to me."

1) My great-grandfather, b. 1833
2) Great-uncle Albertius, b. 1876?
3) Great-uncle Marcus, b. 1878?
4) Grandfather Harold b. 1882
5) Great-uncle Edgar, b. 1883?
6) My father, b. 1909
7) Uncle Rolf, b. 1915?
8) Me, b. 1941

Not only was my father tall, but he was also lean, and at the same time strong, neither skinny nor gangly. These admirable traits— height, muscularity, strength of bone—were among those that had come down through the paternal side of my father's family for at least a century and a half, as if an invisible hollow tendril containing them had run through time and space from one generation to another—until just the moment before it reached me, when it disappeared entirely.

In truth, I did inherit a fair share of my father's strength, although the bone and muscle I ended up with are a good lot shorter than those possessed either by my father or by my forebears. It became clear early in life that I was never going to be tall, and the height I reached by the start of ninth grade—five-six and a quarter—was the height I would keep until such time as I might begin shrinking in readiness for the grave.

•

My father, as I have said, was six-four, making him two inches taller than his own father, the original Harold Reiner and the one of my two grandfathers whom I never met, a consequence of his death by pneumonia in 1923, when he was forty-two. I did, however, meet his three surviving brothers a good number of times when they visited West Tree to call on my great-aunts Marie and Lutie, and I know from direct experience that all three of them were large, strong, and tall. The female side of the line was blessed with equivalent gifts, as typified by Marie and Lutie themselves. I never saw the remaining two sisters, my great-aunts Sigrid (born next after Lutie) or Ingeborg (the youngest of the eight), due to their having died in 1938 and 1927, respectively.

But, still, there are other examples of tallness. My great-grandfather Albertius Reiner was said to have stood half an inch under six feet even though he was born all the way back in 1831. And my father's younger brother, my uncle Rolf (the last of four siblings), rose to a record height of six-feet-six, growing an entire foot in one year alone, his fourteenth, which, as it happened, was 1929.

Finding yourself destined to smallness in the wake of giants is not a fate easily or happily dismissed, though the truly formative power of such a fate would be revealed to me only gradually, and in unexpected ways, as I made my way more deeply into the curious and difficult years of my life.

4

The first memory I have of my father is of seeing him lift my sister Ingie over his head so she could touch the kitchen ceiling.

I can't date this memory with perfect exactness, but there is an airiness and a pleasant autumnal warmth about it, and a sense of there being open windows and doors nearby.

The year, however, must be 1945, and the memory must have taken place shortly after my father's return from the war. This is another reason to place it in late autumn, perhaps toward the end of October or even early November.

•

Like all memories from this period of my life, it lasts only a second and has no suggestion of continuity with anything that might have preceded it or with anything that followed. I stand in the kitchen doorway looking up at my father looming over me, his arms raised, his hands around Ingie's ribs. Ingie, laughing with pleasure, arches her back and stretches upward. I remember the unusual sight of her two hands spread out against the smooth yellow paint of the ceiling.

•

If the faculty of memory is absent, a person is nothing, lacking even a way of knowing he exists. This is why achieving memory in early childhood is like passing through a series of small births and deaths.

•

The experience is universal. It follows a pattern known to everyone: At first you are blind and deaf, unexisting and nowhere. Then a sort of doorway opens and you gaze out into a scene of color, movement, and sound. But for only a second. Then the door closes as abruptly as it opened, and you are isolated again, blind, unhearing, nowhere, not existing.

•

In my own case, this phase of peering out into life and then being pulled back again into oblivion went on for a considerable time, whether longer than normal I don't know. Either way, it extended, with minor changes, from September 1945 into the early winter of 1948, when I was seven years old and had begun second grade.

There's no question but that, between the third and sixth years of my life, a great number of events took place that impinged on the later outcome of my life. Among these were major, widely known turning points such as the war's coming to an end. Then there were far smaller yet still highly influential changes: my family's moving to the farm, for example, and my starting first grade at the Emerson School. Beyond these, though, there remained also countless other events far, far more private, all but invisible to other people, yet profoundly revelatory to me in one significant way or another.

In fact it now seems to me—to touch for a moment on the heart of the matter—that events of the second type possess a significance that actually increases in proportion to the true extent of their privacy and hiddenness. The things least visible or least knowable to others—these are in fact the ones most important, invaluable, and far-reaching. In my own case, this would be true, for example, of my memory of the red pennies (which I haven't yet mentioned), and of the wooden counter downtown (also not yet mentioned). It would obviously be true as well of my memories of the blimp and train whistle. And without doubt it would be true of the time in second grade, in the winter of 1948, when, waiting for the bus after school, I couldn't hold my bowels any longer and lost control of them while sitting on the top step of the north entranceway of the Emerson School.

•

More significant than the memories themselves, whether visible or invisible, was the pattern revealed to me gradually through my accumulating consciousness of them. My early life, after all—just as with every member of universal humankind—contained within it the seed and the shape of my later one. As a result, my early achieving of memory introduced the themes, with all their blessings and sorrows, that were to form, shape, and direct the rest of my life.

The gaining of early childhood memory, thus, brought to me an awareness of the following themes, which I list here in what I believe to be the order I gained consciousness of them, although only in the case of the first is this an absolute certainty:

1)The theme of my smallness
2)The theme of space
3)The theme of time

5

I sometimes wonder what might have happened if the war had broken out at another time than it did, either earlier or later, and in what ways my life might have been changed as a result.

•

My father's return from the south seas, as I've mentioned, catalyzed the sensitivity toward my smallness that was to stay with me throughout my life. But something else about my father and the war also influenced my unfolding sense of self. This was the simple fact that my father had enjoyed his experience of the war very intensely indeed.

In later life, often when he had been drinking, although often enough also when he had not, my father lamented again and again the disappearance of the war years and the bracing wonders they had brought him of rigor, purpose, cleanliness, order, the firm and steady comradeship of men, and, not least, long voyages on the open seas to the farthest reaches of the earth.

•

When my father came back I wasn't yet four, so of course, at the time, I had no understanding of these things. But my father's sense of the war's having raised him, however briefly, to the very pinnacle of what life was capable of offering became only too clear to me over the next decade and a half of my life with him. In the middle and later years of the 1950's, there were many late evenings when my father, having devoted himself for a time to the lyricizing of his blood with gin, would hold forth until the small hours in long and tapestried lamentations for the promise, adventure, and opportunity that the war years had held and that, as my father grew older, had now slipped through his fingers like sand.

6

Over the years, I came by means of my father's monologues to know many details of his life in that long-ago war. Their meaning has undergone curious changes with their gradual withdrawal into an ever deeper past, but their historical—or perhaps their narrative—significance remains unchanged and calls for me to mention at least a relevant handful of them. That my father, for example, was commissioned as ensign in June of 1942, was promoted soon after to lieutenant junior grade, and left the war as lieutenant commander. That he served for slightly over three years as communications officer on transport ships. That although he was never wounded or injured, he sailed through two typhoons, came within range of enemy guns many times, served as offshore support during landing operations, and throughout his time at sea cruised in enemy waters. Twice, he saw ships in his convoy torpedoed and sunk. Afterward, standing at the rail, he saw bodies floating in the sea.

•

My own experiences from this period of history are fewer. They differ also in kind, although not in dimension, intensity, or significance.

Only two memories—not counting my somewhat later memory of V-J Day—can I identify with absolute certainty as having taken place during the war.

In one, I am standing in the side yard of our house, below the same bedroom window of my first memory, looking at two pennies that lie together on my open palm. They are wartime pennies, made without copper, and they are a dullish red. My sisters are with me, looking down at the coins on my hand. All around us there is sunshine.

There the memory ends. And as it does so, I, too, disappear again from existence.

•

In the second memory, I am walking downtown with my mother and sisters. The time must be early spring, since the light is thin, the sun coming through white watery clouds, and the air has the pleasantly fresh near-icy chill of April in it. Downtown, we go into the National Tea Company, where the wooden floors are unpainted, dark, and worn. It is wartime, I know for certain, because I remember watching my mother hand ration cards over the counter to the grocer.

7

The house we lived in was divided in such a way that two families could live in it, each having an upstairs and a downstairs.

Ours was the east side of the house. This meant that while one living room window and one bedroom window looked out over Fourth Street, all the rest (except for a pantry and a kitchen window in back) faced east, onto the side yard and toward the inside of the block.

Greta Nichols was the name of our house-neighbor. Her husband wasn't with her, but whether this was because of the war, separation, or divorce, I don't know. Greta had a daughter named Patricia, better known as Patty, who was six months younger than I.

Our neighbors' rooms were completely separated from ours, and except for one exception in front and one in back, all their windows faced west instead of east. No inside doorway joined the two apartments, and, aside from the basement, the only space in the house common to both was the front porch. The porch was shaped like a letter "L" fitted around the southwest corner of the house. Our front door was at the right-hand end of the base of the "L," theirs at the top of the upright leg. If a person came out of each apartment at the same time and walked straight ahead, the two would meet inside the elbow.

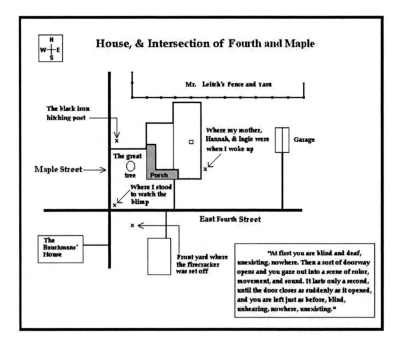

House, & Intersection of Fourth and Maple

Mr. Leitch's Fence and Yard

The black iron hitching post

Where my mother, Hannah, & Ingie were when I woke up

Garage

The great tree

Porch

Maple Street

Where I stood to watch the blimp

East Fourth Street

The Bauchmans' House

Front yard where the firecracker was set off

"At first you are blind and deaf, unexisting, nowhere. Then a sort of doorway opens and you gaze out into a scene of color, movement, and sound. It lasts only a second, until the door closes as suddenly as it opened, and you are left just as before, blind, unhearing, nowhere, unexisting."

The supporting post that stood in the angle of the elbow at the southwestern-most corner of the house, became especially meaningful to me later, after we'd moved away, because I came to think of it as having been the geographical center of my life from birth until the age almost of six.

When I thought back to that supporting post, I would think of strings being tied to it and then drawn out to extreme distances until each one made a connection to some other place with an important bearing on my life. One string, for example, stretched southwestward from the corner post to Honolulu. Another went in almost the same direction but stopped at Archer, Nebraska. A third went south-southeastward, to Columbia, Missouri, while a fourth extended almost due east, to the Bay Ridge section of Brooklyn, New York. Other strings, although more numerous, were much shorter. These reached out, for example, to the top of Old College Hill and the top of New College Hill, connecting with the bell tower that rose atop each college's oldest building.

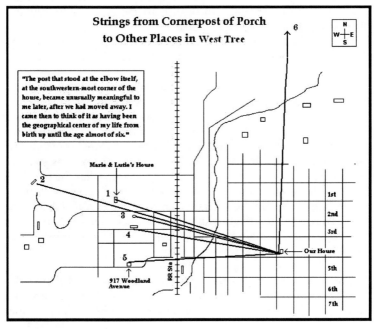

1) Marie & Lutie's House
2) Nordic Ski Jump
3) Wading Pool & Fountain
4) Hospital
5) My Grandmother's House
6 The Farm We Moved To

Other strings extended to the Nordic ski jump, to the kitchen table in my great-aunts' house on Christiania Avenue, to the back door of my grandmother's house at 917 Woodland Avenue, and to the entrance stairs on the north side of the Emerson School on West Third Street. Still another went north-northeastward (bending slightly as it rounded the house) to the farm we moved to, the string ending somewhere in the middle of the front yard there, near a swing made of a rope and an old tire, exactly at the point where, early one morning in 1950, I would stumble on my father sitting naked in a white wooden lawn chair, an experience I later understood as having provided a pivotal and crystallizing moment in the development of my perceptions of space and time.

•

My first memory with its setting on the front porch at Fourth Street, like other memories from this period, had no apparent continuity with anything that might have come before or after it. The memory was like looking suddenly and unexpectedly into a lighted room—into time— and then having that brief glimpse thrown just as suddenly again into darkness, as if a great eyelid had closed.

In the memory, I find myself with my back against the right angle formed by the porch railing, aware not of kissing Patty Nichols but of apparently just having kissed her.

In the two or three seconds that the memory made visible, I saw two women (one my mother, the other Patty's) standing near our own front door. Their heads just then went back in laughter. My sisters, at the same instant, ran away from me and toward them, calling out.

I have no memory of Patty herself in the moment, although I remember her generally well enough. I assume that she was standing beside me, but I have no image of her and no idea what she may have thought about the situation. As for myself, what remains is an unpleasant feeling of self-consciousness, a combination of confusion and embarrassment, as I hear the laughter of the mothers and watch my sisters run away from me, then glare back with accusing faces as they tug urgently at my mother's elbow.

•

The curtain fell, and the universe disappeared again. The only other thing I remember before I became nothing is that I saw the leaves of lilac bushes pressing against the porch railing, sunlight falling through them.

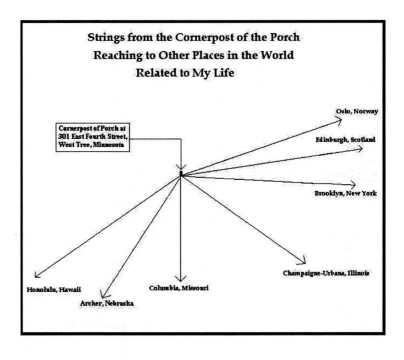

Strings from the Cornerpost of the Porch Reaching to Other Places in the World Related to My Life

Cornerpost of Porch at 301 East Fourth Street, West Tree, Minnesota

Oslo, Norway

Edinburgh, Scotland

Brooklyn, New York

Champaigne-Urbana, Illinois

Honolulu, Hawaii

Archer, Nebraska

Columbia, Missouri

8

By August of 1945, one might expect that I would have grown expert at memory. A full year had passed since I first saw a pattern of light on the ceiling and heard voices below the window. But the achievement of memory is unpredictable and slow, with setbacks occurring often. In my case, there were glaring inconsistencies in the effectiveness of my memory even as late as the autumn of 1945, when oceans of nothingness still surrounded the small islands of increasingly vivid memories that came to me. One of these is my memory of V-J day, which, although early, is almost as detailed as memories from a year or even two years later—similar in quality to my subsequent memories, for example, of the blimp, or of the train whistle, or of Harry Bachman's convertible, or Mr. Leitch's fishpond.

I have come to think of V-J Day as being a watershed memory. It by no means provided my first glimpse into time. But I think it may have been the first incident giving me evidence that time exists not only in one place but in all places simultaneously, throughout the entire cosmos at once.

•

I have been fastidiously careful, looking back into the beginning of my existence, to separate what I know I remember from what I may have been told afterward by others.

Throughout the day the war ended, as everyone knows, people waited for the news over their radios. I have no memory of this happening, however, or, for that matter, of anything else whatsoever from earlier that day. I can verify objectively that the day of radio-listening is a blank simply by noting, for example, that I have no memory whatsoever—not even now—of where the radio in our Fourth Street house may have been placed or what it looked like—as opposed, for example, to the radio later, in the kitchen of our farmhouse, or the one in my grandmother's house at 917 Woodland Avenue, with its neat little row of tuning buttons the size of pencil erasers and the color of ivory, on its table in the southeast corner of the dining room.

As to our Fourth Street radio, however, I draw a blank—I know nothing of its size, location, dial, buttons, knobs, or sound. Nor do I remember, whether from that radio or from any other source, actually hearing the news of the war's end when it finally did come. All I remember is being aware that the news had arrived.

Like most of the days of my life up to that point, Wednesday, August 15th, 1945, would remain completely non-existent if it weren't for the sliver of time that opened up toward evening, allowing me to become aware of myself at the railing of the porch near our front door. I looked out into existing time, I suppose, for three or four seconds, maybe five, certainly not more. Gazing into this opening, I recognized evening through the comfortably soft feeling in the still air and the pleasantly muted light that comes after suppertime. I knew also from the scent and softness of the air that the time of year was late summer. And I knew, of course, that I myself was there, at our porch railing, four or five feet from our open front door, near the wooden steps that went down to the yard.

None of these things, however, were what made the moment unusual. What made it unusual was this: events in it were taking place not just all at once, but all at once and also in separate locations.

The woman from the house east of ours, and another from across Fourth Street and up one, along with her two children, were standing on their front porches cheering while at the same time beating spoons on the upturned bottoms of cooking pots. Through our own front door, I could look in and see my mother. She sat on the ottoman, leaning forward with her elbows on her knees, sobbing convulsively with her face buried in her hands, while Hannah and Ingie moved and fussed around her, touching her uncertainly on the shoulders and head and stroking her hair. The two high school boys who lived right across Fourth Street, Victor and Dexter Easdon, had come outdoors with the intent of setting off a firecracker. Their lawnmower had been left in the middle of the yard, and they balanced the firecracker on the waffled iron rim of one of its wheels. I remember the way their heads came together as they bent over the firecracker, and then, as the fuse threw off its spray of tiny white sparks, the way they quickly withdrew from it, going backward with big steps in two different directions.

Through the evening air around me fell the melodies of churchbells, woven into a curious disorder. From downtown, two blocks west, came the sound of honking horns. Then the shutter fell, silence and darkness returned, and the universe once again ceased to be.

9

The house we lived in was built in 1908, although of course I knew this only long after we had left it.

Our side was larger than our neighbors' and extended farther back than theirs, so that there was one place in the house where we had windows on both east and west. The narrow side room at the back that served as pantry and also as a passage from the dining room into the kitchen was where we had the one west window. Its walls were wainscoted with tongue-and-groove strips. Possibly they had been varnished once, but by the time we lived there, everything from the baseboard up was painted the same light yellow as the kitchen. It was here, looking through the kitchen door with the west window just behind me, that I saw my father lift Ingie up to the ceiling.

When we were outdoors, as I've mentioned, we spent most of our time in the side yard, or on the porch, or in the "front" yard, by which we meant that part of the lawn running along Fourth Street rather than Maple. I do remember going around the corner onto the other leg of the front yard, although rarely, since it was thought of as properly belonging to our neighbors.

A great elm stood near the porch steps on their side of the yard, a tree large enough that the earth sloped up toward its trunk from a considerable distance all around. Because of the deep shade there, the grass on this side of the house was thinner and more fine than elsewhere. Our neighbors' side had actually once been the front of the house. Not only did they have a pair of very large windows in their living room facing west onto the porch, and a stained-glass transom over their front door, but at the curb on Maple Street there stood an old iron hitching post once intended for the convenience of visitors arriving by horse and buggy.

The hitching post was painted black and had an iron ring at its tip that I enjoyed lifting up in order to let it fall down again with a clink against one side of the post or the other. My first memory of my great-aunts

Marie and Lutie is from a summer afternoon when I was standing by the hitching post as they walked past on their way to visit my mother.

The grass underfoot was burned and dry. My father was still away, I'm certain. The feeling of great antiquity that lingers in the memory makes me place it in late July or early August of 1945.

Marie and Lutie approached from the north, walking on Maple Street from Third. In the memory I didn't become aware of them until they were perhaps ten or twelve arm-lengths away. I stood looking at them as they came nearer. As always, they walked side by side. As always, they wore dresses of a thin dark material, open at the neck, belted loosely at the waist, the hems coming down halfway below their knees. As always, they walked in near-unison, with a hint of industry in their steps that fell just short of haste but had about it an air of something greater than ordinary determination. They walked with their heads bent forward slightly, as if they were engaged in a conversation with each other, although a conversation in which neither of them was saying anything, but both instead were listening attentively.

•

I have no other memory of Marie and Lutie ever being at our house on Fourth Street. I learned later, though, that during the war they made a point, every third or fourth week, of walking across town to call on my mother.

•

By the time of this memory, Marie was sixty-eight, Lutie sixty-one. They stopped in front of me and bent down where I stood in the sunlight, on the dry grass, beside the hitching post that, I remember, felt warm from the sun when you touched it.

•

I don't remember what they said, or how long they stood there, leaning with their faces bent down toward mine. But I remember watching them walk away from me, in an image that I understand now was a glimpse through a hole in time.

Having thought back on it countless times, I suppose that a certain kind of perfected or ideal version of that moment may have emerged. But whether this is so or not, I swear that I am faithful to the concrete truth and detail of what I saw that afternoon.

I stood by the hitching post and watched them move away from me to the corner, make the left turn onto Fourth Street, then continue toward the walkway that would take them up onto the porch and then to the front door of our house.

In the memory, as their twin figures move away from me, there is no sound. The afternoon is quiet, the air warm, sunlight falling in leaf-shadow patterns on the cracked squares of the old sidewalk.

•

Not until years later was I to understand what actually happened that moment or how profoundly it would shape and nurture the rest of my life: the fact that one summer afternoon when the world was on the edge of changing forever, my great-aunts passed by, side by side, in long dark dresses, their heads bent slightly forward, one of them—it was Lutie, I'm certain—carrying a cloth-covered basket on her arm.

I know now that at that moment they were not simply my two great-aunts, but a window for me to see through—with the result that, for a brief moment in the summer of 1945, when I was almost four years old, standing near the curb, on the grass, by the hitching post, I looked back through them into the nineteenth century, and was changed forever.

CHAPTER 3

TIME AND SPACE
(1857–1947)

1

In the six years from my birth until the autumn of 1947 I have only two substantially detailed memories of my father. The first, as I said, was watching him lift Ingie up to the kitchen ceiling. In the second—which logically can be placed only in the summer of 1946 or possibly 1947—I am leaning against our car on a gravel road as my father takes a photograph. He stands some distance away, out in a field of tall grass. A black cloth covers his head and shoulders as he leans forward over a wooden tripod.

•

Here is something I have little reason to doubt: that my scarcity of memory is due to unconscious repression caused by
anxiety resulting in turn from my heightened sense of inadequacy due at least in part to my smallness.

The human mind speaks through what it forgets as well as through what it remembers.

•

My memory overall, however, became steadily more active over this period, in keeping with the increased pace of my sensory maturing in general.

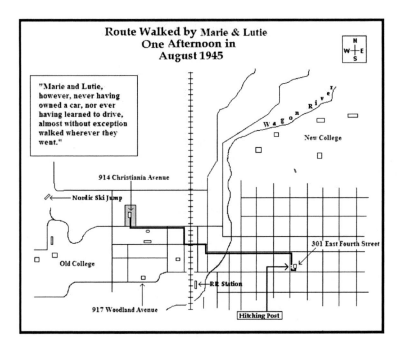

Route Walked by Marie & Lutie
One Afternoon in
August 1945

N
W—E
S

"Marie and Lutie,
however, never having
owned a car, nor ever
having learned to drive,
almost without exception
walked wherever they
went."

Wagon River

New College

914 Christiania Avenue

Nordic Ski Jump

301 East Fourth Street

Old College

RR Station

917 Woodland Avenue

Hitching Post

After my fourth birthday, I began to remember things more frequently, though not yet with any greater extension through time: my memories remained brief, fragmentary, and unconnected with anything coming before or after them.

At the same time, memory did take on one new quality that was to prove of great importance to the development of my life: that is to say, near this time, memory began to provide me with a consciousness of space.

•

Again, the change may have been simply a consequence of maturation in my sensory life, merely a result of my progressively increasing consciousness of color, shape, atmosphere, texture, scent, temperature, and sound. Either way, I know that memories in this period became deeper, wider, and higher than before. It wasn't just that they contained more space or had wider angles of vision, but something more important began taking place in them, something that itself had two logical aspects. To speak very precisely, my memories from this time made me conscious of these two principles:

1) that not just a single place existed at a single time, but that all places existed all the time;

2) and that events, however unrelated from one another they might seem to be, could nevertheless occur at identically the same moments in an infinity of locations.

2

This seemingly minor and obvious development in the nature of my memory was a major turning point in my life and inexpressibly important.

Being aware of existence's occurrence simultaneously in entirely discrete parts of space brought with it immediately an expanded and heightened self-consciousness. The reasoning is as follows:

1) If a person exists in one place but is intensely aware of another, he will be unable not to imagine his existence in that other place.

2) He will, therefore, "see" himself existing elsewhere.

3) As a result, he will have remained no longer only inside the self, looking out through the holes that are in it, but he will find himself to have moved outside of the self, and to be looking back at it.

4) This means that when feeling enters into memory, the rememberer and the thing remembered will have become, in some sense, one and the same.

•

Memory therefore was to be an eye for me. Through it, I would see

1) the enormity of the past;
2) the tone, color, texture, and feel of history;
3) the revealed mysteries of space and time.

3

What I had begun to see was a quality that in fact had been present in all of my memories from the beginning. The difference now lay in my heightened consciousness of it and therefore in the increased emphasis it received.

Obviously, at the age I'd reached by this time, I couldn't yet begin to understand much of what inevitably lay in waiting for me to learn: the near-inconceivable complexity of the relationships among things in space, for example, a complexity that, further, increases not arithmetically but exponentially in proportion to the number of things themselves.

That was something for later, although neither could it be set aside entirely, for whatever length of time, since it was already a part of my consciousness (however shadowy and dim in recollection) and was destined furthermore to constitute, as indeed it has, so vital and ineludible a part of my life.

•

Of memories from this period immediately after the war, I've made mention of the blimp, train whistle, Mr. Bauchman's convertible, and Mr. Leitch's goldfish pond. Of these, the blimp and goldfish pond are the best examples of my emerging consciousness of vertical relationships. The convertible and train whistle are those most successful for the horizontal.

•

Our house was surrounded by lawn on three sides but not at the back, the reason being that only two or three feet of space remained between the back of the house and the property line at the rear. That line itself was identified by an imposing fence made of upright iron bars between brick sentinel-posts that stood at intervals of every ten feet or so. Growing along this fence on its far side was a thick, green, impenetrable hedge.

This barrier stood between our property and that of Mr. Leitch, who was whispered to be a millionaire. Whether he was one or not, I know I was afraid of him because of his reclusiveness, his living by himself, and his reputation for not liking children.

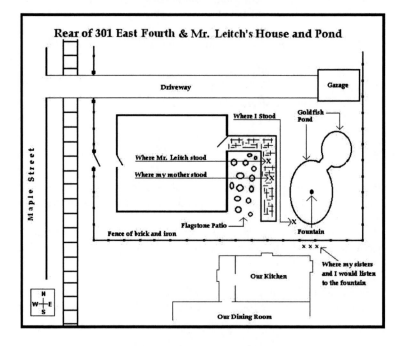

Whether he really disliked them, I don't know, although I'm sure that the notion of his being an eater of children was given color and innuendo mainly by Hannah whenever she had a chance to scare me by weaving those fears into some new story of her own devising. Mr. Leitch's house, like the sentinel-posts of his fence, was made of red brick, and it had a tile roof and leaded-pane windows. Once, as I passed by on Maple Street going toward Third, on the way to my maternal grandmother's house, I saw him peering out from an upstairs window. I was alone at the time, and I remember being frightened enough to turn my face and run.

The most alluring thing about Mr. Leitch, on the other hand, was the sound of water from his back yard—the deliciously cool, enticing burble of water falling onto the surface of the goldfish pond from the fountain at its center. How I knew there was a fountain before I'd seen it myself, I don't know, although I expect, again, that Hannah, in her three-and-a-half-year advantage over me, had been taken to visit it already and afterward took any opportunity to spin its charms into something even lovelier than the reality. I remember the three of us huddling in the green darkness at the back fence and listening to the sound of the water through the hedge. Those were the moments, doubtless, when Hannah would whisper her golden stories.

When I was taken to see the pond, I remember my mother being with me, but neither Hannah, nor Ingie, nor my father. I know that my father was at home again by this time. Therefore the memory comes from the small window between the end of the war and our move out of town two years later.

Of Mr. Leitch, I remember only that he stood on the brick patio behind my mother as I looked at the pond, that he had thin hair, sunken eyes, long legs, pale trousers, and smooth white shoes. I have no memory of what was said, either by Mr. Leitch or by my mother. I don't remember the beginning of the visit or its end. And I don't remember going inside Mr. Leitch's house, the probability being that we came by way of the driveway that ran along its north side.

Of the pond, however, I can recall every detail and curve, every aspect of shape and light and shadow, every color and even every scent. The back yard itself struck me as disappointingly small, perhaps because of the lush greenery pressing in from every direction except along the patio. The patio was also made of red brick, and a path led from it out to the pond, which was shaped like a crude figure eight, a brick path forming a walkway all around it. I suppose that the pond, at its widest point, must have been eight or ten feet across.

A miniature wooden bridge spanned the narrow waist between the two parts of the eight. Lily pads lay on the water's surface, and a short pipe stood upright in the center of each pool, water emerging with just enough pressure to rise a few inches into the air before falling down and making the pleasant sound that we had heard so many times through the hedge.

But most overwhelming in the interest they held for me were the goldfish themselves. Some were huge, ten or twelve inches long, while others were half that size and many a very great deal smaller. Under the water, the largest lay still, only their gills opening and closing, their stabilizer fins moving almost indiscernibly now and then for a fine adjustment of position. Sometimes, on the other hand, the fish would glide suddenly, as if without effort, through the water, disappearing into the darkness under the lily pads. At still other times, with casual flicks of their tails, they would cross the entire pond, then settle down majestically in the darker water along the bottom or in a far corner, frightening away groups of little fish in the process, all of whom would swerve in unison as they swam away from the big, passing fish.

4

I'm certain I was taken to see the pond only once—possibly because Mr. Leitch really didn't like children. But it doesn't matter. What I saw in his back yard is in no way less memorable, in no way less formative either intellectually or epistemologically, for what may have been his dislike of me. My visit, as I said, took place either in 1946 or 1947. I am inclined for a number of reasons to put it in the earlier year, as I am strongly inclined to do also with my memory of the blimp. On the other hand, I have not the least doubt whatsoever that the train whistle and Mr. Bauchman's convertible belong to 1947.

•

Since my memory of the blimp took place one summer afternoon, it has about it—being so different in tone from the memory of the goldfish—a vivid brightness and simplicity, along with a wonderful cleanness of atmosphere and sky. Missing from it, at the same time, are complications like those brought about by the presence of Mr. Leitch himself and my uncertainty about his feelings. Unlike the goldfish pond, the blimp simply appeared unexpectedly in the sky, made its oddly sluggish way overhead, and then, far more quickly than I would ever in a hundred years have wished, disappeared from sight.

•

I was in the front yard, playing one sort of game or another with Hannah and Ingie, when we first heard its low, slightly wavering drone. Trees obscured any view of it at the beginning. Hannah was the first to spot it from where she stood on the lawn, facing southwest, looking up, her arm raised and her finger pointing. For some time I saw nothing through the canopied leaves of the great maples and elms over Fourth Street. But then the blimp, already approaching the zenith, broke into open view above the intersection and was plainly visible—fat, soft, huge, droning, slow, as if just out of arm's reach above the trees, hanging miraculously in the air against a cloudless, perfect, clear blue sky.

For reasons unknown to me, the sight of the blimp immediately released a surge of hilarity in my sisters that caused them to join hands and twirl in circles on the lawn, singing snatches of familiar songs in excited voices as the blimp floated overhead. Almost a perfect opposite of them, I was driven instead by a compelling desire to be as still as possible and simply stare up at the blimp for every conceivable last second that it would remain in view. From my spot near the southwest corner of the lawn, without taking my eyes from it, I crossed the sidewalk going backward, then inched my way backward farther, to the very edge of the curb, where I stood craning my neck and rising up on my toes in an effort to keep this inexplicable and remarkable object in sight. I watched as it glided wonderfully and hugely above our house, keeping to its northeastward course, not even beginning to diminish in size before it escaped from my view. It disappeared behind dense green foliage like a coin going through a slit in a piece of paper.

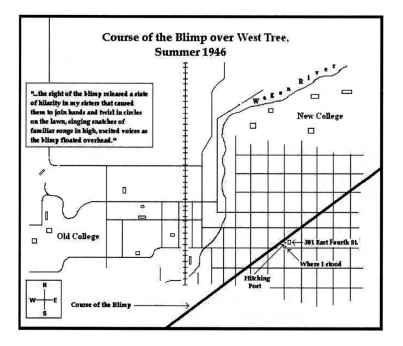

Course of the Blimp over West Tree, Summer 1946

"...the sight of the blimp released a state of hilarity in my sisters that caused them to join hands and twirl in circles on the lawn, singing snatches of familiar songs in high, excited voices as the blimp floated overhead."

Wager River

New College

Old College

301 East Fourth St.

Where I stood

Hitching Post

N
W—E
S

Course of the Blimp ⟶

5

At this time in West Tree's history, a vestige of frontier law remained in effect, making illegal the buying or selling of intoxicating drinks inside the city limits. The one exception to this rule had to do with beer of a certain designated alcoholic content, which was allowed for sale in bars by the glass.

In the countryside surrounding West Tree, a number of small communities found means to turn this archaic restriction to a benefit for themselves. Most such villages or towns consisted of little more than a store, gas station, church, and three or four houses. Usually there was also a bar and grill, however, or a farmers' saloon that offered both on-sale and off-sale, and there would be the assurance of a small but always steady trickle of commerce from West Tree as people drove out into the countryside for supplies of liquor to take back home with them again.

Alcohol was to play a large part in my own life—as it certainly did in my parents'—and it seems fitting enough that it should have been responsible, at least in part, for the earliest memory that created in me a horizontal consciousness sufficiently broad and deep to prove formative and lasting.

This, of course, was the memory of riding in Mr. Bauchman's convertible to the town of Gaylord one summer night, for liquor. As mentioned, I place the memory in 1947 rather than 1946. And as for my placing it specifically in the month of August, I do so because of the air.

•

The ride started out in the evening, when daylight was already giving way to slowly encroaching darkness. The air sweeping over us in Mr. Bauchman's car brought with it a scent more varied and lovely than any imaginable perfume. In it were the sweetness of cut hay and ripening corn, the dry, golden, straw-scent of cropped grain fields, the myriad other smells of approaching harvest: apples, alfalfa, summer foliage, ripening fruits, all along with the faint tang now and then of manure, and always the slightly sweet, soft, full smell of earth itself, coming sometimes from places where the soil was damp and therefore black- and leaf-smelling, as in the valley bottoms, but most of the time coming from the broad flanks and hills of open fields, where the earth was dry and slightly crumbling and still faintly warm.

(I know now that this—the air itself, in its perfumed, oceanic, all-embracing existence—is what would later awaken my earliest consciousness of the interconnectedness of all places, all people, and all things.)

•

I have no memory of arriving in Gaylord, or of waiting in the car while Mr. Bauchman went into the corner tavern, or of the return to West Tree. All I remember is starting out from the curb in front of the

Bauchmans' house, which stood diagonally across the intersection from our own; driving out of town across the bridge that we called the "viaduct"; and then, for an unknown length of time, being on the open road. The sun had just set, and colors were fading out of things everywhere, turning them to monochrome.

•

I remember, before we even drew away from the curb, the unpleasant fact of being too short to see over the sides of the car. I was so low down that I wasn't able to look at nearby things, only more distant ones.

•

I was pressed uncomfortably against the right side of the car by my sisters and three of the Bauchman sons, all squeezed into the back seat. The three Bauchman sons were all older than I was, and therefore bigger, and one of them was older even than Hannah.

The two seats in front, unlike those in our own car, were separated from one another instead of forming a bench. Mr. Bauchman sat behind the wheel. On Mrs. Bauchman's lap sat the one son younger than I was, along with the family's single daughter, then not quite two.

•

I had no idea of it then, but I'm certain now that my father must have disapproved of our riding that way, in so crowded a car. I'm certain that he must have been disapproving also, though more inwardly, of our going on the trip at all, because of his feelings about the character of the Bauchmans.

Mr. Bauchman owned a drug store downtown and, unlike my father, remained devoted to a single thing until it turned out well. In the next decade, he was to open stores in two other towns and move his family to a much larger house in another part of West Tree.

I liked the Bauchmans and envied the festive untidiness and disorder in their lives, although it's true that sometimes I also slightly disliked those same things. I remember hearing the older brothers, from all the way across the intersection, screaming at each other inside the house near suppertime and often again at bedtime. They left their scooters and wagons and other playthings in the yard, and I remember the shabby look of it, especially when the grass began growing up around them, emerging between spokes and through the wickerwork of baskets.

Still, I envied the feeling, which I sensed whenever I went to their house, of there being so much life among them, and I envied the children's being allowed, at least to a great extent, to do as they wanted. Freedom of such a kind had never been a part of life at our own house, and years later I would realize that in a certain way the expressiveness of life at the Bauchmans' house had been my first exposure to anything, excepting my great-aunts Marie and Lutie themselves, in the least way exotic.

•

I expect that my father, in truth, was envious of Mr. Bauchman, with his good-natured impetuousness and his generosity, his cheerfulness and seemingly easy-going way of getting along through life. If we walked downtown after supper and stopped in at his drug store, Mr. Bauchman would give us free ice cream cones, insisting that we accept them. This flamboyance and generosity must have been difficult for my father, who was preternaturally incapable of remaining relaxed, natural, or unconstrained either when giving things away or receiving them—a trait that can have come to him only from some unknown place deep in the lineage of his own family.

•

In every way, Mr. Bauchman was different from my father. Even while driving, he still wore the white shirt and tie from his working day, and for most of the trip, the tie fluttered over his left shoulder. He was slightly shorter than Mrs. Bauchman, and he drove with his chin raised up in order to see over the car's long hood. I liked Mrs. Bauchman very much. Her hair was thick and black like my own mother's, she kept it pinned up loosely from her neck, and she wore long earrings.

Of the trip itself, beyond what I've mentioned, and beyond riding across the viaduct over the railroad tracks, and beyond being on the open road then for a certain time, and beyond becoming aware for the first time in my life of my horizontal consciousness, I remember nothing whatsoever.

•

We would never have gone on the ride, I'm sure, or probably never have been invited, if it hadn't been for the open car.

•

Our own car was a 1941 Ford coupé, small and two-doored. In back, there were only two drop-seats, but my father had laid a cut piece of board across them so I could sit in the middle between Hannah and Ingie.

The triangular windows in back didn't open. Air had a hard time flowing through the car, making it often stuffy.

In the Bauchmans' convertible, on the other hand, air was all around. In their car, with the top down, we were immersed in the air, in the plenitude, depth, and fullness of it, like fish swimming in an ocean miles deep and as big as the world.

The car made its way up one hill and then down another. The air eddied, moved, and swirled.

•

When it happened, I had no words for it, either silent or spoken. It didn't occur to me to think about words.

Like all the other memories up to this period of my life, after taking place it existed solely as image, sensation, and feeling. Only many years later would the question of words arise at all.

•

Mr. Bauchman's convertible was white.

•

Imagine someone in a blimp or light airplane one summer evening in 1947. Far below, they see an open car with ten people in it traveling northeast from West Tree. It follows a narrow blacktop highway across gently rolling hills covered by farmland and punctuated here and there with stands of trees. No other cars are in sight. The highway takes the white car down one low hill and then up the next. From the sky, the car has a way of looking industrious, and the person viewing it from there imagines it working hard to achieve what looks like small progress.

•

In the low spots, the air became chill, then grew pleasantly warm again as we drew up the next hill.

(I would have this same experience four or five years later, riding out with my father on the tractor just before dark to close the chicken houses on the range. On the way back, as we came down from the warmth of the hilltop into the darkening pasture-bottom, there would be the chill of the air that had already flowed down and settled there.)

•

It's possible that what I remember isn't from the trip going out to Gaylord, but is a scrap of memory from the return, when the hour was later, the evening darker, the air cooler. Perhaps what happened is that I fell asleep in my corner of the back seat, propped up by Hannah squeezed beside me. But even if I did move in and out of sleep, I'm certain, even so, that the pieces of memories I do have are accurate and exact. I remember specifically the air, the changes in its scent with the alternating warm places and cool places on the road, then too the feeling of the car moving up and down the hills. And I know with equal certainty that I remember specifically the sense that came to me suddenly—vivid, clear, immediate, powerful, and real—of all circumferent things extending outward around us on a horizontal plane: the road itself, the hills along the road, then other hills beyond those, and still others beyond those. The car would go up one, down another, while the landscape radiated outward around us in every direction and continued doing so, would always do so. Behind us was Gaylord. Ahead was West Tree. And in West Tree, I knew, would be the railroad bridge, then two or three blocks of downtown buildings, then tree-lined streets and sidewalks, with the streetlights shining under canopied foliage, and then our street, and the Bauchmans' house, and, across the intersection, in the gathered shadows, our own house, and our own porch, and our own door.

6

The last memory from this period of my life that had a direct bearing on my awakening consciousness of space is my memory of hearing the train.

Unquestionably simple, the memory nevertheless, with its strongly unifying effect, marks the natural end of a major period of development and points the way toward what was to follow.

•

I place it, again, at a point very late in my family's remaining time in West Tree. It came after the car ride to Gaylord, I know. And I know also that it took place before October tenth of that same year, 1947, since the tenth was the day we moved out of our house and went to live on the farm.

As for the memory's exact place between those points: from what I remember of the scent, warmth, and stillness of the air, and of the feel, texture, and tone of the sounds, I place it either in the fourth week of September or late in the third.

•

I heard the train from the southeast corner bedroom upstairs, the same place where, three years earlier, I'd had my earliest memory, of the pattern of light on the ceiling and voices below the window.

The second time around, here is what happened: I woke in the silence of the deepest part of the night and heard the whistle of the train as it came into town, stopped briefly at the station, then set out again, making its way northward.

•

I don't know what woke me, any more than I know what woke me the first time, in 1944, in the afternoon, when I heard voices under the window.

This time there were no voices, sounds, movement, not the least conceivable thing stirring. I woke into the deepest, most silent hour of the night. No sound came from anywhere, neither from inside the house nor out, not even from Hannah or Ingie, sleeping in their beds across the room. The streetlamp, from where it hung over the middle of the intersection, threw a narrow swath of light across the wall. Except for that, the room was darkness and shadow.

•

This is what I think now: that those few waking minutes were balanced, harmonious, and perfect; that there had been no time in my life before that, and has been none since, when I remembered, or remember, feeling more sheltered, secure, protected, and calm than I did then, in our house, in West Tree, in my bed, in the dark, waiting (though I didn't yet know it) to hear the train.

•

I didn't move. I did nothing but listen and wait. I knew the strength of what I was feeling because I could sense it radiating outward from me, then returning back toward me, from the stillness of the night that reached out everywhere, to the horizons, and then beyond.

•

Again, I associated no words with any of this, nor did I have any sense of their absence, not the least need, feeling, or desire for them.

Admittedly, such an absence made this way of experiencing life a primitive, untutored, solitary one. But from it I gained, even so, a heightened consciousness of the complexity of the relationships among all things. And because of this consciousness, I was to be drawn all the sooner to my life's vocation of pondering the ineffable fact that all things in all places are governed equally and simultaneously by the impenetrable, fundamental, inexplicable, and shaping powers of space and time.

•

From the goldfish suspended motionlessly in the water, then from the blimp hung against a cloudless sky, I received an early awareness of the great range that things in the world could reach on the vertical axis. In the Bauchmans' car, and then in the night hearing the train enter West Tree and depart from it again, I gained an equally strong consciousness of the enormous breadth that was available for things to achieve on the horizontal: as the train, moving out of the station, then out of the town, then through the open farmland until it disappeared, drew my consciousness with it, past the railroad bridge, past the farm we were to move to, then beyond the farm, moving farther and farther northward, into silence.

•

(That night, after the train had gone, I fell back asleep. In the entire universe, no one was aware that I had been awake; that I had taken in the scent of the night; that I had heard the train.)

7

With the result that I discovered in myself an understanding of the nature of life and the study of it—at least insofar as these might have to do with the horizontal and the vertical.

What I didn't know, however, or what I knew but at an insufficiently conscious level to incorporate it yet into my thinking, was this:

1) That if things are capable of appearing (which I knew them to be),

2) then they must be capable also of disappearing (which I knew as well).

3) These two facts, once accepted as true, can never become untrue, not even

a) if the things that appear and disappear exist in a vertical relationship with other things, or

b) if the things that appear and disappear exist in a horizontal relationship with other things, or

c) if the things that appear and disappear exist at a single point in space, or

d) if the things that appear and disappear exist in extension through space, or

e) if the things that appear and disappear exist at a single point in time, or

f) if the things that appear and disappear exist in extension through time.

4) Consequently, it is impossible to prevent the disappearance of things, even through the closest study of their relationships both through and within space and time; and

5) therefore, in conclusion, no matter how hard one might attempt to avoid its being the case, the study of time and space is destined to become, in the end, the study of sorrow.

8

And so I come to the conclusion of this, the first period of my life, at a point not far distant from the end of my fifth year. I have tried, in looking back, to make as clear as possible how it is that I came to be a scholar of space and time, and a scholar therefore also, as I have suggested, of history.

Because history is the only true product of space and time. In the years to come, West Tree (in the short remaining time before its disappearance altogether) was to be a window I would look through into the past, finding testament there to the integrity, completeness, and harmony that history, in at least one brief, fleeting period, had been capable of achieving.

Beyond that, my story was destined, as all lives are, to become a thing of loss as much as of desire.

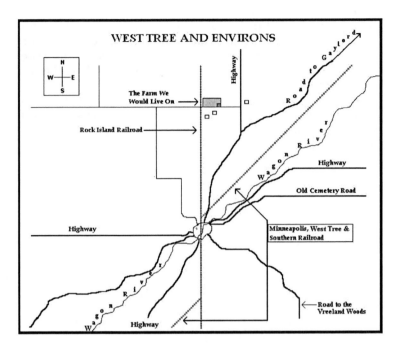

WEST TREE AND ENVIRONS

The Farm We
Would Live On →

Rock Island Railroad →

Highway

Highway

Old Cemetery Road

Minneapolis, West Tree &
Southern Railroad

Highway

← Road to the
Vreeland Woods

Highway

•

On the night of the train whistle, however, when I woke up in my bed, in my room, in the night, to hear the train's arrival and then its disappearance past one road-crossing after another, blowing its whistle at each, I didn't yet know that this was to be so. If I assumed anything then about the outcome of my life, it was that I would go on being a part of all things around me, as all things would go on being a part of me. The foundation for such a hope, without question, was firmly in place. Just as surely as I had seen a pattern of light on the ceiling one warm, quiet, long-ago afternoon; as surely as I had gazed down at the enormous goldfish gliding effortlessly in the lily-ed water of their pond; as surely as I had seen the majestic white blimp hung against the blue sky; had ridden in the Bauchmans' car through an unmoving but undulant landscape; had held red pennies in my hand, gone downtown on a watery April day; seen Marie and Lutie walking away from me to the corner; heard the voices of churchbells woven through the evening; watched a firecracker go off across the street; seen my mother weeping; or watched Ingie being lifted to the ceiling: just as surely as these things had happened, and had had meaning, there would also, as my life continued, be other events, turning-points, and moments that would show me how I, too, like those whose lives had come and gone before mine, would enter into the deep and sustaining current of history, would become a part of history: my life, waterdrop falling into ocean, in this way entering into and becoming a part of all other places, all other things, all other times, all other lives that had ever been, or were, or ever were to be.

•

Or so, for a time, I truly believed; then hoped for; not long afterward wished; subsequently doubted; and now despair of entirely.

SECTION II

MY EARLY LIFE
COMES TO A CLOSE

CHAPTER 4

THE HISTORY OF
WEST TREE, MINNESOTA
(1857–1953)

PART I
I LOOK INTO THE
HISTORY OF WEST TREE

1
WINDOWS

As clearly as I am able to tell, West Tree reached its most perfect historical period sometime after the close of 1915 but before the beginning of 1923. At whatever precise instant the new era's initial moment actually occurred within that span, it was clearly an event of great importance, marking the start of an extraordinarily desirable condition that the town proved itself capable of sustaining for an impressive length of time. Only in 1949—or possibly as much as a year after that, though no more—did the first signs appear of what was very soon to become a steep decline, leading ultimately, as is well known, to the destruction and disappearance of the town altogether.

•

Through the fact of my having been born in 1941, the early part of my childhood overlapped with the last handful of those years still belonging to West Tree's most historically significant era. Given this timing, it was unsurprising that I was to become aware, later on, of having lived through the last moments of an era that, only after it was gone, came to be perceived as invaluable, irreplaceable, and unique.

•

I often think that from the very moment of my birth I must have possessed a heightened awareness of the past. Of course as an infant I couldn't have had any such thing, but by the time I was six or seven, my sense of the world as being composed solely of the past (which of course, in truth, it is) had already begun evolving toward a consistent and objective consciousness. And by the time I was eleven, twelve, or thirteen, it had grown into an omnipresent and ineradicable aspect of my life.

•

In the years of my early adolescence, there existed innumerable aspects, features and places of and in West Tree that provided windows for me to see through, into the past. These included, for example, objects as varied as the wooden paving blocks still remaining in some areas of downtown, on the one hand, and the pitted iron railing (erected there in 1854) on the crest of Old College Hill, on the other. Or they included everything from the smooth deep flow of the river as it curled over the lip of the mill dam to the way the air smelled when it came from the southwest in the sweetest part of a warm autumn, or from the early sound of church bells on lilac-infused spring mornings to the taste of root beer floats in Harry Bauchman's drug store or the way sunlight looked when it flowed down through dense leaves to splash brokenly on old sidewalks in July and August.

Simply to name all such windows, let alone describe them, would approach the impossible. But here, even so, is a list of some of the moments, things, and places that I now think were in one way or another typical, and typically influential, in bringing me in my adolescent years toward an increasingly precise and complete understanding of the world as a creation of the past (and to an understanding, although not immediately, of what place I might expect to have in that world).

Being by its nature arbitrary and to some necessary degree partial and selective, the list nevertheless offers a real and practical usefulness by its inclusion of:

1) My grandmother's house at 917 Woodland Avenue (similar if not almost identical in style to my great-aunt Marie and Lutie's house on Christiania Avenue)

2) The back yard of my grandmother's house, which extended deep into the center of the block, with trees, hedges, and swing; the part of the yard nearer to the house, most significantly with its picnic table

and, at the northwest corner of the house and providing the driveway's terminus, its pitted concrete apron for a car to stand on

3) The basement of my grandmother's house, with, among others, these particulars: the extra toilet in the far southwest corner, behind an improvised wooden wall; the exposed ceiling beams, made of two-by-eights, with smaller angled struts separating and bracing them; the vestiges of the vanished life of my father and his siblings, among these a bicycle frame without wheels, a rusty bicycle pump, three and a half pairs of skis, five bamboo ski poles, a croquet set complete with mallets, balls, sticks, and wickets, albeit the wickets rusted, the colors of all the wooden parts faded, and the handles of three of the six mallets broken

4) The upstairs of my grandmother's house (similar to but considerably larger than the upstairs of Marie and Lutie's house), with its central hallway, its telephone and telephone table, sloping ceilings, and four bedrooms

5) Of these, my father's bedroom in particular, with its window facing north and its ceiling slanted

6) Located a long block directly north of my grandmother's house, the West Tree Hospital and what I believe now to have been the significance both of that building and of its design

7) The park and esplanade reaching north from the rear of the hospital, toward Christiania Avenue

8) The wading pool and sprinkler located in that park, at the Christiania Avenue end

9) My visit to the wading pool in the summer of 1944, although it could conceivably have been 1943 or 1945

10) The figure, personality, and influence of Dr. F. K. Kampfer, nearby neighbor of my grandmother, fellow church member, frequent visitor to her house, and professor, since 1928, of German and physics at Old College

11) The clothing worn by Dr. Kampfer, in particular the hat, soft brown jacket, high socks and baggy shorts that he commonly wore on his walks through West Tree

12) The scent that came from Dr. Kampfer's clothing: a scent composed of mothballs and the smoke of ancient campfires, these mingled with a number of other and much fainter smells

13) The part these smells played at my grandmother's house one Saturday morning in early April 1954, when they caused me, for the first time in my life—through realizing that what I smelled in Dr. Kampfer's clothing were the scents of the past and therefore the scents of what no longer existed—to understand that by necessity the past exists and yet by an equal necessity can not exist.

2

THE GEOGRAPHY OF WEST TREE AND THE BEGINNING OF MY LIFE

As much any other force, natural or supernatural, the geography of West Tree, I believe, is responsible for my being born where I was rather than anywhere else.

I say this mainly because, if the geography of the town hadn't been such as it was, neither Old College nor New College would in any significant probability ever have been located there.

And if Old College had not been located in West Tree, my family would never have come there either. My great-aunt Marie, in the first place, would have had no reason to step off the train on a summer day in 1910. Lutie would not have come four years later to join her. And without my great-aunts as pathfinders, my newly widowed grandmother, with her four children, in June of 1925, would not have chosen West Tree to move to from Brooklyn. My father, then, would not have arrived in West Tree at age sixteen; would not have met my mother and married her; and I, in the last event, would not have come into existence.

•

The south-central area of Minnesota was comprised of gently undulating plains that at one time had been inhabited only by the Sioux, the land consisting of meandering streams, prairie grasses, and abundant wildlife native to the region. By the time I came into being, however, a century or so after West Tree's birth, that state of perfection had long since been changed. Open grassland had been transformed, by the time I was born, into squares and rectangles of farmland punctuated by windbreaks or groves of trees where farmhouses stood (or had stood), those white clapboard structures themselves accompanied by customary arrays of fences, silos, gardens, outbuildings, sheds, and barns.

•

With its two flanking hills as landmarks, West Tree could be seen by travelers from far away, especially if their approach was from the west or south.

These two rounded, weathered hills, left behind by a glacier that had once advanced up to that point before dissipating into meltwaters, would unlikely be considered either notable or massive in the eyes of the broader world. Their particular placement, however, on a flat sheet of rolling plains that extended outward twenty-five miles in every direction, provided them with a different stature than they might otherwise have had. They stood out more than sufficiently to gain the notice of passing wagon trains, for example, on the lookout for shelter, or to hold the attention of straggling groups of idealists and believers who were migrating westward and might find themselves caught, like thistle-down on barbed wire, by the image of promise that the twin hills offered. Rising softly toward the sky, West Tree's hills, after all, would serve to make visible for miles in every direction whatever kind of structure might be erected on their crests.

•

So it was that West Tree became home not to one but two colleges.

The first, invariably referred to by townspeople as Old College, was founded in 1854. Its original building, made of stone and topped by bell tower and flag, was constructed in that year, facing east on the crest of Old College hill, where it was to remain until the end of West Tree itself.

About a decade later, in 1865, New College rose up a mile away, on the other side of the river. Its own first building, on the crest of its own hill, faced west, with the result that the two buildings, holding down the two sides of West Tree, appeared to be keeping watch over all that went on in the valley between.

•

Between the two hills flowed the river. And, spreading outward from the banks and rising gradually up the flanks of the hills was the valley it flowed through. Filling the valley were the houses, trees, sidewalks, and streets of West Tree—where fate determined that I was to be born, and where, in the brief remaining time that this was possible, I would gain all I was ever to know about space, time, history, and the nature of West Tree itself.

3
MY MOTHER AND THE TALE OF THE RIVER

From time to time my mother revealed the pleasure she found in telling stories. Often, however, her stories were better taken as imaginary or symbolic tales than as stories with a basis in actuality or fact.

She told me more than once, for example, that West Tree got its name from the name of the man who built the first mill in the valley between the two hills. His name, she told me, was West, and for his mill he chose a shady spot under the largest tree that at that time was standing on the riverbank. When farmers began bringing their grain in to his mill from the surrounding countryside, they would point their horses toward "the West tree."

•

Unlike my father, my mother was a native of West Tree. Her parents, also, were born and bred there, and the same was true of all except one of her grandparents.

In later years, I became afraid of my father, but this was never so with my mother. I wonder now whether the difference had anything to do with her not having come from someplace else, far away, as he had.

I wasn't afraid of my mother, but I never thought of her, either, as especially mysterious. I see now that this was a very great error, ignorant and short sighted, which now there is no remedy for. The thousand questions I failed to ask her can never be asked now, since my mother, like West Tree, is gone.

•

Thinking back, I realize that I associate my mother with sunlight and warmth more than with coolness and shade. This is a curious thing, with no seemingly rational basis.

Perhaps it comes from my knowing that all the members of her family, up until her own birth in 1908, had been born on outlying farms rather than in town.

•

When I was seven or eight, I asked my mother how the Wagon River had gotten its name. At that moment, she happened to be lifting sheets from a wicker laundry basket and pinning them to the lines to dry. The day was warm and filled with sunlight. The Wagon River got its name, she told me, because once years ago, before there were any bridges, pioneers crossed the river on their horses, or in their wagons, and one time, for a reason no one knows or remembers, one of the pioneer farmers had to abandon his wagon in the water when he was only halfway across. There the wagon stayed. And that was how the river got its name.

•

As with any prairie river, the depth and swiftness of the Wagon's flow varied with the seasons. It was equally capable of widely overflowing its banks in the spring as it was of dwindling to little more than a trickle in dry autumns.

In my own life with the river, I came to think of its most perfect state being its typical late-summer form: when it flowed languidly over its

shallow bed between high-cut banks of farmland, now and then—
especially downstream from West Tree—disappearing into the cool
shadows under stretches of trees.

•

Not only is my mother gone now, but so is my family, our farm, and
all of West Tree, including its history, which of course disappeared
along with it. Only the river itself remains, though the story of its
naming no longer exists, no more than does the wagon that was left
behind. Still, for whatever time is left me, or for whatever time I am
able, I will keep the image my mother gave me that day by the clothes
line over half a century ago. I will continue to see an old grain-wagon
standing halfway across the river, far from any house or farm. The
wagon's tongue slants down into the water like the head of a drinking
horse. Its weathered gray planks have warped one way and the other,
pulling away to leave wide gaps here, overlapping one another's edges
there. The prairie sun rains down warmly all across the fields of grassland that reach away from the banks of the river. Whenever I see this
image in my mind's eye, the level of the river is the same, always just
high enough so that the wooden-spoked wheels of the old wagon are
immersed to their hubs in gently moving water.

4
THE TWO BANKS OF THE RIVER

A curious thing about West Tree was that although the west side of
town was older, it was the east side, in many ways, that seemed so.

The original mill, after all, had appeared on the west bank of the
river, sometime between 1834 and 1842. The earliest settlers' houses
had been there, too, although they were flimsy structures and didn't
last out the century. And of course Old College itself stood on the west
side of town.

When Old College was founded, however, in 1854, nothing stood
on the reach between it and the west riverbank except bare land punctuated with a few squatters' shacks and one or two patchwork fields.
Christiania Avenue was a meandering wagon trail.

On the east side of town, though, by that same year, Main Street
and the town square had already come into existence, and a handful of
numbered streets had begun running eastward up from the river, those
being crossed, in the fashion of a grid, by three or four of the north-
south presidents' streets—Washington, Jefferson, Madison, and so on.

The east side at this time was hardly less barren and empty-looking
than the west side. But it got an earlier start not just in the putting down

of streets and the building of the more substantial houses, but also in the planting of trees that, as they became full-grown over the following decades, were to provide West Tree with its characteristic and wonderful asset of abundant, dense, high, cool, shade-producing foliage.

There were exceptional cases of antiquity on the west side, one of these being the president's house near the base of Old College hill on its southeast flank. This house dated from 1874 and remained standing until the end, but by and large the east side was overwhelmingly favored by earlier and much more sustained building. The east side, in fact, came to be fully settled, in firm possession of all the attendant civic amenities and comforts, as much as four or five decades before the same was true on the other side of the river.

The result of this pattern of settlement wasn't really that one side of town came to be considered superior to the other, even though it did always remain true that the residential "heart" of old West Tree was on the east side rather than the west. The most meaningful result of the staggered development, however, was that the two sides of town came to have the atmosphere, quality, and texture of two very obviously differing historical periods. There is no question but that the east side of West Tree had within it and about it the feeling, tone, texture, and scent of the historical period starting, say, sometime near 1880 and reaching to 1910; while the west side had about it those identical qualities but of the period, instead, that began sometime very near 1915 and continued on through the decade of the 1930's.

•

My own life was changed permanently—in fact it was determined from the start—by this two-sidedness of West Tree.

•

Very early I became conscious of the subtly differing textures, scents, and tone of the different historical eras. This came about partly through the stimulation of passing frequently across the river from one side of town to the other.

I was born on the west side, but only a week later, as I've said, I was taken to the east, where my family lived at that time. And although my first six years took place on the east side, not only my great-aunts Marie and Lutie but also my paternal grandmother lived across the river, where they had originally been attracted, though for somewhat differing reasons, by the presence there of Old College.

I am fairly certain now, in other words, that my awareness of historical periods as existing in clear and observable layers (which can nevertheless become richly if oddly commingled)—I am fairly certain now that the seed of this consciousness, and the power it has exerted on the whole of my life, was planted when I began crossing back and forth from one side of West Tree to the other.

5
VESTIGES

i

Because I lived in the midst of it from the time I was born, I had no name at first for the turn-of-the-century atmosphere that permeated the older sections of the east side. I later understood, however, that the houses set comfortably back on their flat lawns, the sidewalks made of pitted old squares of concrete heaved up where tree roots had expanded under them, even the quiet streets themselves, shadowy in summertime under their cathedral-archways of foliage—I came to understand that all of these, along with the accompanying smells of bark, damp moss, earth, and green grass, were in fact still-existing vestiges of years that had begun as early as 1880 or 1885 and that had lasted until half a decade or so beyond the end of the First World War.

•

With the coming of that important transforming moment, someplace in or near 1923, the character of those many preceding years changed abruptly. The era they had belonged to—the layer of time that they had constituted—ceased then any longer to be a generative and expanding force. From that point on, the layer changed instead into something that was quelled, captured, stilled, but suspended forever inside the continuing life of West Tree.

ii

By the time I myself experienced them, therefore, those scents of bark, moss, earth, grass, and trees both did and did not exist, in exactly the same way as, in the future, in 1954, the scents of mothballs and old woodsmoke were both to exist and not exist in the folds and seams of the clothing worn by Dr. F. K. Kampfer one Saturday morning at my grandmother's house.

•

The same was true also, to mention only one more example, of the iron hitching post on the Maple Street side of our house in West Tree, where I first saw my great-aunts Marie and Lutie, one August afternoon in 1945.

The hitching post existed and was there, of course, proven if only by the fact that I was able to touch it with my hand. But by far the greatest part of its life no longer existed and was not there.

iii

I came to understand, in other words, that the true importance of things lay to a great and perhaps even preponderant extent in what no longer existed about them: their true importance, in other words, lay in their existence not as things but as vestiges.

In West Tree itself, extending even into the early stages of its disappearance, vestiges of this sort were almost literally everywhere, waiting to be perceived in the color and shape, in the texture and the proportion, in the very atmosphere, tone, and scent of the innumerable everyday objects that inevitably surrounded any and all who lived there.

6
THE EPOCH OF WALKING

i

There was an extended historical period in West Tree when walking took place regularly. It was an era during which horses and buggies began, gradually at first, to fall out of use, then to disappear from life almost entirely. Yet it was a time also when automobiles had not yet become commonplace, omnipresent, and overwhelming in number.

With little question, the beginning of this epoch fell somewhere in the vicinity of 1885, when the muddy, rutted streets of the east side first came to be improved by means of sewers, gutters, paving blocks, and curbs—and later through macadamizing—and when sidewalks themselves, for the first time, were constructed routinely throughout that part of town. These improvements made it possible for pedestrians, especially female, to venture out in any season or weather without danger of being (at best) spattered with mud or (at worst) sunk in mire over the boot-tops.

•

During this same period, the hedges, shrubbery, and trees planted earlier in the century having filled out substantially and having achieved much of their height, the streets of the east side took on the inviting, poised, austere, calm, bucolic quality that proved unquestionably to be among the highest achievements, anywhere, in the records of domestic history.

•

As it manifested itself in West Tree, The Epoch of Walking fell across the natural boundaries of a number of other historical periods. It did not, for example, come to an end with the close of the First World War in 1918, nor did it end in 1925 or 1926, when the east side's First Mature Period is generally agreed to have come to a close. The Epoch of Walking, instead, continued robustly on through the decade of the 1920's, and, although admittedly walking had by this time acquired a faint hint of the old fashioned, it continued through the 1930's and managed to survive, although in increasingly vestigial manifestations, all the way into the middle and even closing years of the 1940's.

The Second World War, without doubt, helped prolong the Epoch beyond its otherwise natural life by creating shortages in gasoline and cutbacks in automobile production. In any case, artificially prolonged or not, the Epoch continued to exist even in the very earliest years of my own life. Had this not been true, it would never have come about that my great-aunts Marie and Lutie, as I have described, would have walked across town to our house on Fourth Street one summer afternoon in 1945, when I saw them for the first time: when history came toward me, leaned down, spoke words—then walked away, on the sidewalk, through sun and shadow, toward the corner.

ii

There was one occasion even earlier than that in the Epoch of Walking when it is possible that I saw my great-aunts and remembered doing so. That memory is so distant, however, and simultaneously so complex, that I can't be absolutely certain that my great-aunts are in it.

The memory is of walking across town with my mother and sisters, in what I'm quite certain could only have been the summer of 1944, to the wading pool at the Christiania Avenue end of the esplanade behind the West Tree Hospital. From the excursion that day, I remember green grass, benches, a perimeter of trees, the smell of water-moistened concrete, and the sight of spray coming down on me from overhead in a fine, drifting, sun-spangled mist.

•

This vivid but distant memory, my earliest from the west side of town, took place one hot summer afternoon during wartime, just two-and-a-half blocks from Marie and Lutie's house. I believe, although I can never know it with absolute certainty, that my great-aunts sat on one of the benches watching us as Hannah, Ingie, and I played in the spray in the middle of the wading pool.

If they did, as I believe, sit there on that afternoon, they would have worn dark shoes laced on the front, and dresses that came down just over the curve of their knees when they sat. They would not, by that time, have worn hats. They would have been bareheaded, the better to enjoy the soft, warm, desirable summer air.

7

THE WADING POOL AND THE ESPLANADE

i

Significantly, the west side contained within itself at all moments more than only one layer of time. In this way, it had a complexity even greater than that of the east side.

The wading pool, for example, along Christiania Avenue, dated from the public works era of the mid-1930's: an oval of poured concrete edged by a low wall and surrounded by radiating concrete petals.

Shrubs stood at the edge of each petal, forming backdrops for the benches placed there. I believe that my great-aunts sat on such a bench one afternoon in August of 1944, watching me and my sisters—with many other nameless and now-unexisting children—run in and out of the spraying water.

•

Suppose that my great-aunts were in fact there (as I believe they were), on one of the benches, in the shade, staying for an hour or two of the afternoon. On leaving, they would have climbed together up the stairs to the street (the pool was a distance below street level), then walked along Christiania Avenue to their house. There, they would have gone in through the front door. Then, after some time, they would have come out at the back, one with a wicker basket on her arm and both in wide-brimmed hats, to work for a time in their garden.

iii

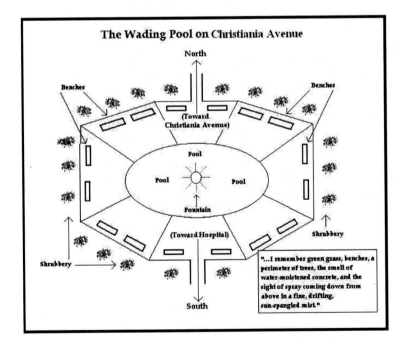

The Wading Pool on Christiania Avenue

North

(Toward Christiania Avenue)

Benches

Benches

Pool

Pool

Pool

Fountain

(Toward Hospital)

Shrubbery

Shrubbery

South

"...I remember green grass, benches, a perimeter of trees, the smell of water-moistened concrete, and the sight of spray coming down from above in a fine, drifting, sun-spangled mist."

Extending southward from the wading pool was a grassy esplanade with walkways, flowers, and trees. Here and there stood park benches of the same old-fashioned style as those around the pool. The esplanade continued for perhaps seventy-five yards, making its way up a gradual incline. At the top stood the West Tree Public Hospital, where I was born.

The esplanade (it had been completed, along with the new hospital, in early 1939) had been conceived not only to bring comfort to patients in the hospital but also to bring them something medically useful. Clearly, it would have been especially helpful for recuperative patients by providing them with sunlight and fresh air as aids in the return of health. Patients of other kinds could also have benefited, including those still in the grip of whatever accident or illness had caused their hospitalization, or those entering unexpected decline, or even those passing through the last scenes of old age and the close of life. All of these and others could have strolled on the esplanade's walkways, or been guided along them, or, as the case might be, wheeled by nurses or visiting members of their families.

The esplanade made it possible for all of these, whatever their status or the stage of their illness, to find some degree of pleasure, solace, and comfort amid the scents of grass, tree, blossom, earth, and moisture, and under the steady and penetrating warmth of the sun.

8
THE MEANINGS OF THE ESPLANADE

i

The esplanade, however, contained meanings that went farther than these, both as to complexity and purpose. These are the meanings that would prove later to have had so deep and lasting an influence on my life.

The esplanade, in short, was an efficient unifying device both of space and of time.

•

At the most simple and rudimentary level of its function—that of connecting one thing with another—the esplanade was eminently successful. Most obviously, it connected the hospital with the outdoors surrounding it and vice versa (a mingling now considered anathema in buildings), to the enhancement of each. Further, the esplanade went on to form a bond between the hospital, at the top end of the hillside, and the wading pool, at the bottom. In this way it revealed an additional and wider connection: an outwardly radiating connectedness with all of West Tree and environs, since it was from the entirety of

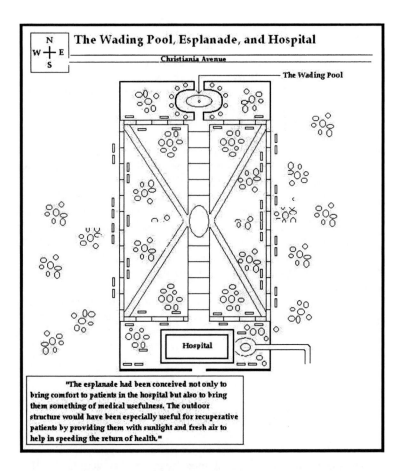

The Wading Pool, Esplanade, and Hospital

Christiania Avenue

The Wading Pool

Hospital

"The esplanade had been conceived not only to bring comfort to patients in the hospital but also to bring them something of medical usefulness. The outdoor structure would have been especially useful for recuperative patients by providing them with sunlight and fresh air to help in speeding the return of health."

this area that visitors converged to make use of the pool, exactly as they converged, when sorrow or necessity demanded, to make, although in a different sense, use of the hospital.

•

Beyond these local relationships, however, there remained other and even more important ones, some having to do with space and others—simultaneously—with time. The choices of style and design in the esplanade's various elements, for example—in the pool and park benches, the landscaping, the hospital building itself—revealed a complex interconnection of places, decades, and eras, so that the esplanade reached across great distances, going as far away as Europe, not only the Europe of this century but of the preceding one as well.

The wading pool bespoke the public- and project-minded 1930's, while the old-fashioned park benches of wood and cast iron near the pool and along the esplanade were particles of life plucked up from Paris in the 1920's or Vienna in the 1890's. The same blending of time and place was created by the gently rising and falling walkways with their flanking beds of tulips, cyclamen, phlox, daisies, ground roses, lilies of the valley, and peonies; the blending was achieved additionally by the chestnut trees and plane trees that lined the walks, along with random clumps of poplar, red maple, pin oak, and ash; and the same mingling of place and time was brought about, finally, by the imagery of the patients themselves, often with woolen blankets over their laps or shawls across their shoulders, sometimes being pushed in wheelchairs along the walkways, or sitting on the benches, in sunlight at some times of the year, at others seeking out the shade, many with an attendant or companion.

•

Then, further still, there was the hospital itself at the top of the hill. It was a relatively low, two-storied, modern building faced with rectilinear panels of lightly streaked limestone. Modern or not, however, it was blessed with abundant windows, all of them multi-paned with frames that opened outward in the manner of small doors. All of these windows, at any given time typically open to various extents and degrees, gave the building a pleasantly busy, warm, and complicated look that was enhanced further by its splendid rooftop solarium. Centered on the building's roof and occupying perhaps half of the space there, this was a structure of faintly green-hued glass panes supported by fretworks of iron beams and ribs. Although it was generally rectangular, its edges and corners were softened and rounded in such a way as to give the impression of its being slightly domed, at once determinedly modern and at the same time suggesting the old-fashioned frailty of, say, a late Victorian train station or turn-of-the-century glass pavilion.

•

The wading pool, esplanade, and hospital, in short, drew together space from inside West Tree and from beyond it, and they contained within themselves, simultaneously and furthermore, a number of layers of time: some from as far back as the 1890s, others from the 1910s and 1920s, another from the 1930s. There was still one other, though considerably more thin, layer, from the 1940s, but it began weakening dramatically in say, the years 1948 and 1949, and after that disappeared very quickly.

And all of this, it mustn't be forgotten, included also another fundamental layer, whether visible at every moment or resident only by implication. This was the extremely deep layer from the bare, dusty, unadorned frontier decades of the 1850s, 60s, and 70s, held in place by the presence of Old College's First Hall, which stood on its hilltop, just two or three blocks away, gazing imperturbably across the town.

9
MY GRANDMOTHER'S HOUSE

i

Suppose that you walked from the wading pool up the length of the esplanade, entered the back door of the hospital, climbed up one flight, let yourself out the main door onto West Second Street, crossed West Second, made a slight correction by turning right, then left again (in order to get around the house at number 916), and after that continued in a straight line, due south, for another hundred-and-fifty yards.

If you had done this, continuing on a line straight south, you would have found yourself approaching the back door of my grandmother's gray stucco house, number 917 Woodland Avenue.

ii

There was no porch on the back of the house, though a tiny shingled overhang was fixed above the door to keep off rain during the scraping of boots, closing of umbrellas, or opening of the door. A square yard or so of pebbled cement served for a terrace, its functional note heightened by the iron foot-scraper imbedded into its right-hand edge. Walkways of cement squares went out both to the right and left from the door. The one to the right met the driveway after only a few feet. The one to the left disappeared around the northeast corner of the house and continued from there along the side yard to up to the front porch and walkway.

I myself once made the journey, going in a straight line from the wading pool to my grandmother's back door. It was in the spring of 1955, when a period of warm weather had brought out leaves and blossoms in a great prolixity of pleasure and scent, and when my father was in the hospital, suffering from a burst appendix.

iii

By then, of course, halfway through the 1950s, there was plentiful evidence not only that West Tree had entered into its decline, but that the pace of decay, without brake or governor, was increasing rapidly.

By then, too, my paternal grandmother's health had deteriorated already to the point where she was confined to a wheelchair, and sometimes for extended periods to her bed.

iv

(My grandmother by this time had lived in the house on Woodland Avenue for thirty years, having arrived there in 1925, the year my father was sixteen. His sisters Hannah and Signe were fifteen and thirteen, his brother Rolf eleven.)

Like Marie and Lutie's, my grandmother's back yard extended deeply into the interior of the block, although unlike theirs it contained no flower beds or gardens. Tall hedges stood along its sides. Grass covered the whole, although it was thin and spare in the areas directly under the enormous elms, whose dense foliage held off the sunlight.

In later years, the yard had about it for me a poignant quality of loneliness, if only because it had once been used and now was untouched and empty.

•

Halfway through the yard and near its east edge was a swing-set that seemed stuck in time. It was made from a frame of galvanized iron pipes arranged like two upside-down letter Vs, their feet anchored in clumps of cement buried in the ground. The swing itself hung from chains that were fitted with sliding metal sleeves. These were attached to secondary chains so that the person swinging, by pulling down on the sleeves with each descent, could accelerate the ride, making it as high or long as might be wanted.

•

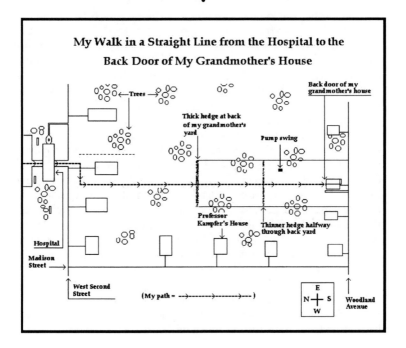

I could never imagine my father having ridden on this swing. For certain, he would have considered it childish or effeminate. On the other hand, it required no effort to imagine him sailing off the lip of the

Nordic ski jump.

I could easily imagine Hannah and Signe on the swing, however, and even Rolf. (Hannah and Signe, in my mind's eye, wore white dresses that flew out in front or behind each time the swing rose or fell.)

vi

It is impossible to overestimate the part my grand-mother's house played in forming my life and influencing its outcome.

At the same time, I don't remember ever having felt happy there.

vii

I can still see the back door of the house perfectly, down to its latch, handle, and screen. The door opened outward, admitting you into a tiny vestibule with tongue and groove walls painted pale yellow. A set of stairs straight ahead went down to the basement. On your left, three steps took you up to the door that opened into the kitchen.

viii

(I remember the kitchen. I remember the dining room, the living room, the foyer, the front closet, the side bedroom, the bathroom, the back bedroom. From upstairs, I remember each room also: the front bedroom overlooking the street, the side bedroom, the two additional bedrooms tucked under the slopes of the roof (one my father's, one Rolf's), the central hallway with its telephone table, the wood-and-dust smell of the crawl space that was called the "attic."

I remember the cellar.

I remember the steep incline of the driveway as it came up from the street, the rectangle of cement at the back corner of the house for a car to stand on, the narrow side yard with its faucet for the garden hose, the unscreened front porch with its square wood columns, the shallow front yard and the short steep embankment going down to the sidewalk, the town park across Woodland Avenue, with its picnic gazebo, and the brick orphanage behind the trees at the east end of the park (and I remember the view from my grandmother's front porch, looking south, of the low land along the Wagon River valley, trees and scrub along its banks, and then rolling farmland beyond, drenched in sunlight).

•

Just as at Marie and Lutie's, I was filled with fascination and curiosity. At the same time, I now understand at least part of the difference between what I felt at the one house and what I felt at the other:

1) At Marie and Lutie's house, I felt the past around me.

2) At my grandmother's house, I felt, for the first time in my life, the past falling away from around me.)

PART II
A FAMILY IN WEST TREE

1
A DEATH

i

My grandmother was widowed in the third week of January, 1923, when her husband died of pneumonia.

•

My grandfather's death came to be associated for me with a variety of place names and with certain other kinds of images. When I thought of those words and images, they had about them a pleasant, distant, antiquarian appeal.

ii

My grandfather died in Cleveland, Ohio, a city he had come to some days earlier from Buffalo, New York. He had been in Buffalo for the annual meeting of the National Lutheran Council, of which he was then president.

The main agenda item in 1923 had to do with the church's role in post-war relief in Europe, and especially in Russia. My grandfather was a strong advocate of continuing aid and had himself been active in the relief effort, only a week earlier having come back from the second of two journeys to Russia. On both trips, he visited St. Petersburg and Moscow, although his main work had been in towns and villages throughout the valley of the Volga River.

He went to Europe by steamship. Once there, he traveled almost entirely by rail. He went by automobile only rarely and for short distances. In the more provincial areas, he traveled as often by horse and wagon as by car.

•

Back home again, he continued traveling by rail. I am very fond of picturing my grandfather on the trains that carried him, say, from New York City to Buffalo, and from there to Cleveland. I am equally fond of observing in my mind's eye the streetcars and trolleys that at that time existed in such cities. It is extremely pleasing to watch my grandfather climbing up onto such a car or trolley, with its straw seats and wood trim and brass fixtures, as he makes his way from one appointment to another and from place to place in fulfilling his obligations as giver of guest sermons.

•

My grandfather, of course, died well before the Epoch of Walking went into its decline. It is therefore accurate also to imagine him traveling on foot.

As a result, I see this tall, large-bodied man in a loose-fitting black suit, sometimes bare-headed and sometimes looking out from under the shadowy brim of a fedora, as he walks with an unhurried and yet purposeful, faintly bear-like pace from one destination to another.

I see him on crowded city sidewalks, or against rows of trees, or passing dense green hedges or iron fences. Or I see him, his briefcase hanging from one hand so that he looks like a salesman or medical doctor as much as he does a man of God, making his way up one flagstone walkway or another, going up to the door of yet another rectory, parish house, annex, or church.

iii

(When the last of three telegrams came to the family's house in Brooklyn, confirming that my grandfather's sudden illness was indeed very serious and growing rapidly worse, my grandmother left her four children with a housekeeper and took a pre-dawn train from Grand Central. She arrived in Cleveland shortly before midday, giving her twelve hours at my grandfather's bed before he died.

He was then forty-two years old. My grandmother was thirty-five. Her children, beginning with my father, were thirteen, eleven, nine, and seven.)

iv

In West Tree, Minnesota, two and a half years later, the afternoon of June 27th, 1925, was sunny, calm, and warm. At that time, a cab drew up in front of a new bungalow-style house at number 917 Woodland Avenue. The house was hardly set back at all from the sidewalk, but it did seem high and tall—even though it was only a story and a half—since it stood on ground six or eight feet above the level of the street. On the roof of the cab were lashed a number of suitcases and pieces of baggage. For a moment or two after the cab drew to a stop, none of its doors came open. If you had been standing on the front porch looking down (as my great-aunts Marie and Lutie were), you would have seen five faces, all craning toward the windows on the right-hand side of the cab, peering back up at you.)

2
DISTANCES

i

The place names I associate with my grandfather are strewn across the face of the globe. They include St. Petersburg, Moscow, Kiev,

Odessa, Bremerhaven, Berlin, and Unter den Linden (because I once saw a postcard sent by my grandfather showing that avenue). Other place names that I associate with him include Brooklyn, Bay Ridge, Fourth Avenue, Sheepshead Bay, the Hudson River, the Catskill Mountains, and Riverside Drive. They include Archer, Nebraska, where he was born in 1882, St. Paul, Minnesota, where he went to seminary (in 1903), and Elmira, South Dakota, where he had his first congregation (in 1906).

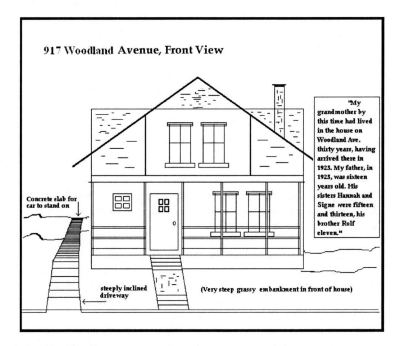

917 Woodland Avenue, Front View

Concrete slab for car to stand on

"My grandmother by this time had lived in the house on Woodland Ave. thirty years, having arrived there in 1925. My father, in 1925, was sixteen years old. His sisters Hannah and Signe were fifteen and thirteen, his brother Rolf eleven."

steeply inclined driveway

(Very steep grassy embankment in front of house)

The places I associate with him also include Elmsford, Iowa, which was my grandmother's home town and the place where my grandfather had his second congregation. My grandmother and he were married, in Elmsford, in 1908. My father was born there in 1909.

•

I associate my grandfather, moreover, with places he was connected to through others, especially through his siblings, but also through other close relatives as well. Columbia, Missouri, is such a place, through the fact of my great-aunt Marie's having studied there. Lincoln, Nebraska, where Marie taught between 1900 and 1910, is another, as is Iowa City, Iowa, where Edgar was professor of medieval literature for many years, up until 1955. Urbana, Illinois, is another such place, where Marcus was professor of classics until sometime past 1960, and Philadelphia, where Lutie had studied cooking in 1901. Congo is another, because of Albertius's long ministry, beginning in 1903, as is China, through the fact of Sigrid (who died in 1938) having lived there as a journalist from 1911 to 1916. And Kansas City, because of Ingeborg—the only one of the four sisters to marry—moving there with her new husband in 1915, and twelve years later dying there.

•

In addition, there was the American west. My grandmother's brother Eldon, until his death in 1937, lived for many years in Casper, Wyoming. My grandfather, who got along well with Eldon, deeply regretted never having made a visit to his brother-in-law there.

That this desire remained unfulfilled at the time of my grandfather's death was the cause, partly, of my grandmother's taking her children, in the summer of 1927, on a car tour out west. The five of them went to visit Eldon, as well as to tour that area of the West in general, making a stop, for example, at Yellowstone Park, with its rustic log buildings, pine forests, mountainous grandeur, natural beauty, and enormous, bright, open sky.

ii

My father, by the time of this trip, was seventeen and just that spring had finished high school. In the autumn, though continuing to live at home, he would enter the freshman class at Old College.

•

On the trip west, my father did most of the driving, though not all of it. My grandmother took the wheel on some stretches of the road, and so did Hannah, who, at fifteen, was the next oldest. Signe and Rolf, at thirteen and eleven, did no driving. From time to time, though, they were given turns riding in the front seat.

My father had learned to drive when he was fourteen and staying with his uncle and family in the Catskills the summer after his father's death. That same summer, in 1923, he took up smoking, which he was to continue, heavily, for the rest of his life.

•

The family trip out west in 1927 exists for me in a number of vivid images, all in color.

I see my father at the wheel of the high, black, old-fashioned four-door car, its spare tire under a metal cover on the back and its long hood tapered to a point in front. My father, as he drives, is bare-headed. He wears a white shirt open at the neck. His elbow rests on the ledge of the window and, much of the time, he drives with only one hand on the wheel.

Beside him sits his mother. Her long, reddish-brown hair is piled abundantly on the top of her head and pinned there. The dress she wears has long sleeves that are puffed out at the shoulders and narrow at the buttoned wrists. A simple white collar closes snugly around her neck, and the dress is secured in front with a vertical row of small buttons.

•

These images of my father and his family, just as if they were photographs, seem to me both old-fashioned and modern, looking both forward and backward in time.

At age thirty-nine, my grandmother is still young, and quite pretty, with neither any sign of gray nor any visible hint of her later crippling disease. With her abundant, Edwardian hair and out-of-date clothing, she is the most old-fashioned thing in the picture.

My father, who has already grown to his full height of six feet four, offers a contrast not only in his clothing but in his manner of relaxed, almost insouciant casualness. Even when he leaves both hands on the wheel, the left one is often connected by means of just one finger, or perhaps two. My father's shirt-sleeves are rolled loosely up above his elbows. His head is tilted back slightly and very slightly to the left, as if he had no care in the world, or as if he were trying to distance himself from the others in the car, or, even, as if it were in his mind to break into song as he drives.

In the distance are the Rocky Mountains, the remarkable landscape, and the blue immensity of the sky—while in the back seat are Hannah, Signe, and Rolf.

Hannah and Signe wear gray pleated skirts and simple white blouses. Rolf wears brown knickers, knee-high socks, and oxford shoes.

iii

(By then, in July of 1927, my mother and father had known one another for almost two years, having met very soon after my father's arrival in West Tree in the summer of 1925, and since then having been classmates at the West Tree High School.

By the time of the trip out west, they were firmly in the habit of seeing one another each day. On those occasions when for one reason or another this was impossible, they would talk on the telephone.

One of the telephones they used stood in the upstairs hallway of my grandmother's house on Woodland Avenue. An old-fashioned model, it was designed in such a way that the ear-piece was held in one hand and the remainder of the telephone in the other. The small table it rested on stood outside Hannah and Signe's door, across from Rolf's, and roughly equidistant from my grandmother's room at the front and my father's at the back.

It was the first telephone I had ever seen in the upstairs of a house.

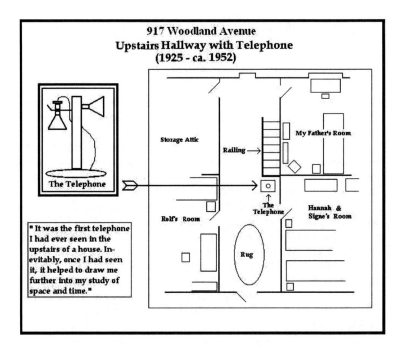

917 Woodland Avenue
Upstairs Hallway with Telephone
(1925 - ca. 1952)

Storage Attic

Railing →

My Father's Room

The Telephone ⊳

The Telephone

Rolf's Room

Hannah & Signe's Room

Rug

" It was the first telephone I had ever seen in the upstairs of a house. Inevitably, once I had seen it, it helped to draw me further into my study of space and time."

iv

I imagine the telephone now, during the family's trip in July of 1927. It stands silently in the empty upstairs hallway as my father and his mother, his brother, and his two sisters, hundreds of miles away, drive on a road that leads them westward, climbing up into the hills away from the town of Cody, Wyoming.

v

The telephone, with an almost perfect inevitability, drew me further into my study of space and time.)

3

THEN

i

Immediately at the top of the stairs, there was a choice: you could turn right, into my father's room; or you could make a hairpin turn to the left and be at the north end of the hall with a view of all the doors leading off it. If you stood in that position, on your left would be the doors to my father's room and to Hannah and Signe's. On your right would be the doors to the storage attic and to Rolf's room. At the far end of the hall, facing you, would be the door to my grandmother's room.

•

My grandmother's house was entirely different from my own family's house on East Fourth Street, and it was even more different from the farmhouse we lived in later.

Unlike our houses, my grandmother's was orderly, neat, and entirely free of dust. Because it was on the west side of town, it was not especially old, but dated from the middle 1920s and therefore had a quality of the modern about it while at the same time feeling faintly museum-like. The woodwork and floors were stained to a moderate darkness and then waxed and polished. This was wholly unlike the woodwork in our farmhouse, which was made of a softer wood and painted in such a way as to give it a look of inelegance and simplicity, even of poverty.

In my grandmother's house, the woodwork was all of oak or rock maple, with sharp edges and a finish that almost gleamed. The latches on every door clicked into place, and the doors themselves fit smoothly into their frames—unlike those at our house, where knobs were often missing, latches frozen or painted shut, and doors skewed, warped, or swollen until they seemed never to have been intended for their own frames.

•

In my grandmother's house, the doorknobs were of glass. The latches and latch plates were of brass. The north window in the upstairs hallway, like the windows in my grandmother's room (when her door was left open), allowed light to fall in across the hardwood floor. The only cover on the floor was a single oval rug near my grandmother's room.

ii

The telephone table was of stained oak. It stood alone, without stool or chair beside it, as if the idea of sitting while talking hadn't yet been thought of. Its small surface, with the phone occupying its center, provided little room even to make a note while talking if one should wish to. To do that would have been difficult in any case, since one hand would have been occupied in holding the horn-shaped earpiece while the other might well have been occupied holding the telephone itself in order to eliminate the need for bending down to the mouthpiece.

When a person hung up, they put the earpiece on the claw waiting for it, and the weight of it closed the connection.

•

It seemed to me that the telephone was fascinating, unusual, and memorable.

•

It wasn't just its being old-fashioned. More exactly, the interesting thing was its seeming, once again, to be simultaneously the height of modernity and indescribably antique.

It was not unfixed in time. What struck me instead was the way time flowed around the telephone, like a stream of water flowing around a stone.

iii

I don't remember seeing the telephone in use. Once, when I was upstairs alone, and when only my grandmother and I were in the house, I picked it up, surprised at finding the earpiece so heavy as I pressed it against my ear. Inside was my grandmother's voice, distant and small but also busy and rapid.

At once, I set the piece back on its hook.

•

This was in later years, of course, 1952 or 1953. By then, my grandmother's illness had forced her to a first-floor bedroom, since she was no longer able to use the stairs.

iv

The most significant era of the upstairs telephone began sometime late in 1925 or early 1926. It continued through 1932 or perhaps some time beyond, into the late months of 1933 or even a very small distance into 1934.

•

The years of greatest importance were the earlier ones. This is because in them there still remained a completeness and coherence of mood, atmosphere, color, shape, and texture that served that particular time fully, nourished it completely, and allowed it to exist independently, in and of itself, without reliance for meaning or sustenance upon either an earlier or a subsequent period.

•

Evidence of this temporal integrity and aesthetic-historic coherence can be found in any number of commonplace occasions, moments, or scenes.

For example, for many decades I have looked back closely at a winter evening somewhere in the first or second week of February 1928. The scene takes place in the upstairs hallway. The time is somewhere near seven-thirty. Dinner has been prepared, served, and eaten. The dishes have been stacked, washed, dried, and replaced in the cupboards. My grandmother is downstairs. All four of the children, however, are upstairs.

Rolf, at twelve, is the least likely to use the telephone, and in fact he almost never does. However, in keeping with an increasingly familiar pattern of making himself irritating, he leaves the door to his room open so that from his desk, where he does homework, he can overhear the others' conversations. Signe, who is good at math and has already been placed ahead into trigonometry, gets two or three calls from other students asking for help. Hannah makes calls to classmates about organizing rehearsals for glee club and madrigals. A boy calls her once. His name is Paul Rasmussen.

In the case of my father, two calls arrive from college classmates. Then, later, my father comes out of his room to make a call of his own. This is a call to my mother on the other side of town, where, instead of staying in a dormitory at Old College, she lives with her parents in an apartment upstairs from the movie theater that they own and operate. As my father stands talking, he holds the earpiece in one hand and the telephone itself in the other, keeping it close to his mouth so he can speak at a low volume and still be heard by my mother. As he stands there, he leans with his right shoulder against the wall. His left knee is kept stiff but he allows his inside knee to unlock. He wears cuffed wool trousers, a white shirt, and a V-necked sweater that has no sleeves. The sweater is knit in an argyle pattern of interlocking black, gray, red, and white diamonds.

My father is tall enough to make the hallway seem low-ceilinged and almost crowded. As he leans there, very slightly turned in toward the wall, his height is accentuated also by the way he holds the telephone up to his mouth and yet at the same time bends down toward it as he talks.

•

The hallway is lit by four sconces fixed to the walls, two on each side. Their electric bulbs glow through small orange shades that are shaped like lilies.

•

My father pauses, saying nothing for a long moment. During this time, my mother describes to him what her own feelings were as she watched him stand at the top of the Nordic ski jump that afternoon, then race down the face of the jump and sail off the lip into space. My father answers her by promising that he won't go down the jump again. He will in fact go back on his word several more times that winter, until the weather is warm enough so that the snow covering the apron of the hill below the jump begins to deteriorate.

•

He tells my mother that he will see her in forty-five minutes. This will give him time to finish the chapter he is reading and then walk over to meet her. They will go to the café downtown that is their favorite.

PART III
MY GRANDMOTHER'S HOUSE
AND THE END OF THE EPOCH OF WALKING

1

CHRONOLOGIES

i

By the time I became aware of my grandmother's house, the past had fallen away from it almost completely. What was left provided me with my first intimate and extended experience of absence.

ii

A chronology of the departures of family members from the house on Woodland Avenue:

1931, August: My father, having graduated the previous June from Old College, moved out of his upstairs room and away from West Tree. (He attended seminary but withdrew after a year, changing to graduate work in literary studies. He came back to West Tree in June of 1933, married my mother, then stayed there for the rest of his life. He was the only one of his siblings to remain in West Tree.)

1933, June: Three weeks after graduation from Old College (and a week after my parents' marriage), Hannah left for Philadelphia to study voice.

1934, August: Signe, finishing Old College a year early, moved to New York City to study mathematics and accounting at Columbia University.

1936, June: Rolf graduated from Old College and left home to become a divinity student at Holy Theological Seminary.

1956, August: My grandmother, thirty-two years after her arrival, moved out of the house. Crippled badly by her disease, she went to live with my aunt Signe—who had never married and had no children—in her small but comfortable bungalow outside of Baltimore.

•

A chronology of the deaths of family members who, between 1925 and 1956, had lived in the house on Woodland Avenue:

1963: My grandmother, age 75, in Signe's house near Baltimore.

1966: My father, age 57, in the West Tree Public Hospital.

1973: Hannah, age 62, in Signe's house in Baltimore

1980: Signe, age 67, in her house in Baltimore

1997: Rolf, age 82, in Los Gatos, California.

2
THE END OF ANTIQUITY

i

Of my grandmother's house I remember the shape, texture, atmosphere, quietness, and scent, and also the more powerful quality of absence: the presence of the attitudes, things, spirits, sounds, and feelings that were no longer there.

ii

I was taken in my infancy to my grandmother's house for visits (photographs show this), and I know that I also went there in early childhood. But I don't remember these visits.

Exactly when I became aware of the house, I'm not certain. I have early imagistic memories of high trees, sunlight, cool grass and shade, and the smell of moss. My first more expansive memory with any clarity is of a picnic. Not far away from the back door stood the picnic table, laden with food and surrounded by a large number of family members both standing and sitting.

•

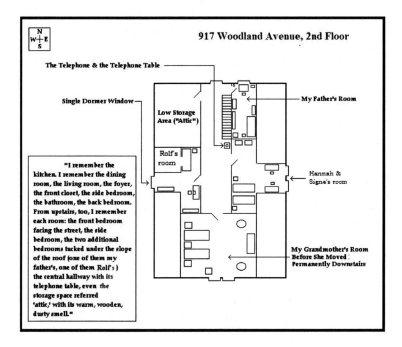

917 Woodland Avenue, 2nd Floor

The Telephone & the Telephone Table

Single Dormer Window

Low Storage Area ("Attic")

My Father's Room

Rolf's room

Hannah & Signe's room

"I remember the kitchen. I remember the dining room, the living room, the foyer, the front closet, the side bedroom, the bathroom, the back bedroom. From upstairs, too, I remember each room: the front bedroom facing the street, the side bedroom, the two additional bedrooms tucked under the slope of the roof (one of them my father's, one of them Rolf's) the central hallway with its telephone table, even the storage space referred 'attic,' with its warm, wooden, dusty smell."

My Grandmother's Room Before She Moved Permanently Downstairs

That picnic took place in 1946, the summer after my father's return from the war. Like other pivotal memories, its importance lay in providing me with a window into the past, whether indirectly or directly.

•

The picnic guests included not only Marie and Lutie, but also, since the event was a reunion, all of their siblings who were still living at the time. This meant that the gathering, which was quite large, included my great-uncles Edgar and Marcus, along with their wives Klara and Nora. It included as well my great-uncle Albertius, who by then was the oldest living member of the family, and his very tall and extremely beautiful wife Karen.

•

Those who were there from the next generation included my own parents and my aunts Signe and Hannah. Hannah, who at this time was very recently divorced, had her two children with her, my first cousins Eldon and Charlotte.

In addition, of course, there were Hannah and Ingie and me.

iii

This gathering was not the last, but it was coming unquestionably closer to the last time when Marie and Lutie would be gathered in the company of all of their remaining siblings.

If it were possible, I would go back to see it again and to listen to the conversations of this group of people whose origins lay in the century before my own—figures who were tall, strong-boned, and self-assured; who were glamorously old-fashioned, the women wearing long dresses, the men loose-fitting trousers and linen jackets. Represented among them were depths, realms, and reaches of knowledge beyond any that I was ever to approach or master: the world's histories, entire literatures, the lexicons of Greek, Flemish, Latin, Icelandic, German, Mandarin, Italian, Norwegian—making up sounds, music, and languages that I myself, living in the slowly disappearing world that was to follow these august forebears, would never know, hear, or see.

•

(In my earliest memory of her, I am walking with my grandmother on Woodland Avenue from her house to the neighborhood shop known as Mrs. Peterson's store.

I date the memory in the summer of 1945. It is distant but extremely vivid. In it, my sisters aren't present. There are only my grandmother and me.

The afternoon was hot and bright. Moss grew in the cracks of the sidewalk in the shaded places, but where there were no trees the moss disappeared and even the grass beside the walks was coarsened and brown. On our left as we walked, there were houses, raised up on their embankments, and on our right, across Woodland Avenue, was the park where the orphanage stood back behind the trees.

The walk to Mrs. Peterson's store was a quarter of a mile or so. From it, I have no image of my grandmother's face. I remember her clothing, which was dark, loose, and seemed to me very plentiful. I remember her cane, which was brown, varnished, and placed firmly by her on

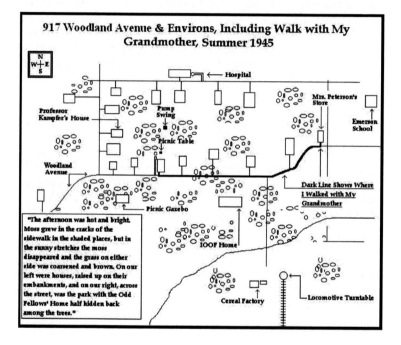

917 Woodland Avenue & Environs, Including Walk with My Grandmother, Summer 1945

the sidewalk in advance of each step. I remember very clearly the general impression of my grandmother's body. Her fingers and hands were gnarled, she had grown very large in the hips, and she was unable to stand straight, but remained bent cruelly forward, as if cemented, from the waist.

My grandmother had already become an old woman.

I have other memories—though very few—of my grandmother when she was still able to walk, although even then she was able to do so only with great difficulty, and never again with only a single cane.)

3
THE END OF THE EPOCH OF WALKING

i

After Rolf, the youngest, left 917 Woodland Avenue to study theology, the house still did not become empty immediately. People continued to arrive and depart, with the result that, at first, things did not seem entirely changed. Gradually, however, these comings and goings diminished in frequency, and as time passed, the house grew increasingly museum-like. Very faintly at first, signs appeared of its being kept less fastidiously organized and clean. In 1957, with my grandmother in the full grip of her illness, the house was left behind.

ii

The years of my own consciousness of the house began in 1945 and ended, of course, in 1957. The most influential years, however, were the first five or six of those, when a stronger remnant of the past remained than it did later. After 1950—or 1951 at the latest—the decline in the presence of the past was extreme. In this period, the history of the house drew rapidly toward an end, as the Epoch of Walking simultaneously entered its own final stages.

iii

(The dates having thus been established, only a small number of matters with regard to the history following June of 1936 remain to be mentioned, along with certain details, which, although they precede June of 1936, have pertinence.

As:

I.

Each school day morning between September of 1925 and June of 1927, my father walked to the West Tree public high school across town on Maple and East Second Street. His sisters Hannah and Signe, who at that time were two and three levels behind him in school, respectively, did the same. The three (the girls walking together, my father alone) returned for lunch at noon, walked back to school, and of course came home again in the evening. The distance each way was exactly nine-tenths of a mile, so that a day's walking amounted to nearly four miles. Rolf, who was a fifth and then sixth grader during those two years, walked slightly more than a quarter of a mile to school. Twice a day he followed Woodland Avenue past the orphanage and Mrs. Peterson's store, then went a block more to the Emerson School. And twice a day, of course, he made the same trip in the other direction.

•

Beginning in the spring of his junior year and continuing through his senior year, my father would stop on his way to school each morning to meet my mother at the corner of Washington and East Second, where her parents' apartment was, then walk with her the additional two blocks to school.

In the winters, my father frequently went cross-country skiing, often covering considerable distances, especially when he set out on day-long treks south from town, following the river for two or three miles and then verging to the east up into the large wooded area known as the Vreeland Woods.

Often he went on these skiing expeditions alone, though frequently also with friends, most especially his high school classmates Karl Halbrunn and Haken Swenson, who were also to enter Old College in my father's class. After their first year there, however, the three did not remain close.

In his first year in West Tree, my father became a scout member and with small groups went on outings both out to the northeast of town and also southwest along the river. Two or three times a year, my father also went on overnight and weekend camps in the Vreeland Woods.

In addition, for three weeks or so each summer after his junior and then senior years—that is, 1926 and 1927—and then again after each of his first two years in college, my father took work on outlying farms during harvest, mainly during grain threshing in mid July and early August, when labor was in strong demand on the farms. An exception to his pattern of farm work came the time he drove out west in 1927.

In high school, my father excelled in all subjects. He was especially praised, however, for his excellence in Latin.

•

(My grandmother's house, although becoming steadily more vacuous, never entirely—until its disappearance—lost all vestiges of its history. As late as 1952 and 1953, even some distance into 1954, I continued exploring the house when I was there alone (with my grandmother, of course, who by then was confined to the downstairs) for traces, colors, and moods of the past.

This was the period when I would go to the basement, for example, where I found the extra toilet built into the southwest corner, secluded behind its improvised wooden partition. Leaning against the basement walls and hanging from exposed ceiling beams were other vestiges of the lives of my father, Hannah, Signe, and Rolf: a bicycle frame with no wheels, for example, and another with no front wheel; a rusty tire pump; three and a half pairs of skis, each pair a different size from the others; the croquet set with faded colors and broken mallets; and five bamboo ski poles, all five of differing lengths, the leather netting torn and half rotted away.

On the second floor (the stairs going up were carpeted, to me a remarkable thing), I always looked into my father's room first and saw his cot still in its place tucked under the slope of the roof. It was made up neatly under an olive drab scout blanket stretched tightly. In the storage attic across the hall from my father's room were six tennis rackets in wooden presses, though with their gut strings loose, dried, and broken.

In the hallway itself, outside the door to Hannah's and Signe's room, was the telephone table, and, standing on it, the black, old-fashioned telephone.

•

(In 1948, almost exactly twenty years after Rolf had been a student at the Emerson School, I was a second-grader there and lost control of my bowels at the top of the north entranceway stairs. Sitting on the top step, I felt my entire weight raised upward slightly, so powerful were the expelling muscles in their final, relieving spasm.

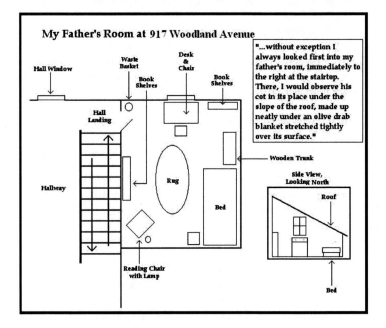

My Father's Room at 917 Woodland Avenue

Hall Window
Waste Basket
Desk & Chair
Book Shelves
Book Shelves
Hall Landing

"...without exception I always looked first into my father's room, immediately to the right at the stairtop. There, I would observe his cot in its place under the slope of the roof, made up neatly under an olive drab blanket stretched tightly over its surface."

Hallway
Rug
Bed

Wooden Trunk

Side View, Looking North

Roof

Reading Chair with Lamp

Bed

When Rolf, in 1927 and 1928, attended the school, I don't know whether he went in and out using the north entrance. I don't know, either, whether my grandmother, when she came for class-room visits or teachers' conferences, went in through that door. Perhaps both she and Rolf used the west entrance, or the east, these being the only other possibilities, since there was no entrance on the south.)))

II.

My grandmother's house, clearly, was most filled with life between 1927 and 1936. In the following five or six years, however, frequent visits occurred—from Hannah, for example, who in 1934 and 1935 made summer trips from Philadelphia during breaks in her music studies. She returned again in 1936, this time for her own wedding to Roger Arthur—from whom she would be effectively although not officially separated after 1943 and from whom she would be legally divorced early in 1946, when my cousins Eldon and Charlotte were nine and seven years old.

Signe, who was never to marry, spent the summer of 1936 at home after finishing her master's degree. In 1937, she took a position as instructor in a business and secretarial college in Delaware, and after that she traveled home for some part of each summer, always by car.

Others converged on West Tree from various distances to visit my grandmother's house or—in those years equally often—Marie and Lutie's house. These included my great-uncles Albertius, Edward, and Marcus, most often with their wives. Once, in 1936, even my great-aunt Sigrid, whose death would come two years later, was included among them.

During the period that began in 1933 or 1934 and extended through the first year or two of the Second World War, the tradition of family gatherings in my grandmother's back yard flourished most strongly. These were the years of the almost annual summer gatherings of my tall great-uncles and their tall wives, of my tall great-aunts, and of my parents (my sister Hannah was born in 1938; my mother brought her to the picnic in a bassinette that year). The women at that time often wore hats with wide brims of various sizes, and everyone, men and women both, dressed in the loose, draped clothing that was in keeping with the period and that gave the events (there were snap-shots, although infrequent) an inescapable look of elegance. These, in sum, were the years when the large family gathered out on the lawn, under the elms, around the table, when food and iced tea and lemonade and dishes of various kinds were brought (by Hannah, by Signe, by my mother, by Nora, by Klara) out through the back door from the kitchen, invariably including, toward the end of the afternoon, a whole watermelon and a choice of flavored sherbets.

III.

(When I was born, history still existed and was visible, although I was unable to see it. When I emerged out of the universal blindness of my infancy, in 1944 and 1945, history was still there, surrounding me like a cawl, though I saw it only in glimpses and fragments. Then, just as my seeing of it gained consistency and wholeness, history began to disappear. A tiny sliver of time, three crucial years—1947, 1948, and 1949—constituted a single moment when history still existed and when I was also able to see it. This experience, in my entire lifetime, was never to be repeated.)

IV.

In early winter of 1946, my grandmother took in two orphans who stayed with her until the spring of 1949. From a distant branch on the maternal side of her own family, the two had lost their father during the war, and shortly afterward their mother had died also, under circumstances never known by or made clear to me.

They were a girl and a boy, a year apart in age, both in high school. Each of them stayed with my grandmother until graduation, two years in the case of the boy, three in the other. Their names were Christine and Victor Olvestad, and they were from Seattle, a city that I had no image of at the time but came to think of later as exotic, western, and densely green.

After she finished high school, Christine went to nursing school in Washington State, and Victor, after graduating a year before her, joined the army. Eventually, he went to Korea. I remember my grandmother once reading a letter she had gotten from him while he was there. By this time my grandmother was unable to walk, or even, without help, get up from her wheelchair into bed or into a car. Before this point, of course, she had moved from her front upstairs bedroom to the side bedroom downstairs, which was smaller and, because it had windows on the west rather than the south, less filled with light.

•

When my grandmother read the letter from Victor, she and I were alone in the house. I have always assumed that she read it to me aloud so that she could leave things out, but perhaps that wasn't the case. She shook her head sadly and clucked her tongue at Victor's using the word "gooks" when he cited the number of Koreans his unit had killed the day before.

•

This memory comes from 1951 or 1952, when I was ten years old or near that. When Victor was discharged from the army, he did something criminal—I was never told what, but I suspected robbery of some kind—and was sent to prison, I don't know for how long.

•

What became of Victor and Christine in later life, I don't know. They disappeared, went away, moved elsewhere, drew out of touch, left no trace. I assume they stayed in touch with my grandmother for some years, but as far as I was concerned they had ceased to be.

V.

(One of the indications that history was beginning to disappear came in the form of a series of summertime visits from my aunt Hannah and her children, Eldon and Charlotte.

•

Even before Roger Arthur returned from the Pacific in August of 1945, my aunt Hannah had initiated proceed-ings for divorce from him, on the grounds that he had been seeing other women. As I mentioned, she became legally divorced shortly before the summer of 1946.

For the next five or six years, toward the end of each August, she drove from Boston to West Tree for a two or three week stay, bringing Eldon and Charlotte.

•

My first cousins were both taller than I was. I knew that this was not only because they were older—though Eldon was five years ahead of me, and Charlotte four—but because they were in the process of inheriting, through their mother, the trait of tallness that had traveled historically down through my father's family but that had stopped at me.

•

There were other differences between them and me that caused tension and often a chill between us. By the time their visits began, my family had moved from West Tree into the country, but the idea of "country" meant something very different to my cousins from the rolling farmland they saw surrounding West Tree.

Every summer before coming to visit West Tree, they would both hold jobs in the Berkshire Mountains, in the same camp where their mother taught music. This meant that they arrived in West Tree each August more tanned and long-limbed than the year before, their hair bleached an even lighter brown by the sun, while they brought clothing with them that looked enviably rugged—hiking and tennis shorts softened by use and sunshine, and boots that were scuffed from real rocks, trails, climbs, and outings—not to mention, in addition to all this, that they arrived every summer with a yet more advanced knowledge of woodlore and survival, campfires, ropes, tents, canoes, compasses, and jackknives, of how to start fires without matches, or notch trees so as never to get lost no matter how deeply you made your way into a forest.

I knew nothing of any of these things—things from the worlds of scouting and sport—beyond the vestiges of them, of course, that I'd found in my grandmother's house—the pile of tent pegs and ropes, for example, stuffed deeply into the storage space across from my father's room, where I'd also found the half-dozen old tennis rackets. That world had been known to my father, and now it was known to my cousins, but for me it had already disappeared.

•

With what seemed their natural tendency toward aloofness, and with the habit of moving their large and strong-boned bodies in slow, calculating, studiously casual ways, my cousins showed little curiosity about me, and no interest in initiating me into the exotic realms of what they knew. Instead, whenever the impulse might come upon them, they were more inclined without explanation to throw themselves on a sofa, drape themselves over an easy chair, or fling themselves through a doorway, disappearing wordlessly into the outdoors.

•

My aunt Hannah herself was no less improbable a figure for me to imitate or find guidance from in my desire to understand as much as possible of the world as we drew closer to the conclusion of history.

My aunt Hannah, perhaps as a result of her training in vocal music, seemed always to hold herself fully erect, her spine straight and head thrown slightly back, a little bit as though she were greeting a sunrise. She had a quality also of steady and almost unmitigated cheerfulness. I could never understand where this might have come from, especially considering that she was a sibling of my own father, whose moods swung constantly, hugely, and with great inconsistency, plunging often into the deepest and most despairing gloom and anger.

Whatever else may or may not be said of my aunt Hannah's character, however, I know that I never had reason to find her unkind or cruel. I attribute this virtue in part to her possessing a thoughtful intelligence that, while nowhere near the extraordinary level of her younger sister Signe's, was nevertheless in a slight but measurable degree greater than her own children's.

• • •

MEMORY-NOTES
917 Woodland Avenue, West Tree, Minnesota, 1950–1957

1.
My cousin Eldon (as had the orphaned Victor before him) slept in my father's old room, on the cot-sized bed with its olive-drab wool scout blanket, nestled under the slant of the roof.

In the earlier years of their summer visits, when my grandmother still slept in the big bedroom upstairs, Charlotte would stay in the little room that had been Rolf's, and my aunt Hannah would take the room across the hall that had been hers and Signe's when they were girls.

During later visits, however, when my grandmother had moved downstairs, Charlotte took the side bedroom upstairs and my aunt Hannah stayed in the northwest corner bedroom downstairs. Eldon, however, remained in my father's room at the top of the stairs, through the doorway to the right, on the cot-sized bed, under the slant of the roof.

2.

The driveway at 917 Woodland Avenue climbed up very steeply from the street, then leveled out as it went along the west side of the house. At its terminus, under the window of the back corner bedroom where my aunt Hannah slept, a cement slab had been laid just large enough for a car to stand on. Normally, none stood there, but when Hannah came with Eldon and Charlotte, her car would be parked on it.

•

The cement slab always seemed to me extremely old, something out of the antiquity of my father's childhood. It was badly pitted, and tiny half-buried pebbles kept trying to rise up out of its grip. It lay in the shade, and from its edges large areas of thin moss spread inward. The sight of this encroaching moss invariably released in me an overwhelming sense of the unused, old, and forlorn.

•

Although I never saw it, this is where the high black car would have stood that my father and his family took on their driving trip out West in the summer of 1927.

•

The car my aunt Hannah drove from Boston was a black Chevrolet, squared off in back, but still with the spare tire hidden inside the trunk. The car had four doors, running boards, and a pointed hood that opened up like birds' wings from the sides. I stood beside it one day as Eldon raised one side of the hood. As we lowered our heads to look in at the engine, he pointed out to me that all twelve of the head bolts were fitted with polished chrome caps.

I looked and saw the twelve caps shining in the complicated darkness under the hood.

•

The engine, Eldon said to me another time, was "a straight six." Then he added, as he turned his back and walked away, that of course I wouldn't know what that meant.

Suppose that this memory took place in 1951. Eldon would have been fourteen. I would have been nine.

3.

The quality most surprising in my aunt Hannah, and least understandable to me, was her habit of bursting frequently and unexpectedly into song. My sense of uneasiness when this happened may have been due to the fact that at my house neither my mother nor my father sang at all, let alone unexpectedly. Hannah, however, did so commonly and with no sign of warning. She might trill forth suddenly while simply walking through the doorway from the kitchen to the dining room. Or she might rise from silence into song as she stood with her hands submerged in dish water, or as she disappeared up the stairs, so that one would hear her voice ascending—sometimes she warbled nothing more than scales and exercises—into the distance.

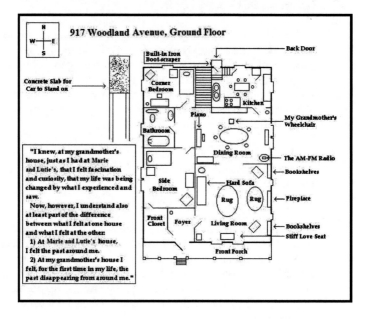

917 Woodland Avenue, Ground Floor

Back Door

Built-in Iron Boot-scraper

Concrete Slab for Car to Stand on

Corner Bedroom

Kitchen

Piano

My Grandmother's Wheelchair

Bathroom

Dining Room

The AM-FM Radio

Bookshelves

Side Bedroom

Hard Sofa

Rug   Rug

Fireplace

Front Closet   Foyer

Living Room

Bookshelves

Stiff Love Seat

Front Porch

"I knew, at my grandmother's house, just as I had at Marie and Lutie's, that I felt fascination and curiosity, that my life was being changed by what I experienced and saw.

Now, however, I understand also at least part of the difference between what I felt at one house and what I felt at the other:

1) At Marie and Lutie's house, I felt the past around me.

2) At my grandmother's house I felt, for the first time in my life, the past disappearing from around me."

Over time, it became clear that Charlotte, prone to periods of deep sullenness, had no temperament that would cause her to follow in her mother's path of song. Equally clear, however, was that Eldon would compensate for the smoldering touch of rebellion in his sister through the doubled intensity of his own enthusiasm for voice.

Each year, he sang more readily and more often than the year before. By the time his visits came to an end, he was not only at a new peak of singing ability but old enough to drive legally. This was a combination that gave rise to a phenomenon both memorable and unpleasant to me, his habit of driving and singing at once.

My grandmother, in the much earlier years of the late 1920s and early 1930s, when she still had her old car and was still able to drive, was fond of taking her family for picnics on Barn Bluff, twenty miles or so east of West Tree, overlooking the Mississippi River. In the summer of my cousins' last visit to West Tree, when my aunt Signe and her close friend Josephine were also visiting, a final picnic on the bluff was proposed. Because Signe was there, two cars were available instead of one. As chance would have it, I was designated to ride in my aunt Hannah's car, but with Eldon driving. My sister Hannah sat in front beside him. My own place—unwisely chosen, as it happened—was in back between my aunt Signe on the left and Josephine on the right.

Eldon's singing, like his mother's, was a characteristically unpredictable mix of the religious and the secular. As either one of them walked through the rooms of 917 Woodland Avenue, they might be as likely to break forth in "He Is Born, the Holy Child" as in "I'm Gonna Wash that Man Right Outa My Hair." Or "Upon This Rock Our Faith Will Stand" might as likely burst forth as "Swannee River" or "Boogie Boogie Bugle Boy."

Halfway or so to the picnic site, Eldon decided to take the lead and passed the other car. That car was Signe's, of course, though with my aunt Hannah driving, and I remember, as we pulled alongside, seeing her for a moment, an arm's reach away, behind the wheel, smiling over at us, her dark reddish hair blowing in the wind. Her chin was raised up slightly, accentuating her long white throat, and I could see that she was singing, though with the movement of the cars and the rushing of air through the open windows I could hear no words.

Hannah's face, in fact, was one of the few things I did see during that trip. Because of my sitting between Signe and Josephine, and because of my being short, the only things I could see were either very nearby, like Signe's and Josephine's bare arms, or very far off, like one of the ranges of flat-topped hills in the distance. The seatback in front of me, meanwhile, kept me from seeing anything at all ahead of the car, so that for me it became a matter of faith alone that the road was still ahead of us, and free of obstacles, and that we were proceeding along it properly.

The result of these uncertainties, along with the swerves and movements of the car itself, which, being blinded, I was unable to see coming and thus brace for, feeling them instead only after they had occurred—the result of these conditions was that I became carsick.

Years before, when I'd ridden in Mr. Bauchman's convertible, sitting low in the back seat, I hadn't been troubled with sickness—but the car was open, the evening was late, I was younger, and I may (as I suspect) have spent a good part of the trip asleep. Now, however, things were different, and when the sickness (until then I had thought I could keep it in control) violently overtook me with an extraordinary suddenness, I flung myself like an arrow released from the string across my aunt Signe's lap. She thought for a moment—she said afterward—that I was about to throw myself out of the open window entirely.

•

Once near that time I watched my father adjust the ball cock in our toilet tank. I was pleased by the way it worked—the floating ball, as it rose, closing the flow of water, and, as it fell, allowing the flow to open again.

Later, I was to think of Eldon, at the wheel of the car, as having a float-valve of such a kind somewhere inside him, since it would explain so well how he worked. When the level of a certain kind of spirit—the divine, the operatic, the comedic, the dramatic—fell low enough, he would burst into song of the appropriate kind, and, when filled once again, he would just as inexplicably fall silent.

4.

(Now, of course, all of it is absent, gone, vanished, as if never having existed—the singing, the voices, the drive, the picnic, the sky, the sun, the afternoon, the view of the Mississippi majestic and far below, winding and bending southward, the white curve of my aunt Hannah's throat as she smiled over at us from the wheel of Signe's car, Eldon, age sixteen, behind the wheel of the car I was in, holding his head up as high and straight as his mother held hers. Eldon is gone, Charlotte is gone, my aunt Signe is gone, her friend Josephine is gone, my sisters, my parents, my grandmother, my aunts, my great-aunts, my uncles, my great-uncles. Of all who once were, I alone am left, being transported slowly through whatever may remain of my life.

I remember:

i. My grandmother's kitchen, its way of seeming unused, museum-like, half abandoned even by the time I first became aware of it. The cabinets and woodwork a pale yellow. The sink without a cabinet, its two iron legs letting you see the curving drainpipe where it hung underneath and disappeared into the wall. The built-in wooden drawers with the everyday silverware in them—thinking of my father himself removing spoons, knives, forks when he was sixteen, seventeen, eighteen. Christine and Victor doing the same. And now—although seldom—my cousins and my sisters and me.

ii. On the morning of the picnic (an hour or so before we left in the cars), with all three kitchen windows open wide and the cool morning air coming in, helping my aunt Signe make chicken sandwiches at the table. Charlotte coming in through the door from the back yard with my sister Ingie. The two of them standing for a minute to watch, and Ingie saying to our aunt Signe, without thinking, "Oh, that's why you're so fat. You put butter on both pieces of bread."

iii. Eldon making friends with the boy from two houses away, Meredith Tonsager, the same age as Eldon, thirteen or fourteen. When they went down into my grandmother's basement because they were making a soapbox car and needed parts. I being outside the back door as they emerged, on their way to Meredith's house. "We needed an axle," Meredith said. I asked him what they needed it for. Eldon spoke for him, saying "You wouldn't know what an axle is."

iv. Charlotte and my sisters together in the back yard under the high elms and taking turns on the swing. The way they sometimes twirled around the poles while waiting for their turn, or helped push the swinger, or just sat on the grass nearby. The way they began swinging two at once, facing one another standing up. Charlotte and Hannah, for example, and then Ingie and Hannah, swinging higher and higher, shrieking on the descent. Then Eldon coming out of the house, where he had been lying on the cot in my father's room, reading. He pushing the two swingers from behind. Then their getting off and he going up by himself, sitting down. After a time, at the topmost point, at the instant the swing was motionless, his letting go, sailing outward as the suddenly-lightened swing jangled and tossed behind him and the air was full of shouts and voices and pleasure, and the trees were high and thick and green and the sky above, higher still, was flawless blue.

v. And then life leaving, draining away, disappearing, the house falling empty. The day in autumn when I came with my mother to see my grandmother (by car, of course, the Epoch of Walking having by this time come to an end). The empty and unusual feeling of being at my grandmother's house when Charlotte and Eldon weren't there, aunt Signe and aunt Hannah weren't there, even my sisters weren't there. It being neither summertime nor Christmas time, and it consequently having such a feeling of emptiness.

My grandmother in the dining room, at the table, in her wheelchair. My mother at the table also, her back to the twin windows. As they talked, my opening the door to the staircase and going up. As usual, looking at my father's bed and dresser and bookcase and desk and window (it looked out toward the swing), at the tennis rackets and tent pegs across the hall, and then at the telephone table, which now had a different kind of telephone on it. My going through the other rooms, liking Hannah and Signe's because of the twin windows in the dormer, creating a kind of small room of its own. Disliking the front bedroom and knowing even then that I had always disliked it because it seemed oppressive and vacuous at once. Remembering my grand-mother lying on one of the twin beds, I disliking even the twin beds themselves, though I knew they were antiques and had come from Brooklyn and that my dead grandfather had slept on one of them.

Going downstairs and through the kitchen and down the other stairs to the dry woody smell of the basement. Having seen the coal bin and dusty toilet and skis and poles and bicycle frames and rusted pump so many times before that I felt I had memorized them, then going up the stairs and out the back door into the warm, gusty mid-morning. Someone having raked a large pile of leaves together near the middle of the lawn, and I lying down in the center of it, on my back. Lying there for a long time, looking up at the half-naked arms of the elms high overhead, their crooked fingers stirring uneasily against a sky of milky blue, while all around me were the sounds of the warm autumnal wind lamenting and whispering and sighing through the trees and over the earth and around the corners of houses, and it seeming to me then, as it has seemed to me ever since, that at that moment what I heard was the sound of emptiness and absence, of loneliness and abandonment, of hollowness and loss, of all that had once been and now was no more, of nothingness and sorrow, of death.)

VI.

During 1948 and 1949, my grandmother's illness worsened rapidly, and from that time on she was able less and less often to leave the house or go outdoors. One by one, a large number of activities disappeared from her life. Among them was going to church. From the time she first came to West Tree until as late as 1949, she had gone to St. Peter's Lutheran church every Sunday—and, in the earlier years, on other days of the week as well, owing to her involvement in various congregational organizations and affairs. The church was not quite a half mile away, not far past Mrs. Peterson's store, but the walk soon became impossible for my grandmother. For a time she went by car, getting rides from neighbors or friends, but before long she was forced also to give up even that way of travel, due to the increasing difficulty and pain, and the slowness of being transferred from her wheelchair into the car, and from the car into the church, and then the same again in return.

My own religious career, short and unsatisfactory it may have been, began too late, in any case, for me ever to have seen my grandmother inside the church.

•

My aunt Signe, when she came for her visits to West Tree, was dutiful about taking my grandmother on outings, although doing so required a great amount of organization, energy, patience, hard work, and time. I remember being taken along on some of these outings. I remember one in particular, which consisted of an after-dinner ride through the lilac groves along the meandering roads on the east side of New College Hill. The lilacs were in bloom—they were the reason for the outing—and I remember sitting in the back seat of the stopped car, Signe behind the wheel, my grandmother in front beside her, all of the windows rolled down, and the sweet scent of the blossoms filling the car as evening gradually arrived and color faded out of everything.

•

(My grandmother came out to our farm once or twice even when Signe wasn't visiting, being helped into the car and out of it again, in Signe's absence, by my father. These visits must have taken place after Marie and Lutie's deaths in 1953 but before 1957, when my grandmother left West Tree to live in Baltimore with Signe. Even by 1953, my grandmother was very badly crippled. Her hair, which had once been reddish-brown and voluminous and thick, and which she'd once worn pinned up abundantly on top of her head, was now gray and, from her medicines, thinned out almost to nothing. I remember her, on the front lawn of our farmhouse, in her wheelchair, saying again and again how pleasant she found the summer breeze that was flowing steadily from the southwest.

•

Less and less often was it practicable for her to leave the house, especially in the winter months.

•

Her disease was remorseless, twisting her body cruelly and distorting her hands, fingers, knuckles, limbs, feet.

HISTORY:

i.

Memories of my grandmother receiving visits from others, since by then it had become almost impossible for her to be taken out of the house.

•

Pastor Bordum among these, whose visits I hadn't understood at first, thinking they were only social. Then passing my grandmother's door one day on my way to the bathroom and hearing him not just praying, but praying in the same incantatory way as in church, after which I understood that he was carrying the service to her, since she couldn't come to it.

•

My glimpse into history as I glanced in through the door. Pastor Bordum sitting on the bed, his big rounded back toward me. His heavy head, like a tired bull's, bowed forward. His hands holding my grandmother's hands as he prayed. My grandmother's eyes being closed. I not knowing whether Pastor Bordum's eyes were closed or not because of their being turned away from my view.

•

In that moment, in the size and shape of him, in his sitting on the side of the bed, in his bowed head, his clasped hands, his low and droning voice, I saw back into history and for a moment there before me was my dead grandfather returned: the man whom I had never seen but who had had this same shape and same voice and black suit, the man whom I imagined walking on the streets of Brooklyn and Erie and Buffalo and Schenectady, carrying a briefcase, in 1913 and 1916 and 1920 and 1922.

ii.

For a certain period in sixth grade, I had clarinet lessons once a week after school. When the lessons were over, I would walk to my grandmother's house and wait for my father to pick me up there with the car and take me home. I remember those afternoons as taking place always in damp and chill weather, when darkness gathered in the rooms early in the day. Because of her interest in international peoples, my grandmother subscribed to the National Geographic. I would sit in the living room on the small hard sofa with its back to the front windows and look through the magazines for pictures of women with uncovered breasts.

•

For as long as she could, my grandmother kept up correspondence with friends and colleagues of her dead husband, and with old members of his congregations. She would sit in her wheelchair at the dining room table with her supplies in front of her—fountain pen, paper, envelopes, stamps, letters not yet answered. From the radio in the corner, with its row of little ivory buttons, would come classical music from the station at Old College.

By this time, my grandmother's hands were like bundles of broken sticks at the ends of her arms. With her left hand, she managed to thread the pen in among the fingers of the right in such a way that it would stay there, and then she would write painfully and slowly. When envelopes were ready for mailing, she would summon me from the couch. My penis by then would be like a small stick of pine. In a transparent charade to make it seem that I was unaware of my arousal (and to make it go away), I would give a false yawn, stretch my arms overhead, and then do a cartwheel across the living room on my way to pick up the envelopes from my grandmother at the table.

The letters were addressed to places in Missouri and Iowa and New York and Taiwan and Berlin and Congo. I took them as far as the corner of Woodland Avenue and Poplar Street, where I dropped them in the mailbox.

iii.

On the wall behind where my grandmother sat were cabinets with glass doors, the good china stacked inside: cups and saucers, plates, gravy boats, bowls, creamers. The everyday dishes were kept in the kitchen on papered shelves behind painted wooden doors.

To me this seemed elegant and old-fashioned and exotic, having two sets of dishes, since at home we had only one. Like so many other things at my grandmother's house, I thought of it as something left behind, a relic, something intact and untouched, dating from the 1920's.

iv.

Pastor Bordum's large body, his big head, his un-usually wide face. He isn't fat but bearlike, and he is tall, just as my dead grandfather had been. He sits behind his desk in the parish house and I sit across from him.

Pastor Bordum never speaks, it seems, except in the first person plural, and only with very great rarity does he change the intonation of his voice. We are sinners, he tells me, and if, when we die, we are still outside the redemptive grace of the church, there is nothing we can do to prevent being cast into hell. Hell, he explains, is like the pain of being immersed in liquid fire, for eternity.

•

I agree to begin confirmation classes. At this time, I am near the end of seventh grade, and I am much too ignorant to defend myself against anything Pastor Bordum might tell me. Also, I have never been more terrified in my entire life.

•

(One night my father gets drunk and says that Pastor Bordum is a goddamn liar. Because of the amount my father has had to drink, he gives free rein to his anger, and also to his intense dislike for Pastor Bordum. Cursing freely, my father tells me that in actuality I'm already saved, that I underwent the sacrament of baptism after I was born, that being baptized is what saves you from hell, not confirmation, no matter what kind of self-serving bullshit Bordum might try to unload on me.

My angry father has been skeptical and rebellious all his life, though at the same time he has also been indecisive and weak. When I'm in seventh grade, however, I know little of the history of these things, nor do I understand them clearly.

On the night when he gets drunk, for example, and comes to my aid by assuring me that I won't go to hell, he nevertheless immediately afterward falls under the influence of his weak side, chooses to be indecisive, abandons his assault, tosses up his hands, turns away.

After all he has said about Pastor Bordum, about hell, heaven, sin, baptism, and fire, my father ends up by telling me that, like Hannah and Ingie before me, the decision is mine. I'll have to decide for myself what to do. As a consequence, I feel abandoned by everyone, on whatever side.

•

At this time in my life I am intensely and equally afraid of three things, these being death, pain, and eternity. As a consequence, at age twelve, I follow Pastor Bordum's medieval and non-empirical absolutes. I turn my back on the post-Enlightenment liberal relativism of my well-intended but weak and uncertain father.

As a result of this decision, there is brought into existence the relatively brief period when, at my grandmother's house, I feel more intensely than ever before that the past has disappeared from around me entirely. And the period, also, when I meet Professor F.K. Kampfer.

v.

This period began toward the end of February 1954, went on through March and April of that year, and came to an end near the middle of May. At that time, I dropped out of confirmation classes and never returned, leaving the church forever.

vi.

(First and second year students had their confirmation classes at staggered times on Saturday mornings, first-year confirmands at eight-thirty and those in their second-year two hours later. This meant that I was dropped off at the church sometime after eight o'clock, while Ingie went on to my grandmother's. At ten o'clock or so, when I was let out of class, I would walk uptown, past the Emerson School and Mrs. Peterson's store, to 917 Woodland Avenue. Sometimes I would meet Ingie, who would be coming in the other direction on her own way to class.

•

Because she was there earlier, Ingie sometimes had breakfast at my grandmother's house. She told me that most often the meal consisted of pancakes, adding that when she first came in through the front door, the house would be filled with the smell of them cooking.

I didn't believe her. The idea of pancakes at my grandmother's house was inconceivable, though I was afraid of making the direct accusation that Ingie was lying.

•

At this time, a nurse came to my grandmother's house for an hour or two each morning, again at midday, and once more in the evening. On weekends, the schedule was slightly later than on weekdays, so that the nurse was often leaving just as I got to the house. She would already be wearing her coat, about to go out the back door. There was no sign anywhere of pancakes having existed. The dominating smells in the house were soap, rubbing alcohol, and camphor.

•

On her good days, my grandmother would be left in her wheelchair at the dining room table. On her poor days, she would stay leaning up against pillows in the west bedroom, where the windows opened onto the driveway.

She often talked on the telephone, whether in bed or at the table. She wrote a great number of letters. She also read, although somewhat less often. She subscribed to Time, Life, The Saturday Review, and, as I mentioned, The National Geographic. The bible was always nearby, either beside her bed or on the dining room table, although I seldom saw her actually reading it. Beside her bed there was also a green-covered book of sermons by my uncle Rolf entitled *By the Spirit Guided.* A bookmark had been left in page 179, out of 408. It was on one of the Saturday mornings when my grandmother had stayed in bed that she read Victor Olvestad's letter from Korea.

Unlike the upstairs room with its windows overlooking Woodland Avenue, this one was small and crowded. An upholstered chair stood in the corner diagonally from the bed, and against the east wall stood another, smaller, chair that was easily brought to the bedside. There was a hospital-style table, on wheels, that could be rolled over the bed for meals or for reading and writing.

My grandmother sometimes asked me to draw the table over for her, and whenever she asked, I did it quickly.

vii.

(I had nothing to do. The house was empty, hollow, dreary, vacant, abandoned.

Time didn't move. In the living room I looked up at the rows of books on their shelves behind glass doors flanking the fireplace. I went into the basement. I came up again, went through the kitchen, then the dining room, and climbed the carpeted stairs to the second floor. I stood in the hallway near the telephone table and looked from one end of the hall to the other. I went into each of the rooms and came out of them again, including my father's room and the storage room with the tent pegs and tennis rackets in it.

My grandmother reads. She writes letters. The house is quiet and no one is in it. My grandmother sometimes listens to the radio. In her wheelchair at the dining room table she almost always does so. On Saturday mornings when I am there, the station from Old College broadcasts selections of music interspersed with periods of talk and discussion. I pay little attention to it. The sound of the radio seems to me dreary, vacant, and churchlike.

viii.

(Professor F. K. Kampfer most often came in through the front door. He would give the bell a quick double ring, open the door himself, put his head inside, then sing out the word "hello" in a way that was less interrogative than declarative. He sang the second syllable in three extended tones that I thought of as forming an undulating string of letter "o's" that came into the house, wending their way through doors and around corners into my grandmother's ear.

•

If the weather was at all wet, snowy, or muddy, Professor Kampfer's ring would be more distant because he would come in at the back door instead of the front. He would step into the wood-paneled vestibule, take off his boots and leave them on the mat there, then come up the three steps, open the kitchen door and sing out his "hello." Invariably, as though imagining that he still had on wet boots, or muddy ones, he would tiptoe across the kitchen floor, appearing at the entry to the dining room with only thick wool stockings on his feet.

•

My grandmother clearly seemed pleased at the attentions she received from Professor Kampfer. She received him eagerly, with smiles and an awkward, brief half-embrace, for which he leaned down to her. In spite of the fervor of these visits, I remember them as normally lasting little more than ten or fifteen minutes. This kind of brevity, however, was in keeping with one of Professor Kampfer's most pronounced traits, which was the impression he gave of being always in very great haste.

If my grandmother was in her bedroom, he would go in immediately and, after the embrace, draw up the small straight chair to the side of the bed. If she was in the dining room, he would sit at the table where my mother had sat, with his back toward the windows.

He brought items of food for my grandmother—breads, cakes, muffins that he had made himself, small jars of his own preserves from the raspberry bushes in his yard. With very nearly each visit, too, he would return reading materials that my grandmother had given him, commenting without fail—whether or not the two went on to discuss the matter further—that what he'd read had been "very interesting." In turn, he often brought items for my grandmother to read. Sometimes these were books with certain chapters set off by markers. More often they were articles in popular magazines or in alumni or church newsletters. On the following Saturday's visit they would make their exchanges again.

•

(From the beginning, I found Professor Kampfer a curiosity but at the same time faintly unsettling. There was a quality in his appearance—partly the result of his eyebrows, which were dark and bushy and seemed to be held up by tiny invisible hooks—that gave him a look of constant surprise.

In the time I knew him, I doubt that he and I spoke more than twenty words. I know, however, that I had more than twenty moments of uneasiness when, for no apparent reason, I would notice Professor Kampfer staring at me fixedly, as if I were a mystery in need of solving, or—thanks to his eyebrows again—as if I had just done something so alarming as to render him shocked and speechless.

I had no idea that Professor Kampfer was later to play so significant a role in my life. He, too, I'm sure, would have been equally surprised to know the same thing.

•

The pleasure my grandmother took in his company must been due in some part simply to the length of their acquaintance. Professor Kampfer, after all, had lived around the corner (or through the block) on Poplar Street since 1928, the year he began teaching at Old College. This meant that my grandmother had known him and his family—a now-deceased wife and a son grown and gone—for over a quarter of a century.

My own curiosity about Professor Kampfer was less personal than my grandmother's but no more limited. Unquestionably, he was strange both in appearance and behavior. There were his startled eyebrows, his perpetual haste, his rapid speech, the bird-like quickness of his movements,

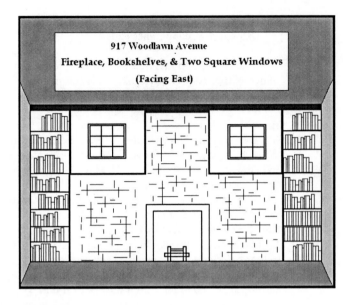

917 Woodlawn Avenue
Fireplace, Bookshelves, & Two Square Windows
(Facing East)

and, most noticeable of all, his curiously asymmetrical mouth. Not only was its left side higher than the right, but a tic had chosen to make its home somewhere within that same left lip. Whenever the tic became active, the top lip jerked suddenly upward—as if tugged by another tiny hook—and exposed the long yellow canine residing behind it. The fleeting appearance of that tooth gave Professor Kampfer an oddly sinister look, as if a civilized face had been ever so briefly unmasked to reveal a glimpse of the speechless carnivore behind it.

ix.

(I can't be absolutely certain which of the following is of the greatest significance, either in and of itself or in its relationship to the future:
1) the clothing worn by Professor Kampfer
2) the mingled smells that sometimes arose from Professor Kampfer's clothing
3) the fact that Professor Kampfer existed seemingly in a different plane of time from everyone else, since he continued

to dwell within the Epoch of Walking when, for all others, that epoch had long since ended

The three, I do know, are of equal interest insofar as all concern themselves obviously with the mysteries of space and time.

x.

Like anyone else's, Professor Kampfer's clothing varied with the seasons. It differed from other people's, however, in being so clearly old-fashioned, as if he had received it from storage in some previous era.

Whether his appearance seemed more unusual in summer or winter is difficult to say. In the cold months, wearing black leather boots that came slightly more than halfway up his calves, a Russian black fur hat, a greatcoat that hung below his knees, and oversized fur mittens, he would walk out in any and all weather. He did so even in the most fierce of blizzards, when he would also put on dark goggles with small round lenses. In the drift-bound, below-zero weather that followed the storms, he could be seen moving through the unpopulated silence on snowshoes.

In summer, on the other hand, he was distinguished by being the only male in West Tree over six years of age to wear short pants. Sometimes these were authentic lederhosen, though most of the time they were belted, baggy, multi-pocketed gray shorts of soft thick cotton. In addition, he wore a pair of dusty oxfords and knee-high socks, an open shirt under a four-buttoned brown jacket (the latter omitted in hot weather), and on his head a Bavarian felt hat with the tail feather of a pheasant set in it at a rakish angle. In this season, he always carried with him a dark, knobbed, slightly crooked walking stick.

•

(He was wearing these clothes one unseasonably warm Saturday morning in April of 1954 when he came in at the front door, crossed the living room, passed the dining room piano, and came to a stop at my grandmother's elbow to look down at something she was reading. He stopped at her elbow at precisely the same moment that I, having been upstairs, where I hadn't heard him arrive, opened the staircase door and came into the dining room.

This coincidental timing placed me very close to him, and it was necessary for me to draw even closer as I stepped behind him (and my grandmother) in order to go into the kitchen. It was at just that moment, as I squeezed between him and the china cabinet, that I caught the scent that made its way out from the folds and creases of his summer walking clothes, perhaps mainly from the brown jacket. It was a smell made up, as I've mentioned, mainly of the scent of mothballs and of very old woodsmoke, these mingled with three or four other traces, much fainter.

I know now that it was the scent of the past, of what had been but was no more, of what had existed and now did not. The scent brought to me, with an overwhelming immediacy and power, a flood of lost things from abandoned years like 1923, 1927, 1931, 1934, and 1938; the vanished remnants of days spent hiking, of backpacks, dust, trails, pine needles, forest floors, of streams and rods and reels and fish-knives and tents and creels and canvas and campfires—an impression so overwhelming to me that, as I left the dining room and went in through the kitchen door (Professor Kampfer, scarcely disturbed, gave me this time only a second's incurious glance before he turned back to my grandmother's reading material), I took with me for the first time in my life the sudden understanding that the past does exist but that the things in it do not; that the scent of old woodsmoke was the scent of something no longer there and that therefore does not exist and yet does exist; and that the mysteries of space and time must indeed be the mysteries holding the answers to all things and yet at the same time remaining, and showing every promise of remaining always, out of reach, impenetrable, and insoluble.

Four Notes on Time and Space

1.

In third grade, I once missed the school bus by going into a hiding place until the bus left without me. At the time, I didn't know why I did this. I think now that it was a test to see whether I could alter my father's life by causing him to come and retrieve me.

Something is a test only if it's possible that it might fail. Somewhere in my mind, I suspect now, was the idea that this one, too, might fail, that very possibly no one would ever come for me.

•

By this time—the autumn of 1949—my family had lived outside of town for two years. The Epoch of Walking was still in existence, but only in its very last stages.

Like Marie and Lutie, my mother had never learned how to drive, so if anyone came for me it would have to be my father.

•

I don't remember planning my strategy in advance, but I clearly remember executing it. The Emerson School was a perfect square, with entrances on the east, west, and north, as I have said. Extending from its south side, a low, flat, windowless projection had been added as housing for the school's boiler plant. This projection was almost as wide as the school's south facade, but it was physically connected only at the southeast corner. For the rest, an alley five or six feet wide was left so that daylight would still fall into the basement room that was used alternately as a gymnasium and lunchroom. The alley was blind at its deep end, and that's where I chose my hiding place.

If someone did come to get me, there would be revealed a connection between one point and another, between the farm where my family lived and the alley where I hid, just as though a string had been drawn out between them. And if my father was the one who came, it would show a connection, in turn, between him and me.

•

The autumnal afternoon was warm, soft, and still. I lay at the back of the alley, on my stomach, my feet to the blind end and my face sideways, resting on my layered hands. The janitor used the alley as a holding place for furniture on its way to be burned, so it held a piled clutter of old schoolroom desks lying unceremoniously in broken and ungainly postures. One desk, resting on its side, provided a blind for me. I lay on the bare ground behind it, able to peer out through its empty inkwell without being seen.

I went into hiding at the last possible moment, with a glance over my shoulder in case anyone was watching as I slipped into the alley. The bare, packed earth felt cool through my clothes. If I craned to look upward, I saw only a rectangle of cloudless blue sky. Immediately in front of me, in the old cracked varnish of the desk I hid behind, were age-old inky tracings like the bare branches of trees.

The sounds of voices outside the alley gradually became more distant as students went off to get on their buses or, if they were town-students, as they left the school grounds on their way home. I heard the engines of the buses, one after another, as they pulled away from the north and east sides of the school. The last cluster or two of town students walked past the alley, their voices and laughter slowly dying away to nothing. After that, from inside the building, I heard the final bell of the day ringing in the hallways.

And then nothing. Time stopped. The sense of emptiness, melancholy, and loneliness grew unbearable.

•

Suppose that imaginary threads had connected me with the departing school buses. Those threads would now be growing longer, more tenuous, stretching to near-invisibility as the yellow buses grew smaller and smaller, then finally disappeared.

•

The air grew cooler, and the light around me diminished faintly. The pleasant autumnal warmth was fading out of the day. The dirt of the alley floor began to feel cold through my clothes.

•

(Through the inkwell-hole in my desk, I saw my father stroll past the mouth of the alley, conversing with Miss Henningson, who was wearing a brown skirt and, as usual, a white blouse open at the neck. She was ten or eleven inches shorter than my father, who bent down to hear what she was saying, a posture that gave him a look of extremely polite attentiveness. He held his hands clasped behind his back as he walked at her side. Just before they passed out of sight, Miss Henningson, who held her arms folded together in front of her breasts, turned her face up to his as she spoke.)

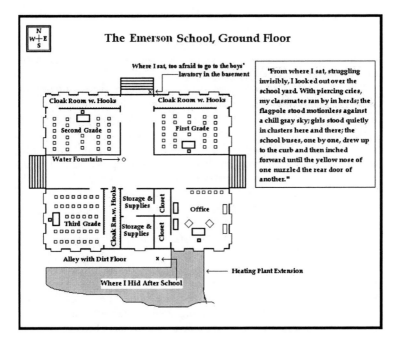

The Emerson School, Ground Floor

Where I sat, too afraid to go to the boys' lavatory in the basement

Cloak Room w. Hooks

Cloak Room w. Hooks

Second Grade

First Grade

Water Fountain ——> ○

"From where I sat, struggling invisibly, I looked out over the school yard. With piercing cries, my classmates ran by in herds; the flagpole stood motionless against a chill gray sky; girls stood quietly in clusters here and there; the school buses, one by one, drew up to the curb and then inched forward until the yellow nose of one nuzzled the rear door of another."

Cloak Rm. w. Hooks

Storage & Supplies

Closet

Office

Third Grade

Storage & Supplies

Closet

Alley with Dirt Floor

Heating Plant Extension

Where I Hid After School

2.

From the beginning of my time at the Emerson School, I disliked the building's basement rooms and was afraid of them. These included the lunchroom and also the boys' bathroom, where my experiences were invariably and powerfully unpleasant.

•

Constructed in 1897, The Emerson School was a square building with rooms in each corner and two hallways crossing at the center.

The basement was given over to varied uses, while the learning parts of the school rose proudly two stories above it. The ground floor housed the first, second, and third grades—and the principal's office—while the three higher grades occupied the second floor. When my uncle Rolf was an Emerson student, therefore, from 1925 through 1927, he would have been on the higher floor. The second floor felt to me more spacious than the floor below it. I thought of it as being flooded with air and light.

In my own three years at the school, I remember only one visit to that floor. It was at Christmas-time, when the lower grades were brought upstairs to carol the upper grades. I stood there, in the light-dazzled hallway amid my second-grade classmates, trying vainly to stay in tempo and in tune while staring at the unfamiliar openness and enormity around me.

Classroom doors opened and the upper students crowded into them to stare out at us as we sang.

•

The stairs to the basement were narrower than the others in the building, and of course they were more dark.

The smells in the lunchroom were a deterrent to the taking of pleasure there, and so was the quality of the light. The daylight that came in through the high windows (along the alley where I'd hidden) was weak, and on dark days the overhead globes went on, making the room seem the more shadowy and giving it an unpleasant brownish hue. We ate at collapsible tables made of chipped composition-board that was mapped and darkened with years and years of spilled liquids. The benches we sat on had warped over the years, so that one end jumped up into the air when someone sat down at the other.

•

The lunchroom had its more demonic counterpart in the boys' lavatory across the hall.

The lavatory was in the northwest quarter of the basement. Enormous, high-ceilinged, and dungeon-like, it had massive walls that were rough-hewn as if carved from rock. Dampness pervaded the place, and—the feature most unsettling to me—throughout the room was invariably the sound of water dripping onto water. The origin of that sound was invisible to any eye, but it could be seen all too clearly by the imagination, and I was tormented by the certainty of there being, under the stone floors, vast, dark, water-filled caverns into which a boy could very easily fall, or could be dragged, for that matter, through one drain-like opening or another, or through an unexpected structural collapse.

As in the lunchroom, there was a row of windows high under the ceiling, though, in the interest of privacy, their panes had been paint-ed brown. Against the resulting gloom, twin bulbs hung on twisted black cords from the ceiling. The light they produced was insufficient to sweep shadows out of distant corners or, even more unnerving, to penetrate into the Stygian darkness of the cabinets housing the row of toilets, with their wide-mawed openings to the below.

In winter, the painted windows remained shut. In these months, the hiss of steam from a massive iron radiator bolted to one wall—it was rectangular and coiled, like huge rusty intestines—accompanied the sound of the dripping water. In spring, however, the janitor used a long pole with a metal nipple at its end to open the latches, allowing each window to tip inward eight or ten inches, where it would be held by a chain from coming farther.

The period of open windows—a few weeks in autumn, maybe a month in spring—allowed some amount of light and air into the room but changed things too little to remove the fear the enormous room held for me. The lavatory—it was referred to by no other word—was designed on a scale inexplicably gargantuan. There were three enor-mous urinals (their brown-hued ceramic fretted by networks of sub-dermal cracks), and in front of each, on the floor, were two shoe-prints indicating, presumably, the distance from the urinal, on the one hand, and, on the other, the degree of open-leggedness that were considered the universally correct ones for successful urination. These alarm-ing shoe-indentations (hadn't dead people stood in them?) were so large that my own feet filled little more than half of each, and, if I ac-tually did step into the two of them, my legs were forced absurdly far apart. The urinals themselves, meanwhile, were twice my height and loomed overhead as I stood there, holding onto my un-urinating penis and fearing the sudden push from behind that would propel me into this stone coffin, where I would be sucked down, like phlegm, though a black drain and into the cavernous chambers below, where I would slowly drown in the horror of darkness, cold, fetor, and slime.

The urinals, even so, were less fearsome than the toilets. In a toilet, being not only alone but out of the sight of others, a person would be even more defenseless against and more exposed—both through pos-ture and nakedness—to a drain far larger than in the case of the urinals and therefore one allowing transport all the more easily down into the watery and terrifying regions below.

·

In first and second grade, I still had no meaningful awareness of my penis, though my bowels were another matter. Their expressive power held me in a state of uncertainty, since I couldn't predict when they might all of a sudden bend me again to their will. So far, I had been lucky: neither in first grade nor so far in second had an urge come to me requiring that I go into one of the toilet stalls. Such luck was extremely important, since I had made up my mind that I never would go into one of them, no matter what might happen or what the alternative to it might entail.

I know that at least a certain number of my classmates shared this feeling and that they, too, preferred anything over leaving the comfort and warmth of the classroom to descend in solitude to that chill, dark, threatening, rock-hewn underworld. Not with great frequency, but perhaps four or five times a year, always at an unexpected moment—when we were scissoring shapes from paper, doing arithmetic, listening to a story—the powerful smell of new feces would arise from somewhere in the room, faint at first, then rapidly overwhelming. The victim was invariably a boy, never—ever—a girl, and he could be identified easily by merit simply of his being whichever boy in the class was just then the most earnestly absorbed in whatever work happened to lie on his desk—so absorbed that he alone seemed to notice no terrible smell, he alone not raising his head to look around the room in search of its origin. Saying nothing, but walking with a seemingly casual directness over to that person, the teacher would bend down, quickly whisper something into his ear, then raise him gently by the arm and escort him quickly from the room. Within only a moment, she would return as if nothing had happened, having left the boy somewhere behind—exactly where, and in what ruined misery and humiliation, I could only too well imagine.

·

I prayed that such a thing would never happen to me, but it was a prayer against destiny. My own moment came at the very end of a day, when class had already been dismissed. There had already been snow, then a thaw, and then cold weather, so that the school yard had a dirty, trodden, bare appearance under a gray sky.

It was a chill and damp kind of weather, in other words, the air not far above the freezing point. All of us wore rubber boots, winter coats, hats and mittens, though the mittens were carried mainly in pockets, as, much of the time, were the hats. The rubber boots were invariably left open, resulting in a jingle of the metal clasps when we ran.

I don't remember when I first sensed danger, but I do remember the moment of decision, when I fell away from whatever game we were playing, its main element being our running in a herd across the school yard. It may have looked as though I'd been struck by an arrow, the way I dropped suddenly out of the running pack, which swept on without me, noticing nothing, and then was gone. I walked—as casually as I was able—around the school to the north entrance. There, I climbed up the stairs, as if I were about to go inside. Instead, when I reached the top step, I sat down.

•

It must have been almost three-thirty, that being the time when the school day officially ended. From where I sat, I watched the first two or three buses turn the corner from Third Street and lumber up to the curb on the east side of the playground. Soon more of the yellow buses would arrive, and park, and people would begin climbing up the three steps made of puckered iron and getting on.

•

I think now that I went up the stairs in order to gain height. Doubtless, the basement toilets were in my mind, but in it just as certainly was the knowledge that, no matter what, I would be incapable of forcing myself to go there. What I needed most, therefore, were height, elevation, altitude, eminence, symbols of strength.

•

That I sat down, thus diminishing my height by whatever small extent, was a result of the logical instinct to meet internal pressure with counter-pressure from outside, the weight of my body being the only means available to me of slowing the inevitability of what was about to happen.

My winter coat, too, was placed between me and the historic old step I sat on—and I felt certain it would somehow, by its substance and thickness and weight, help resist the force pressing from inside.

But I was wrong, of course; nothing was going to help. Paralyzed by the power inside me on the one hand and my craven fear of the underground toilets on the other, I was destined for isolation, humiliation, and shame. Still, the location where this was about to take place made the experience of it greater in meaning than it could have been otherwise, even if I wasn't to understand this fact until many years later. But from where I sat, struggling invisibly, I looked out across the school yard. My schoolmates ran by in flocks and herds, giving off piercing cries and yells amid the jangle of boot clasps; the flagpole stood motionless against a chill gray sky; girls stood off talking in clusters here and there; a school bus, then another, and another, drew up and stopped at the end of the row of buses. I watched all of these things happening. I heard, behind me, the 3:30 bell marking the end of the day. And, unable to hold out for even another instant against the overpowering force of my own body, I gave up. I failed. I lost. I let go.

And then, for a brief but ecstatic moment of indescribable pleasure and relief, I felt myself being elevated, being raised up above the world spread out below me.

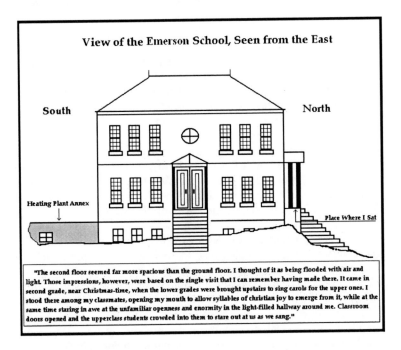

View of the Emerson School, Seen from the East

South

North

Heating Plant Annex

Place Where I Sat

"The second floor seemed far more spacious than the ground floor. I thought of it as being flooded with air and light. Those impressions, however, were based on the single visit that I can remember having made there. It came in second grade, near Christmas-time, when the lower grades were brought upstairs to sing carols for the upper ones. I stood there among my classmates, opening my mouth to allow syllables of christian joy to emerge from it, while at the same time staring in awe at the unfamiliar openness and enormity in the light-filled hallway around me. Classroom doors opened and the upperclass students crowded into them to stare out at us as we sang."

On that step, in those surroundings, at that moment (I came to understand this only much later), everything within me and around me converged in such a way as to unite me with all times, places, and people: so that I was connected not only with my grandmother, who undoubtedly had walked across this very step, and through her with her children and through them with the rest of my family and therefore with the history of my family, with my father and grandfather and great-grandfather, with all great-aunts and all my great-uncles, with all the distant parts of the world they had gone to and come back from, all the knowledge they had gained and the languages they had learned—so that I, rising up now in my own mute, helpless, and unlearned way, possessed no language yet every language, no knowledge yet all knowledge, no understanding yet all understanding, being, seeing, and feeling in this one singular place and yet able to be, feel, and see as if in all others—as the athlete, for example, would see and feel from his giddy place at the top of the ski jump in the last disappearing instant before pushing off—with the result that tendrils reached out ahead of me, and around me, and behind me, in every direction, uniting and connecting me (certainly this was so) with everything in the world and with all of time.

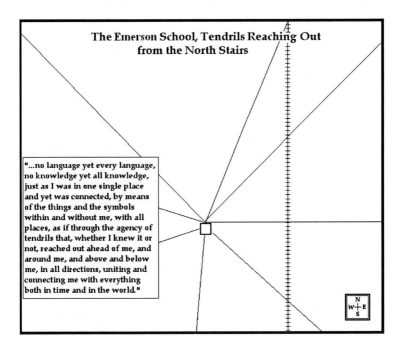

The Emerson School, Tendrils Reaching Out from the North Stairs

"...no language yet every language, no knowledge yet all knowledge, just as I was in one single place and yet was connected, by means of the things and the symbols within and without me, with all places, as if through the agency of tendrils that, whether I knew it or not, reached out ahead of me, and around me, and above and below me, in all directions, uniting and connecting me with everything both in time and in the world."

3.

(After my grandmother left West Tree in May of 1957, Professor Kampfer continued in his role as the solitary living vestige of the Epoch of Walking. As for myself during this period, I traveled around West Tree and environs mainly by means of my bicycle.

Riding one place or another, I would often meet Professor Kampfer on outlying roads or trails, though sometimes catching sight of him only in the distance. With his dusty oxfords, baggy shorts, knee-high socks, brown jacket, knotty walking stick, and Bavarian hat, he would commonly walk out into the countryside, and it sometimes seemed almost more than by chance alone that I would either meet or overtake him at one of the eight entryways into West Tree—the shaded road where it curved below the Nordic ski jump, for example, or the southeast entrance as it came in past the high school football field, or the seldom-used southwest road that had been a main artery in the last century, or even—my favorite entrance—the almost unused northeast road that passed a country cemetery a few miles out before it dipped down into the willow-shaded stream bed on the east edge of the New College campus, climbed steeply up the east side of New College Hill, and emerged thereafter as East First Street.

We knew one another, of course, and yet we never spoke when we met or passed. Sometimes, it's true, we were too far apart to observe amenities, but usually this wasn't so. I might be pedaling south on the same road that was taking him north, yet even then, as we passed within a foot or two of one another, our greetings consisted of a polite nod on my part and, on his, of nothing at all except a fixed stare until I had passed, so that I carried away with me the image of his raised eyebrows, his startled eyes enlarged behind their thick lenses, his asymmetrical mouth, and the long canine exposed by the upward jump of his lip.

I don't know when Professor Kampfer retired (he may have been retired already when I saw him at my grand-mother's house), and I have no idea when he died. As late as 1957, I know, he still taught Sunday school at St. Peter's, and I know also, at least through 1954, that he still offered his Old College "science club" for interested high school boys. I know this because I went to it once, when he demonstrated a cloud chamber.

•

Considering the powerful influence Old College had on the direction and focus of my life (not to mention its influence on my coming into existence at all), I spent a very small amount of time there. Even so, two indisputably important memories did take place there, each with a pivotal bearing on what was to become my life's study of space and time.

Both memories seem to me now almost equally distant, although in fact a considerable time separates them. One took one place in 1949 and the other not until 1955, when I was in eighth grade. This was my crucially important memory of Professor Kampfer and the cloud chamber.

•

I went to the meeting through the influence of Allen Torvald, whom I'd known since kindergarten but became close friends with only in junior high school. Laconic, droll, extremely near-sighted, and extraordinarily intelligent, Allen had already been a part of the science club for a year or so, along with one or two other classmates whom I didn't know as well. I ought to come to the meeting, Allen told me. It was going to be out of the ordinary. Professor Kampfer was going to demonstrate a cloud chamber.

•

Lilledahl Hall of Physics and Chemistry wasn't one of the college's handful of earliest buildings, but dated from 1912. That was early enough, even so, for it to have taken on the qualities of antiquity. It was made of large rough granite blocks darkened by age, and the ivy climbing its walls had closed in around many of its deep, multi-paned windows, adding to the gothic and medieval air of the building.

Inside, however, I was carried back not to the middle ages but to the decades of the 1910's and 1920's. The wooden floors were deeply worn and poured out lamentations of creaks and groans under a person's feet. Just going in through the doorways into classrooms took me back to the world when my great-aunts Marie and Lutie had been young, when they had walked day after day through these same doorways or others like them.

The room where Professor Kampfer held his demonstration was large—cavernous, in fact, considering the handful of eight or ten students who attended. Writing desks rose in tiers up toward the distant back wall. Down at the other end, where the instructor would stand, there was a blackboard on the wall, and in front of the blackboard was not a lectern but instead a slate-topped counter with faucets over a square sink at one end and at the other three silver petcocks standing at attention, like toy soldiers, with their small heads thrown back.

•

I didn't know what a "cloud chamber" was, but the strangeness of the phrase itself appealed to me. When Allen Torvald mentioned it, I thought of clouds in a blue sky but had no idea how they could be contained in a "chamber." Nor did I understand Allen's reference to "rays" or to their being made visible in the "chamber," a word that reminded me only of "gas chamber."

The Old College lecture room had in it a powerful feeling of emptiness, with its tiers of unoccupied seats rising up to the back wall and the darkness of night pushing against the tall windows. The darkness seemed more heightened than dispelled by the yellowed glass globes that hung from the ceiling.

Professor Kampfer stood behind the counter at the front, his appearance familiar to me in every way except for his wearing of a white laboratory coat. His eyebrows and mouth, however, his thick glasses, upper lip, and canine tooth were all as I remembered them from our many previous meetings.

On the slate counter in front of him rested an object the size, say, of two or three cigar boxes stacked one on top of another. The construction had walls of what looked like very thick glass held together and sealed at their edges by strips of metal and thick windings of tape, giving it a blunt and sturdy look that reminded me of the windshield of a B-17. A piece of rubber hose came out from one corner of the box and ran to a vacuum pump. The cloud chamber itself—for this indeed is what it was—rested in a small rubber-lined tub and was nestled in among broken chunks of quietly smoking dry ice.

Pushing in around the counter with the other boys, I looked down through the top of the chamber, seeing nothing. And then, from that nothing, a diagonal line appeared, thinner than a white thread from my mother's sewing basket—a trail of fog left by a passing cosmic ray in the hyper-cold vacuum inside the box. The trail held there, suspended for some brief moments before fading away. In the meantime, another appeared, on a different angle and seemingly from a different direction entirely. After it, and sometimes concurrently, were others, thin, ductile, fine, gray-white lines that appeared again and again out of nothingness and remained a moment or two before fading: the cobweb-trails of criss-crossing particles and rays moving in every direction simultaneously from one far edge of the universe to another, passing through any and every substance as if it were nothing, as if the rays were heedlessly busy with the job of knitting all things together, and yet at the same time were wholly unregulated and unconfined, either by space or by time.

4.

(In the spring of 1949, besides operating our farm, my father took a job, part time, substituting for an English instructor at Old College.

I was eight years old, and because 1949 was still the year before the Epoch of Walking was to begin ending in earnest, time still existed all around me: For a brief period longer, it would remain as omnipresent and nurturing as the air, and as impossible for one not to absorb.

Through this continued existence of time, certain aspects of richness in the world, and certain aspects of depth, could still be experienced, qualities that also revealed through the concomitant and continued existence of color, texture, mood, scent, implication, and feeling—a wealth of qualities resident within experience that all too soon were themselves going to begin disappearing altogether.

•

At the base of Old College Hill, Christiania Avenue abruptly lost its name and turned simply into a one-way road curving up the steep east slope of the hill. Often enough, I rode there with my father on errands up to Old College. As the ascent began, I could look out the left window and see a limestone retaining wall sliding by only feet from my eyes; or I could look out the right window at a sheer drop, where the road was held in place by another retaining wall, this one below road level. After we'd crested the hill and made a hundred-and-eighty degree turn, I could look out the back across a broad vista of prairie rolling westward. Then, a moment later, as the car moved slowly under tall trees, I could look out from any window and see sidewalks, lawns, and buildings—some of red brick, some of limestone, one of wood—that made me think, as I always did, of the hilltop campus as being a small separate town in itself.

•

(Late spring, a cloudless day, warm and still. It was finals week in the spring semester of 1949—near the end of the week, so that there were few students on the walkways or on the lawns reading, most having finished their exams and gone home.

My father had another errand to run—turning in his grades, meeting a student for a make-up exam, I don't know—that took him to First Hall. My sisters hadn't come along.

My mother and I stayed in the car outside First Hall as my father went up the stairs and in through the front door. The car was parked up fairly close to the west façade of the old building. My mother and I sat there looking at it, with its tall windows and high floors. If I put my head out and looked up, I could almost see the pointed bell tower and flagpole on the roof.

The windows of First Hall were all open wide because of the day's warmth, and on the second floor you could see heads bowed forward as students worked on their exams. One of them sat close enough to the window so that he could rest an arm on the sill with his hand out in the air. Between the fingers of that hand he held a lit cigarette.

My mother laughed quietly and clucked her tongue in a mock-stern way that told me that she and my father had done the same thing themselves when they were students at Old College in the late 1920's and early 1930's. "Well, he's breaking the rules," my mother said, but in a school-yard way, making it into a song and holding the last word through two falling tones.

Perhaps the instructor looked up, or came back into the room just then, because the student dropped his cigarette, letting it fall from the second floor window. And in that moment, in the time it took for the cigarette to drop from window to the ground, I saw into the past. I may not have known it at the time, but I did see, through layer after layer after layer, down into the past itself.

•

Things fit together and didn't fit together. In that brief moment, as the cigarette dropped through the sunlight, all time was one.

•

I leaned forward with my elbows on the seat-back in front of me and looked at my mother. Her hair was still perfectly black, and she wore it pulled back tightly, almost severely, and shaped into a bun. She had on a flowered shirt with the sleeves rolled loosely, and over it a faded pair of farmer's denim overalls with straps over the shoulders. On her feet were ankle-high boots with garden mud caked on them.

•

When my father went up the stairs and into First Hall, he'd had on wing-tip shoes, flannel slacks, a tie, light-blue shirt, and tweed jacket.

At home, later that afternoon, he would have on a khaki shirt with the sleeves also rolled up, and khaki pants. He would have on boots like my mother's, but they would be caked not only with dried mud but also with manure from the barn.

•

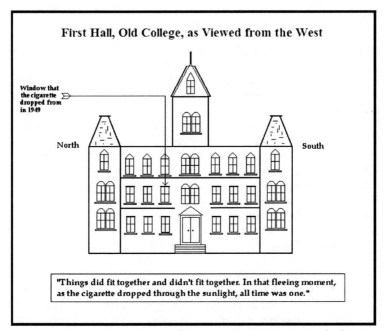

First Hall, Old College, as Viewed from the West

Window that the cigarette dropped from in 1949

North

South

"Things did fit together and didn't fit together. In that fleeing moment, as the cigarette dropped through the sunlight, all time was one."

I was eight; my mother was forty-two. Seventeen years before, in this same season, she had graduated from Old College, a year after my father. Twenty-two years earlier than that, in 1910, my great-aunt Marie had come to West Tree. Fifty-six years before that, in 1854, First Hall had been built—at a time when there were no buildings on the west side of town but a shanty or two, Christiania Avenue was a wagon trail, the wading pool didn't yet exist, or the esplanade, or the hospital, or its solarium, or Marie and Lutie's house, or its upstairs bathroom, or its back yard, or its garden tools in the shed, or my grandmother's house with skis and bicycle pump in the basement and tennis rackets in storage upstairs and the telephone on its table in the hall.

And the same was true going in the other direction as well: things that were going to exist after 1949 hadn't come into being yet or been imagined. At that moment in May of 1949, in our car, with my mother, in front of First Hall, during the time it took the cigarette to fall from the second floor window to the ground, I hadn't yet come upon my father sitting naked on the front lawn, hadn't yet visited Marie and Lutie's upstairs bathroom, hadn't yet begun to fear death or fire, hadn't yet begun hiding in the linen closet to escape my fear of death raining down from the skies, hadn't yet seen Professor Kampfer's cloud

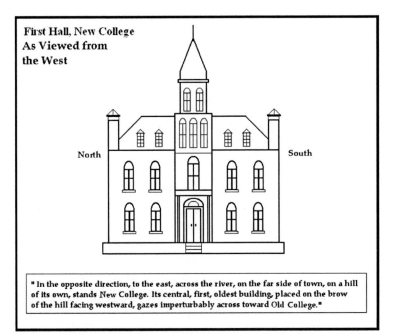

First Hall, New College
As Viewed from
the West

North

South

" In the opposite direction, to the east, across the river, on the far side of town, on a hill of its own, stands New College. Its central, first, oldest building, placed on the brow of the hill facing westward, gazes imperturbably across toward Old College."

chamber, hadn't walked in a straight line from the hospital to my grandmother's house, hadn't discovered unexpectedly the unifying function of my penis, hadn't fallen in love with Marietta Streetfield, hadn't taken her up the Nordic ski jump, hadn't begun to receive even the very first of my perceptions that the world around me was diminishing inescapably into a phenomenon of absences rather than a phenomenon of presences, the first of my perceptions that history was coming to an end, that West Tree was beginning to disappear, that not even the forces of space and time, those forces that governed all things while remaining themselves impenetrable and ungovernable, would be sufficient to keep this last, terrible, and catastrophic thing—the annihilation from the face of the earth of life as I knew with absolute and fervid and uncompromising certainty it once had been—from occurring, from taking place, from happening.

CHAPTER 5

THE END OF THE EPOCH OF WALKING
(1857–2010)

PART I

I
September 1947

One afternoon late in September of 1947, my father pulled our car to a stop on the edge of a gravel road a mile or two north of West Tree. In the passenger seat beside him sat my mother. I was squeezed in between Hannah and Signe in the back. For a moment no one spoke. We all looked out at the farmhouse that, in a few days, would be the place where we lived.

•

The afternoon was soft, warm, and quiet. The air seemed to be infused with a pale gold color as the sun fell down into the west. You could hear the ticking of the car engine as it cooled.

•

The moment was gravely historic for me, although I had no sense of its being so then. I was two months short of six.

•

A list of the three most important things that, over the next few years, were to happen to me:

1) Beginning almost at once, I was to enter into and then pass through my years of perfect seeing. This period would begin, that is, in the autumn of 1947 and come to an end at an unknown moment somewhere in late 1950 or early 1951.

2) Early one summer morning, in 1950, I would come upon my father sitting naked on the front lawn. At this time, I would by no means understand the meaning of the encounter. Later, however, through the experience of it, I was to become able not only to pinpoint the first moment of decline in my early life but also to complete my understanding, at last, and however inevitably flawed, of the nature of space and time.

3) I would, in good part as a consequence of the preceding two items, grow to witness, in the years coming after 1951, the beginning of the end of history, first by its slowing, then by its gradually collapsing, and finally by its disappearance entirely.

II

The House We Lived In

Our farmhouse stood forty or fifty feet back from the road. The driveway—just parallel tire-tracks with grass between them—went

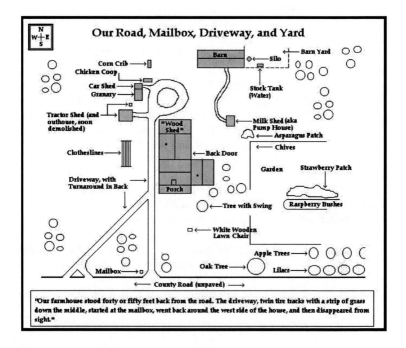

Our Road, Mailbox, Driveway, and Yard

"Our farmhouse stood forty or fifty feet back from the road. The driveway, twin tire tracks with a strip of grass down the middle, started at the mailbox, went back around the west side of the house, and then disappeared from sight."

from the mailbox past the west side of the house and then, turning, disappeared from sight.

Four or five box-elder trees stood along the drive on one side or the other, their branches leaning out in a canopy over it. To the west of the driveway was a large area shaded by enormous elms well spaced from one another in wide rows, where they must have been planted by a farmer a hundred years before. Under them, in the shade created by their high, dense foliage, grew long, light green, fallen-over grass. Still farther away from the house to the west and north was an L-shaped area of denser growth and smaller, more closely-standing trees, a number of them pines. These, with their close growth, formed a windbreak against the northwest winds, which, in the winter, were invariably the strongest and coldest.

The house itself was of white clapboard and shabby in appearance. The roof was pitched steeply, and the upstairs windows—you could see two pairs of them from the road—were set as tall narrow twins. On the ground floor, across the west half of the façade, was an open porch. It had no railing, and its floor sagged in the middle. Three posts, painted white, held up the porch roof.

Near the southeast corner of the house, there was a medium-sized tree with a rope tied to one of its horizontal branches and an automobile tire hanging down from it. This improvised swing hung two feet or so from the ground, and an area of the lawn under it had been worn away to bare dirt.

•

The house once stood in an entirely different location, a mile or so to the east alongside the Wagon river. Built there in 1857, it was moved twenty-five years later to its new location. Before the move, the house was cut into two pieces for ease of transport; at the new location, these two pieces were set at right angles to one another, and in the space between them a new section was added that would later be our dining room, with my parents' bedroom above it.

After those changes, the house had the shape of a letter "L," with the older parts forming the extremities and the newer parts tucked into the elbow.

•

Before my family moved in, there was no central heating, no indoor bathroom, and no water other than what came from a hand-pump in the kitchen. I myself was never inside the house before heat and plumbing were installed. My first memory of the interior is in fact from the day we moved, on October 10th, 1947. By that time, an electric pump and pressure tank had been installed in the bottom of the well, new pipes had been laid underground from the well to the house, a bathroom had been built, and laundry tubs had been put into a section of the pantry, off the kitchen.

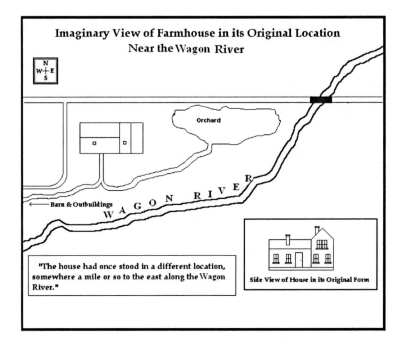

Imaginary View of Farmhouse in its Original Location Near the Wagon River

N W+E S

Orchard

← Barn & Outbuildings

WAGON RIVER

"The house had once stood in a different location, somewhere a mile or so to the east along the Wagon River."

Side View of House in its Original Form

Before we moved in, the house had had three bedrooms upstairs and one downstairs. My parents, however, divided the downstairs bedroom in two, converting the front half—which had the window—into our new bathroom and earmarking the back half for what was intended to be my father's darkroom.

Over the years that we lived there, although we went on calling it "the darkroom," the space came to be first one thing and then another, exactly as my father himself did, chameleon-like, changing from one interest to another while falling bit by bit more and more deeply into despair.

•

The day we moved in, carpenters and plumbers were still at work. The smells of sawdust, pipe compound, and hot flux were mixed in with the unnamable smells of history, antiquity, and previous lives.

When the house was moved from its earlier location, cellars had been dug under two parts of the new location, but they were never finished up with masonry. The exposed earth of the cellar walls was tan and clayey, sometimes pierced by streaks of jet black. Spade-marks were still visible where the diggers had made glancing cuts when they were shaping the walls. For strength, the walls stopped five or six feet short of the foundations and were left curved inward at their bottoms,

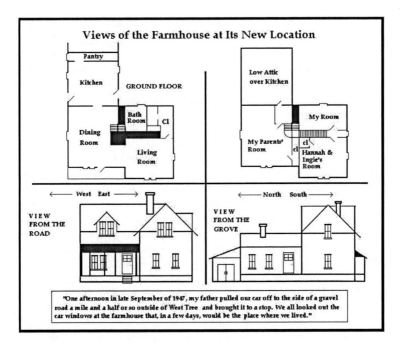

Views of the Farmhouse at Its New Location

GROUND FLOOR: Pantry, Kitchen, Dining Room, Bath Room, Cl, Living Room

Low Attic over Kitchen, My Room, My Parents' Room, cl, Hannah & Ingie's Room

← West   East →

VIEW FROM THE ROAD

← North   South →

VIEW FROM THE GROVE

"One afternoon in late September of 1947, my father pulled our car off to the side of a gravel road a mile and a half or so outside of West Tree and brought it to a stop. We all looked out the car windows at the farmhouse that, in a few days, would be the place where we lived."

making the already crowded cellar even smaller. Overhead were the hand-trimmed beams that held up the ground floor. Some had small branches and twigs still showing. Foggy-gray growths of cobwebs stretched between them and were always visible up in the basement corners.

The cellar had two rooms, the larger one under our living room, the smaller under the dining room. In the first, under the wooden steps that led the way down, a new water heater rested on cement blocks. Wires sprouted from its top and led to a gray metal box attached to a beam nearby. Also from under the stairs, two small copper pipes carrying water disappeared into a black crawl space under the kitchen.

In the middle of this same cellar room, filling it almost entirely, squatted our coal furnace. Great fat ducts wrapped with white asbestos bandages came out of its top and crossed under the ceiling before disappearing up into the dining room, kitchen, bathroom, and living room, where they re-appeared in the baseboards as forced-air ducts. There was no heat on the second floor, although square cut-throughs had been made in all the upstairs floors when the house was built. These were fitted with iron grills so that heat from downstairs would rise into the rooms above.

The second basement room was entered through a low doorway, and in this room there was no lighting, not even a hanging bulb, like in the other room. It was very small, with warped shelves placed against its north wall for storing food in the winter. In the opposite wall, a root cellar had been dug into the earthen wall. It was fronted with a wooden door perhaps two-and-a-half feet square, which in turn was fitted with small hinges and an old-fashioned latch. Sometimes I opened the door and leaned in. I found nothing inside except silence and the smell of earth and clay.

•

In spite of the changes my family made in the house, antiquity remained present everywhere. In all of the upstairs bedrooms, the ceilings sloped downward with the angle of the roof. The glass in their windows was ancient and thin, filled with distortions: ripples, swirls, and thin, elongated bubbles. The windows themselves were simple and plain, tall and much more narrow than those we had had in town.

In Ingie and Hannah's bedroom, the small initials "R. S" were etched into a corner of one of the panes, and beneath them the number "82." After we moved in, Hannah and Ingie and my mother found out that the initials stood for Rose Shisgall, the mother of our neighbor Helen Shuha. Helen Shuha, with her husband Harve, lived on the first farm to the west of ours, a third of a mile away. They lived there alone, having long since raised their own children, who were now grown and gone.

Helen Shuha said that her mother had lived in our house when it still stood over by the river, and that she had gotten married the same year the house was moved. Until then, she had shared this room with her sisters, one older and two younger. Before she left home, she etched her initials and the number for the year 1882 in the glass with her engagement ring.

By the time she told this story, in 1947, Helen Shuha herself was well past fifty, a small, slight woman with a sweet wrinkled face and a manner so polite as to make her seem timid. Like most of the farm wives who lived around us, she always wore a dress (unlike my mother), even on working days. You would see her bent over in her garden, picking or weeding, or in the orchard west of her house, reaching up to gather apples, but either way wearing a dress, as always.

•

From time to time, when my sisters weren't in their room, I would kneel on Hannah's pillow at the head of her bed and look at the scratches in the glass. Then I would fluff the pillow back into shape to disguise my having been there.

•

So far as I knew, Harve Shuha and one other farmer in the neighborhood were the only ones who still used work horses. The other was Harve's older brother William, who lived on a farm to the east, near the river.

Harve's two horses were named Betsy and Flossie. They were enormous, slow, gentle animals with abundant hair in their manes and tails, and at their ankles, and with hooves almost as big as dinner plates. Most of Harve's land lay straight south across the road from our house, and in the spring he would plow with the horses. Holding the plow-handles and at the same time the leather reins, he would walk behind the team, making his way back and forth down one furrow of blackening earth after another.

Not much later, because of their age, he began using the horses only for hitching to wagons and pulling lighter loads. You would see them on the road or in the fields less often. Soon they were gone altogether. For pulling and fieldwork after that, Harve used his John Deere.

And now, of course, the old tractor is also gone, along with Harve, and Helen, and the garden, and the orchard, or any other remaining evidence that the farm was ever there in the first place.

III
My Years of Perfect Seeing

During my years of perfect seeing, I was able to remember in perfect detail even the smallest stimulus that came to me either through sight or any other sense.

This important and intense period of exactness, I now think, came about from my having begun to grow intellectually before having reached, or even begun nearing, puberty.

Without sexual desire, in other words, life did not yet have any additional purpose for me beyond the existential phenomenon simply of existing within it. Consequently, it was as though the farm were water, and I were the fish swimming in it.

·

Inside and outside the farmhouse, history existed everywhere.

·

In the attic over the kitchen—little more than a crawl space, really—were the remnants of a chimney that had once led up from a wood-burning stove below. The bricks of this chimney—it seemed as I touched them—still carried the presence of the hands that had laid them. It was the same way with everything in the house, though more dramatically in some cases than others. Obviously it was so in the case of the sharply angled ceilings upstairs, for example, and in the case of the floors there. Because these were made without tongue and groove, but of plain boards laid down and nailed side by side, cracks would open up between them, especially in winter, wide enough to collect decades' worth of beads, earrings, trinkets, and even coins, like the old penny Hannah dug out one time, dated 1908.

Only half aware that I was doing it, I explored the house in such a way as to find those places that took me back most directly into history, giving me the physical feel of the past and allowing me to breathe its air. Such places included some of the curious nooks and crannies that had been created by the house's having been cut in two and then added to—like the cubby hole upstairs, a cube of space you could crawl into and be suspended directly over the place in the staircase—once straight but now T-shaped—where it split east and west. Other such places belonged to the older but unaltered part of the house—the square window, for example, at the top of the east stairs between bedrooms, set at floor level inside its own small gable.

In the cellar, I drew my fingers over the scars left on the walls by the glancing cuts of spades three-quarters of a century before. In the smaller room, I opened and closed the door of the root cellar, noting the neat working of its hinges and observing its flat-toned, iron-colored latches.

•

The closet behind my father's darkroom, where I often went to hide, was another spot in the house that felt especially rich with layers of history.

It was windowless, and on a clothes pole along its east wall hung a large collection of dresses and coats. Included was the fur-collared coat

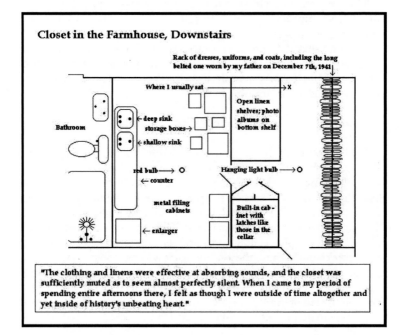

Closet in the Farmhouse, Downstairs

Rack of dresses, uniforms, and coats, including the long belted one worn by my father on December 7th, 1941

Where I usually sat → X

Open linen shelves; photo albums on bottom shelf

Bathroom

← deep sink
storage boxes →
← shallow sink

red bulb → O
← counter

Hanging light bulb → O

metal filing cabinets

Built-in cab-inet with latches like those in the cellar

← enlarger

"The clothing and linens were effective at absorbing sounds, and the closet was sufficiently muted as to seem almost perfectly silent. When I came to my period of spending entire afternoons there, I felt as though I were outside of time altogether and yet inside of history's unbeating heart."

that my mother had worn the day in 1941 when I was brought home from the hospital, and the voluminous belted coat that my father wore on the same occasion. Two navy uniforms also hung there, one white and one navy blue, along with many other items of clothing, some of which I recognized and many not. Built into the southwest corner of the closet was a floor-to-ceiling cabinet whose doors were hinged and latched in exactly the same way and with the same kind of fixtures as the door of the root cellar in the basement. In the northwest corner were four wide shelves that also went up to the ceiling, these piled with towels, sheets, tablecloths, napkins, and linens. The bottom shelf was used for other things. It was piled with pieces of photographic equipment, some boxed and some not, and with stacks of oversize books, especially my father's photography annuals, which began with volumes from the middle 1930s and then, year by year, continued up through the end of the war.

Because there was no window, the closet seemed especially isolated, though still clearly harboring its layers of history. Partly because of the clothing that hung there, and the linens piled on the shelves, sounds were so effectively absorbed that the closet seemed perfectly silent, and when I came to my period of spending entire afternoons there, I felt as though I were outside of time altogether and yet inside history's heart.

•

The kitchen, which was also part of the original house, nevertheless differed greatly from the closet. It had two windows, for one thing (a third if you counted the pantry), two interior doors (both joining it with the dining room), and two outside doors. The east door—the one we called "the back door"—was the one we used most often. On the wall behind it were hooks for coats, scarves, and hats. In all seasons, newspapers were spread out on the floor under the hooks for boots to be set on. This back door (though not in the case of my own early morning outings) was the door people used when they were going out to the back yard or garden, or to the barn, or the milk shed, or the chicken coop or granary or tractor shed, or anywhere else out back of the house.

Deep in the corner behind the door leaned my father's 22 and his twelve-gauge shotgun in its leather case with fleece lining.

At one time there had been a porch on the west side of the kitchen, facing the elm grove. It was now gone entirely except for a few hanging boards, and the west door of the kitchen—which in fact was painted shut—would have opened only onto a four-foot drop into a bed of lilies of the valley.

•

From the beginning it was clear to me that certain areas of the kitchen were more completely filled with the past than others. One of these was the east window, to your right as you faced the sink. My mother had planted morning-glories under it and had put up strings for them to climb on. In the summer, as a result, the window framed a picture of the green vines and their blue, bell-shaped flowers. After the sun had gone over to the other side of the house, the light that came through the east window was muted and cool, similar to the light that had come through the vines in my great-aunt Marie's study in West Tree.

The morning-glory window, like the west door, was painted tightly shut. For curtains it had only a fringe at the top, of blue and yellow checks made from feed sack. From time to time, my mother would fill jelly glasses with sprays of wildflowers or bits of blooming grasses. She would set these on the middle ledge, where, after their water evaporated, they would dry out and stay untouched for long periods of time. In the later years, when my father was beguiling death to an early embrace by drinking more and more intensely, he would set empty bottles in the same place, where they would remain until they gathered coats of dust—an akvavit bottle, a frosted-glass genever bottle, two or three brown bottles emptied of Irish stout.

•

Other especially time-saturated places in or near the kitchen:

1) The corner cupboard. Fitted into the northwest corner, and filling it, was a cupboard made of painted tongue-and-groove slats. Its single door was hinged on the left, and its small spring-latch, again, was identical to the latches on the cabinet in the closet and on the door of the root cellar downstairs. There were four triangular shelves inside the cupboard, the top one too high to be accessible (even for my mother or Hannah, although of course not for my father) except by standing on a stool. Built under the cupboard, and appearing at first to be a part of it, was a flour bin. Hinged at its bottom, it was fitted at its top with a finger-grip as an aid in tilting the bin outward.

2) The pantry. Passing through a doorway placed between the corner cupboard and the sink brought you, on the right, to a windowless utility space and, on the left and through one more open doorway, to the pantry. This was a tiny room, perhaps six by seven, with a full-size window in its west wall.

Most of the width of the crowded little room was taken up by hanging cabinets on the north and built-in shelves on the south; on both sides, as well, were flat counter-tops, with cabinets also below them. Except for the presence of the window, the effect was like that of a ship's galley. The pale yellow paint of the woodwork, however, was less reminiscent of the sea than of sunlight and summer heat, or straw and blowing chaff, or the rolling hills of our fields as they lay in the sun under stands of drying oats.

As for the pantry window itself, it, too, had been painted shut sometime before we moved to the farm. Never in my life did I see it open. One result was that the pantry, even though it was filled with goods and staples, its shelves lined three and four deep with jars of sauces, fruits, and home-canned vegetables, had about it a confined, melancholy, closed, and airless feel. How much better it would have been if a gentle draft of air could have come in through the west window. This is an absence that I now see clearly (although I did not see it then) to have been a sign, however infinitesimal, of time and history's having begun already the first imperceptible stages of moving toward their ends.

•

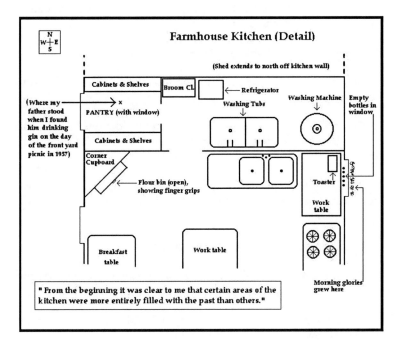

Certain important things were not meant by this feeling of past-richness, past-density, and past-vividness. In no case, for example, did it mean:

1) that the presence of the dead lingered at such past-rich spots; or

2) that the aura of the dead remained in such locations, whether at all or whether just slightly more than elsewhere; or

3) that the ghosts of the dead were felt to be nearby, if these, indeed, existed at all, which I assume and believe they did not.

The feeling, more accurately, meant the following:

1) that the past itself, unpersonified, seemed to be dwelling in such a location more intensely, completely, and with greater continuity than elsewhere;

2) this not in the form of ghosts, auras, or presences, but in the form of the actual physical object in question;

3) as, in the case of the cupboard, in the thickness of the coats of paint on its shelves and door;

4) in the pleasant resistance of the small spring latch;

5) in the feel and fit of the cast-iron finger-grip as you placed your fingers behind it;

6) in the feel of the flour bin itself as you tipped it outward, its balance being easily maintained whether the bin was full, half full, or almost empty;

7) in the sight of the pale, smooth, yellowish, unpainted panels that constituted the bottom and sides of this cunning, ancient, triangular invention that

8) had been in use without hiatus for almost a century and that

9) bore mute witness to every now un-existing hand that had opened it during that time, and to

10) every pair of eyes that had ever looked down into its reserves either of brown or of snowy white flour.

IV
My Years of Perfect Seeing, Continued

My years of perfect seeing can't be understood for what they were without certain additional facts also being clear. During my years of perfect seeing,

1) although I saw things around me in what I believe now to have been very nearly complete and perfect detail, I nevertheless

2) had no intellectual understanding of the meaning of what I saw, nor, even if such understanding had existed, did I have or would I have had sufficient vocabulary to express it. The crucial facts, then, are that

3) I sensed (because of the intensity with which I saw them) but didn't understand the importance of the things I saw; and, for this same reason,

4) during the brief, edenic period that I now call my years of perfect seeing, I felt a complete but unspoken oneness with all that I saw, a perfect harmony with whatever was around me; with the consequent and attendant result

5) that I began to understand these feelings (and therefore to sense, however faintly, the approach of their loss), on the early summer morning in 1950 when I came upon my father sitting naked and smoking a cigarette in the white wooden lawn chair on our front lawn.

•

(The fact is that in the brief but intense years of my perfect seeing, it was the sound, texture, atmosphere, scent, timbre, color, nuance, and feel of things as much as simply the look of them that made them vivid to me and caused them to remain in my memory forever, long after they themselves were gone.)

V

Our Buildings

If inside the farmhouse time still existed in various layers, and with differing qualities and degrees of intensity, how much more true this was outdoors, where an almost unlimited supply of living antiquity was to be found.

The outlying sheds and buildings alone, for example, had their own ways of containing and bespeaking the continuity of history and the existence of its layers.

•

Of these, the closest to the house (attached to it, in fact) was the lean-to shed off the north wall of the kitchen. Its double door (just wide enough, my grandfather said, for a model T) would no longer shut completely due to its dragging on the ground, a result of the shed's having sagged. As for the smaller door on the east side, it was coming off its top hinge and so was left always a foot or so ajar, allowing us to slip in and out rather than opening and closing the door.

Whether originally intended for a car, sleigh, or buckboard, or for each of these in different eras or seasons, the shed was now little more

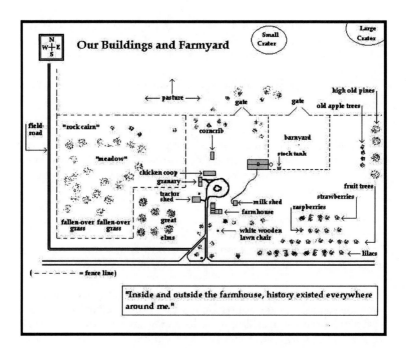

Our Buildings and Farmyard

N W E S

Small Crater

Large Crater

← pasture →

gate   gate

high old pines

old apple trees

field-road

"rock cairn"

corncrib

barnyard

stock tank

"meadow"

chicken coop
granary
tractor shed

milk shed
farmhouse

strawberries
raspberries

fruit trees

fallen-over grass   fallen-over grass   great

white wooden lawn chair

elms

lilacs

(— — — — — = fence line)

"Inside and outside the farmhouse, history existed everywhere around me."

than a repository for leftovers and refuse. We called it the woodshed, for lack of a better name. In it there was in fact a tall pile of old boards that had fallen in on itself, but also a stack of old red bricks, all with burn marks on one side, along with our own lawn mower and garden tiller, which were pushed in through the double door just far enough to be out of the rain. Our post-hole digger was also there, and, leaning against a wall, five or six old window frames with approximately half of their panes broken.

Nailed into the dirt-gray clapboard that formed the outside back wall of the pantry was an array of Minnesota license plates from as long ago as 1929 and as recent as 1942. Overhead, the unpainted wooden rafters were hung with rags, masses of twine-ends, and tangled strands of rusty baling wire. Hanging from nails on the north wall were empty gallon tins, more rags, two rusted sickles, a crowbar, a full-length scythe (it was exactly like the one that hung in the crook of a small tree along the driveway), a long-handled hoe, two or three small trowels that for some reason were tied together with twine and hung over a single nail of their own, and two big coils of cracked green garden hose. Heaped up in the northeast corner were pieces of white garden lattice, some of it broken, some curved, some flat, all of the pieces tangled together. Nesting on the cool dirt under these, our farm cats often produced their litters.

There was a smell in the shed that I liked, made up of a damp mustiness combined somehow with the old smells of the junk itself, perfumed with the tang of gasoline from our garden tiller, all put together with the darker scent of the oil that had, over the years, soaked into the dirt floor, making it now hard as rock.

·

Compared with some of the other buildings, the woodshed lacked in subtlety, in fact was even clumsy, in its way of revealing and expressing the present pastness of time. Though filled with more objects than some of the other buildings, it was, even so, historically narrower. Its rundown, ramshackle, and jumbled character suggested the qualities of the farm's previous owner—a ne'er-do-well man with wife and children (whom I'd seen but never met) known to me simply as "Mr. Beaupré"—as vividly as it did the long, infinitely deeper history of the farm itself.

·

Of the free-standing sheds, the one nearest the house was what we called indiscriminately "the pump house" or "the milk shed." It was the only out-building with anything at all modern or new about it.

It was a ten by ten square with a peaked roof of blue shingles, white clapboard sides, a window in its east and south walls, and a heavy sliding door (windowless) on its west. Renovated to pass dairy inspection rules, it was fitted with a cement floor that sloped inward from all sides toward a drain at the center, and with a milk cooler that would hold up to eight ten-gallon cans. In the bottom of the well, which could be climbed down into through a covered trapdoor in one corner of the cement floor, were our new electric pump and pressure tank.

Modern as it was, the milk shed stood in this particular spot only because the well had been there before it. In 1882, at the very latest, the well had been dug down past thirty feet, to a depth where clear water moved silently all year long, seeping noiselessly through fossiled limestone layers and gathering in sweet dark pools that had been there since pre-history and that had made it possible for the farm, like all the farms everywhere around it, to come into existence in the first place.

·

Across the yard, on the other side of the driveway, stood the next most recent out-building, the tractor shed. Its walls were also white clapboard, but their paint was flaking and in some spots gone entirely, leaving the wood below exposed and grayed.

The tractor shed's east side had no door but was simply an open way for driving a tractor in and out. In the center of each of the other three walls was a square, four-paned window that didn't open.

Alongside the tractor shed, only two or three feet from its north wall, had been the outhouse. Early in the October when we moved, it had been pulled down and the hole underneath filled in.

•

The chicken coop was of the same vintage as the tractor shed, or very nearly so. In shape it was the conventional horizontal, low, semi-cylinder, its roof covered with tarpaper. The front and back were of white-painted wood, and there was a smallish door at the center of each, flanked in turn by two large square windows that tilted out at the top.

These two buildings, as best as anyone could guess, dated from the middle or late 1920's. Twenty or so feet past the chicken coop, however, toward the pasture, stood the old double corncrib, which was another matter entirely. Its weathered gray wood had passed through seventy-five summers and winters, so that now its very color and the deeply eroded grain of its wood, even in the absence of any other ornament, sign, or indication, expressed the entire accumulation of that span of time: mutely, it held every sound that had been heard in that particular spot throughout three-quarters of a century, and eyelessly it contained every sight and movement that had ever passed by.

•

So it seemed to me, in any case (and does still), even though I had no words to express the feeling then, in the sixth, seventh, and eighth years of my life. I sensed the same truth even more strongly in the case of the final outbuilding (not counting the barn). This was the granary, with the extension on its north side that we called simply "the car shed."

The granary and car shed were constructed of the same weathered, gray, unpainted wood as the corn crib, but about them there was a look and feel of even greater antiquity. The car shed, crowded up so closely against one corner of the chicken coop that you could scarcely pass between the two, had an open front that allowed a wagon, sleigh, or car to be pushed or driven inside (although even our own small car's trunk remained outside).

The unique importance of the granary itself, however, as a thing separate from the car shed, was that it possessed a balance and harmony that occurred in none of the farm's other buildings in exactly the same way.

Its front was windowless, although a doorway—lacking a door itself—was placed exactly in its center. If you stood in the yard, out in the middle of the turn-around, and looked in, you could see straight through the interior to a square, perfectly centered window in the rear wall with no sashes, crosspieces, panes, or glass. Through that square, you could see leaves pressing up, and sometimes coming in, from the trees that grew up close behind.

The granary was wooden-floored, its interior consisting of no more than a central walkway with one bin on either side. The inside walls of the bins were high in back and cut down in steps as they came toward the door. In the back wall of each bin, high up, was a square loading hole, protected against the weather with a wooden hatch-cover.

Other than the barn—or the house, of course—the granary was to become the most important to me of the farm's buildings. It had no openings for light besides the window in back and door in front, but numberless cracks, gaps, and widened spots in its weathered and dried walls let in narrow sheets and pencils of sunlight that reached down into the very corners of the shadowy bins. In the morning, the floor just inside the entrance received the full light of the sun, and with the proper weather and season the whole interior seemed to glow faintly. The farm cats, especially when the temperature began dropping, and sometimes even in the very heart of winter, would curl up and sleep the morning away in the sun just inside the door.

Many years later, after the Epoch of Walking was gone and long forgotten, when I was the only member of my family still alive, and when neither the farm nor its buildings any longer existed, I would, whenever I came on the lines

> *whoever seeks abroad may find*
> *Thee sitting careless on a granary floor,*
> *Thy hair soft-lifted by the winnowing wind,*

think again of the gray weathered wood, the pencils of sunlight angling through dust-motes down into the bins, the cats curled at the door, the warmth of the air, the stillness of it, and the presence of the farmland itself extending outward all around, rolling hills lying quietly under the sun.

In the wall of one of the grain bins, just high enough from the floor so you could get a bucket under it, someone had fabricated a chute for the grain to pour out of if the bin were full enough. The chute was fitted with a sliding piece of wood as a cover so you could increase the flow of grain or shut it off. At the top edge of the sliding cover there had been drilled three finger-holes, well worn as a result of decade after decade after decade of use. During my years of perfect seeing, whenever I happened to be in the granary, or whenever I was near enough to make a quick detour and go inside for even a minute, I would put my fingers snugly into those holes and feel the rounded smoothness in their bottoms, where they had been worn and touched, and touched and worn, by generation after generation after generation before mine, all now silent, now gone:

· ·
·

V
The Chair on the Lawn

i

Fleeting and few, my years of perfect seeing went by with extraordinary speed. After I had reached, say, the age of twelve or thirteen, nothing was left of them except an extraordinarily vivid yet increasingly attenuated memory.

•

I lived in a more perfect union with my own senses, during that handful of years, than was ever be the case again.

To some extent, my awareness of this unity was carried to greater or lesser degrees of intensity by changes in the seasons. My consciousness tended to diminish somewhat, for example, in the months of gray skies, ice, snow, howling winds, and long weeks of efforts to keep warm. By contrast, in the sweetly nectared air of spring, or the soft golden afternoons of autumn, or, most especially, in the perfect, glorious, warm heart of summer itself, I was more conscious than at any other time of being fully alive and at one with all that was around me.

•

That I didn't consciously know this until it was no longer true; that I had no intellectual understanding of it until it had begun slipping away from me already and forever; that my happiness was destined therefore to exist only in my memory of it: these are the facts, universal in childhood, that are among those most responsible for having caused me throughout my life to dedicate myself to remaining a student of space and time.

•

But that I knew the significance of none of this when it was actually taking place did not diminish or alter its importance in any way. The same was true—that at the time it happened I didn't know the real importance of it—of the morning I stumbled upon my father sitting naked on the lawn.

ii

The youngest in the family, I was in general also the first to go to bed. This was true especially in the long days when summer was at its peak. Before the light outside had darkened much beyond the palest gray, I would have gone upstairs and gotten into bed, where I would fall immediately into an unbroken sleep regardless of what noise my sisters and parents, still awake and active downstairs, might be making.

At the first start of the day, however, the roles were reversed, and I would be up and awake while the others went on sleeping.

Even my father slept longer than I did, which is part of the reason I was so surprised the day I found him on the lawn.

•

In the very early morning, the house had a quality of silence unlike that at any other time, and the air too, especially in the peak of summer, moved through the house in a different way than at any other time. With the house entirely open upstairs and down, the outdoor air that had finally cooled in the hours past midnight would gradually find its way in through the doorways and windows below. As the hot air flowed at last out through the upstairs windows, the cooler air from below would be drawn in a gentle current up the stairs and into the rooms above.

I could dress quickly in these years, since there were no decisions to make about my clothes. In summer, I wore the same pants for two weeks, the same tee shirt and underpants for one. I changed my socks every three days or so, since otherwise they grew stiff overnight from being imprisoned during the day in my ankle-high boots. After pulling on my other clothes, I would dangle the boots from two fingers as I sneaked past my sisters' open doorway and down the stairs, placing my feet carefully, sometimes even skipping a step, to avoid those places where the old boards creaked when you put weight on them.

On the bottom step, in the small dark space by the bathroom door, I would sit down and put on my boots. After that, my way out of the house was to go left, left again at the telephone, then straight across the dining room to the front door, which, as I've said, would be left open so that only the screen door remained for me to go through as quietly as I could. Then I could step out across the porch.

From the porch I jumped over my mother's bed of narcissus, pansies, and marigolds and out onto the front lawn itself, where, on the grass, it didn't matter any more how much noise I made with my running feet.

•

People said that the front doors of farm houses were never used by anyone except the preacher and the undertaker. But ours was used sometimes almost as much as the back, especially in summer.

•

On the morning when I discovered my father on the lawn, I thought at first he was a tramp or a hobo who for some reason had chosen to use the chair on our lawn. This thought can be attributed to my mother, who cautioned us repeatedly, when we moved out of town, to be on the watch for hobos and tramps. There was an especial danger of them, she was certain, because of the Rock Island tracks that ran only half a mile away from us, at the west boundary of our property.

Never, my mother said, should we talk with a hobo or tramp. And never, ever, no matter what, should we ever let one of them touch us.

•

That it was my father, though, and not a hobo or tramp, became clear to me almost at once.

The clue wasn't just the cigarette smoke that rose above where he was sitting and drifted slowly to one side. The greater clue was that from the front door I could see one shoulder, arm, elbow, and hand of my father. This meant that I could also make out my father's entirely familiar posture: elbow resting on the arm of the chair, forearm vertical, cigarette between two of the long, slightly-curved fingers of the raised hand.

•

He had dragged the white wooden lawn chair from its usual place near the trunk of the swing tree and placed it almost exactly in the middle of the lawn. There he sat, facing south, his back to the house. The high fan-shape of the chair's back obscured him except for the top of his head and that one shoulder, arm, and hand.

But it was more than enough. I closed and latched the screen door quietly behind me. Then I leapt from the porch over my mother's flowers and bounded swiftly toward him. I didn't yet know that he was naked.

VI
The Trouble with My Father

1

There seems to me no understandable reason for my father's having moved to the farm other than that he knew that the Epoch of Walking was coming to an end. What reason, after all, could there have been other than that he hoped to escape the effects of the end—unless he believed also that by moving into the country, somehow, he could prevent the end from coming at all.

•

Any effort of that sort, though, was clearly doomed. It was too late for a reversal of fate, and The Epoch of Walking, as expected, came to its final end in or near October 1952. At that time, as well, in a way too subtle to understand but too overwhelming to ignore, time and space themselves also changed slightly.

2

In our own particular case, or in the case of my father and his last hopes, the farm failed too soon to prove itself of any real use in attempting to hold off the end.

And one of the causes of that failure was that none of us—especially my father—ever really did fit in on the farm.

This was the simple fact, no matter how much any of us might have wished, hoped, or pretended otherwise.

•

Unlike other farmers in the neighborhood, for example, my father hadn't learned farming through the long experience of doing it, but through reading books. This may or may not have been a handicap—I believe, in fact, that my father was a good farmer—but it suggested, as with everything else he did, that farming wasn't something either in his blood or in his bones. As a result, we were much too late. We weren't, after all, rooted deeply in the neighborhood, not having lived there for decades, or for generation upon generation, in the way, for example, that the Shuhas had.

•

These differences were enormous, and there were others, both large and small. My family, for example, spoke differently from others in the neighborhood, never using "ain't" or "she don't," though these were commonplace and natural among everyone else. In my father, differences of these kinds were by far the most pronounced. He dressed differently from others, behaved, held himself, even moved differently from the way they did. A majority of the other farmers had pot bellies and weren't tall men, while my father to the very end was slim, tall, upright, and straight—even, as often as not, imperious. Other farmers in the neighborhood invariably wore hats or brimmed caps when they were outdoors, but my father just as invariably went bareheaded, in summer, winter, sunlight, or snow. He wore shirts and trousers of wheat-colored khaki, not the faded blue denim or green twill worn by the others, and he never once had a pair of overalls. He lit his cigarettes not with matches but with a zippo lighter that had the letters "USN" and the emblem of an eagle soldered to its front. He wore a belt, too, not of leather but of khaki webbing that could be set to any girth, while on the front of its flat metal buckle was soldered an emblem showing an anchor against a background of coiled ropes. Unlike any other farmer anywhere in the entire neighborhood, my father wore sunglasses. Unfailingly, he carried the scuffed leather case for them attached to his webbed belt on the left side, above his hip. These glasses were in the aviator style, their lenses a deep green, though my father never referred to them either as "sunglasses" or "dark glasses" but only as "smoked glasses." Their lenses did nothing but filter out light and glare, making no correction in vision. This was because my father's eyes remained sharp and clear throughout his life, until very late, when, perhaps as a result of his despair, he went blind quickly, and almost entirely.

•

And yet of course, in spite of many and often great troubles with my father, I clung to him, followed him, begged him to let me help in whatever task or chore my size and abilities would permit.

•

The jobs that I was in fact able to do, however, never amounted to many, in part because the farm came to an end so soon and in part because I remained so small.

By the time my father sold our tractor and equipment and gave up tilling the fields, I still hadn't been allowed to do spring plowing by myself, or to plant, harrow, reap, or mow, these being tasks that only my father had the strength and focus to manage successfully—even though he always looked slightly absurd, much too tall and long-legged for our little gray Ford tractor. I rode along with him much of the time, standing on the running board beside him and leaning against the tractor's curved gray fender. I watched what he did until I knew I could do the same if given the chance, or if my legs would just grow enough so that my feet could reach the clutch and brake pedals. Only one time before the end of everything did I do a piece of work alone. It was a blustery, gray, cold, cutting afternoon in March, and I disked our farthest field, in the northwest corner of the farm. It wasn't planted yet, so I couldn't do any harm, and I managed to reach the pedals by slipping down from the seat and standing up.

•

Other jobs I wished I could do were closed to me also, especially in the barn. At six, seven, or eight, I still had too little strength to carry silage to the manger in front of the cows without the feed-fork twisting in my grip and spilling the load too soon. I didn't have the strength or weight to press myself against the flanks of our herd of eight milking cows with authority enough to keep them calm while hooking milking machines to their udders, and certainly not enough to lift the canisters up off the floor once they were full. I didn't have the height or strength yet, either, to carry the stainless steel buckets of fresh milk up the pathway from the barn to the milk shed (even if I could have lifted their weight, one in each hand, their bottoms would have hit the ground). I didn't even—although it was nearer my abilities—have strength enough to do a really good job of cleaning the gutter behind the cows by broom-pushing the heavy soup of manure, straw, and urine toward the door and scooping it from there out into the barnyard.

I wasn't entirely helpless, however. I did have strength and coordination enough to sweep the floors around the calves' and heifers' pens and also the wet floor behind the cows after my father had cleaned the gutter. And I could scatter lime, the last chore to be done before leaving the barn.

It was a job I loved. The lime came in hundred-pound bags that stood near the Dutch door against the south wall. I would fill a three-pound coffee can and then, taking out handfuls of the cool, dense, white powder as I walked, I would scatter it evenly across the floors as if I were sowing seed. The lime had a fresh white look like a dusting of snow, and it left a clean smell. Most of all, I loved the quietness and the feeling of calm that settled over the barn during the time I scattered it. Always the same in that it was calm, lime-scattering was a moment that nevertheless differed according to the season. In the summer, my father would release the cows from their stanchions and they would make their unhurried way back out into the barnyard, confer lazily with one another there for a few minutes, possibly stop over at the stock tank for more water, then amble back out through the gate into the pasture to spend the night. In winter, there was the same sense of a pleasant conclusion to things, though in a different way, since then the cows stayed overnight in the barn. By the time I began scattering lime, up one aisle and down another, the cows would already be contented and half-sleepy after having been milked and fed. They would stand in their stalls, absently-mindedly chewing their cuds, breathing calmly, one or another of them sighing deeply now and then, or giving a low, placid, bassoon-like moo, or rattling a stanchion lightly, or tossing a head just one more time before my father pulled the lever on the metal box up under the ceiling, filling the entire space with darkness. Then he and I would leave the barn, close and latch the top and bottom halves of the door behind us, and, leaving it all alone, walk back up to the house.

•

I'm sure now that my father's outbursts of rage, which I once thought were caused by some great sorrow in his own childhood, in fact came about from his recognition that the Epoch of Walking was nearing its end; that nothing could avert it; and that even during this small handful of perfect years between 1947 and 1952, the inevitable moment of absence and collapse was approaching rapidly.

Because of the almost perfect clarity of it, I'm fairly certain that the memory I have of my father kicking the pail of milk is my first memory of such an outburst.

The pail, at first, stood at the east end of the feeding aisle, in front of the silo door. It waited there, as usual, to be joined by a second full pail so that my father could carry the two, one in each hand, up to the milk house to be poured into cans that would then be immersed in the cooler's deep running water.

That isn't the way it happened this time, however. What triggered the moment I will never know, but what I believe is that a thought of the Epoch's end flickered through my father's mind and, intolerable, pushed him into a rage of sorrow and despair.

I remember that I saw him striding fast down the feeding aisle past the cattle's lowered heads and toward the pail, and that then, with no break in motion, he swung his long leg, at the same time counter-swinging his arms out back for balance and increased thrust. When his foot connected, the pail lifted up slightly from the floor, and the milk in it rose up in a thick white luscious arc that hung in the air for an instant, like in a stop-action photo, before splashing down into the dirty litter of silage and straw below.

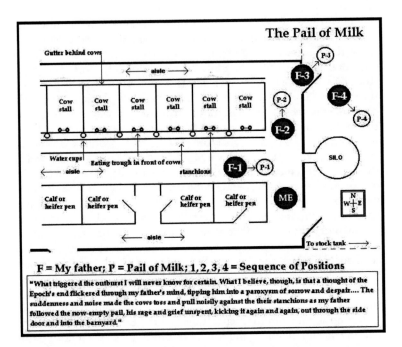

The Pail of Milk

Gutter behind cows

← aisle →

P-3
F-3
F-4
P-4

| Cow stall | Cow stall | Cow stall | Cow stall | Cow stall | Cow stall |

P-2
F-2

Water cups
Eating trough in front of cows
← aisle →
stanchions

F-1 P-1

SILO

Calf or heifer pen | Calf or heifer pen | Calf or heifer pen | Calf or heifer pen

ME

N W+E S

← aisle →

To stock tank →

F = My father; P = Pail of Milk; 1, 2, 3, 4 = Sequence of Positions

"What triggered the outburst I will never know for certain. What I believe, though, is that a thought of the Epoch's end flickered through my father's mind, tipping him into a paroxysm of sorrow and despair.... The suddenness and noise made the cows toss and pull noisily against the their stanchions as my father followed the now-empty pail, his rage and grief unspent, kicking it again and again, out through the side door and into the barnyard."

At the noise and sudden movement, the cows tossed and pulled against the chains of their stanchions as my father followed the now-empty pail, his rage and grief still unspent, kicking it again, and then again, until he drove it out through the side door and into the barnyard.

Afterward, the cattle settled down and the barn fell gradually quiet. Soon, half a dozen of our barn cats, creeping out from the corners where, like lightning, they had disappeared into hiding, slunk forward cautiously and began lapping industriously at the spilled milk. Now and then they paused to check for danger before lowering their heads again to the milk.

VII
I Begin to Learn, Without Knowing It, of My Desire
to Hold Things Together

1

It's clear to me now that summer mornings in those years—in 1948, for example, 1949, and 1950—were the last of their kind. Mornings afterward were to become increasingly inexact and adulterated replicas of the true thing, until, at last, experience of such a kind as I knew in my years of perfect seeing was to disappear altogether and fall away gradually from the universal memory.

•

Nor is this to say that during my years of perfect seeing themselves, in the very last moments of the Epoch of Walking, there were no hints or signs of the coming breakup.

•

My father himself was a sign, if only in his way of failing to fit in—going without a cap, wearing khaki pants and webbed belt, referring to "smoked glasses." Where, after all, did this leave me, supposing, for example, that I myself were to choose later to become a farmer? If that were to be the case, would I imitate my father, or would I imitate our neighbors, who, like me, were generally small in stature, even though I wouldn't gain a pot belly yet for some years? Would I, though, wear denim overalls with shoulder straps, hats with brims, and say "he don't"? Or would I wear khakis, carry an eagle in my pocket, solder the letters "USN" on a zippo lighter, and say "smoked glasses"?

Doubts and unknowns of such kinds could be nothing if not signs of coming breakage in the world, at least in the world as I was being asked to experience it. Why, after all, did my father wear eagles and anchors even though he was working far from the sea, in the heart of the continent, tilling soil and reaping crops under hot sun amid the dust and chaff of dry grasses and grains? And how could I myself ever successfully become a farmer unless I turned away from him entirely and managed somehow—the way the other neighborhood farmers did—to make my neck as deep red as fired brick and my forehead as pallid as the stomach of a frog, and learned also how to chew tobacco, curse, hawk, and spit? And then, in turn, how could I possibly go on doing these things, or being these ways, at picnics in my grandmother's back yard, or—even more unimaginably—at dinners at Marie and Lutie's house?

And yet again, at the same time, how could I, being as short as I was, hope really to imitate my own father with his smoked glasses and khakis, his eagles and letters and ropes, his trim and slender tallness, his elegant way of holding himself, and his slow, courtly way of moving? If I couldn't even reach the pedals, how could I ever emulate his way of looking spider-legged and over-sized on our small Ford tractor? Or how could I, being myself uninterested in reading, ever succeed in carrying on his habit of collecting books—he having gathered enough of them already to fill two walls of our living room (although admittedly it was true that I did privately enjoy, in the silent, lazy, long, hot, humid afternoons of the dog days, the curiously pleasant scent of mildew and dampness that the books added to the still air of the living room, where, unknown to anyone, I spent hours lying on the carpet, on my back, doing nothing but breathing it in)?

•

Discontinuities, disjunctions, eccentricities, along with still more disunions existing inside of these, as in the case of in my father's outbursts of rage, his equally inexplicable risings into states of apparent bliss, and his tendency, with increasing frequency, even in these early years, to turn to large amounts of alcohol. During alcohol—that was when his episodes of bliss took place, during the drinking of it, episodes of rage coming in the aftermath. Certainly none of these things gave me any sense of stability, unity, security, predictability, or harmony, nor did any of them imbue in me any confirmation whatsoever that the Epoch of Walking would in fact not end but instead go on, continue, remain a nurturing and guiding force.

I must have sensed even then the necessity for caution in everything I did; the necessity to guard myself against whatever it might be that the future held in store for me; and in one way or another I must have been aware of something steadily approaching that could not do otherwise than result in discontinuity, collapse, and loss.

•

(This was the period in my life, in other words, when the first conscious foundations were laid for my becoming a student of space and time.

The truly formative episodes of this period were by no means restricted only to the warm months of the year, although, without question, summer remained the most memorable season for them. In the summer, too, it was also clear that mornings tended toward a greater degree of significance than did other parts of the day.

2

The only dog we had while we lived on the farm was a mongrel named Ganges. She was affectionate and good-natured but sufficiently unintelligent as to be almost incapable of learning. In fairness, it may be that she had suffered from bad training (or from none at all) before she became ours, which was at a late enough point in her life so that further training was not possible.

If left alone and untied, Ganges would chase cars along the road, although for some reason only those traveling east, never west. She would burst like a cannonball out of the dirt trail she had worn behind the lilac bushes and, leaping the ditch onto the road, race at breakneck speed beside a rear wheel, nipping at the flicker of speeding hubcap.

An additional failing in her character was that she showed little discretion about other animals, large or small, but would happily pursue almost any such creature that happened to catch her eye. She one time went after a skunk and, judging from the putrid stink that clung in her coat for weeks, must have made an attempt to corner it.

For reasons like these, it was essential that she be tied overnight in the back yard, or, in cold weather, locked in the barn.

As a result, the first thing I did on summer mornings during my years of perfect seeing, after letting myself out the front door, was to run around the house on one side or the other and let Ganges off her leash. I had successfully trained her in one thing only, which was not to bark when I came to untie her. When she was new to us, I would grab her snout and clamp her jaws shut while swatting her as sharply as I could bear to on the haunch, staring her in the eye and saying "no." Finally she stopped barking when I came to untie her, but she never did stop jumping up on me. She would try to lick my face, expending such energy that her back feet would leave the ground. The only way I could stop her was by setting off on a run, and, partly for that reason, every morning began with a run as hard as we could go in one direction or another.

•

Without question, I loved Ganges enormously. Even though she was barred from coming inside, she was a faithful companion to me like no other, bounding cheerfully and running with me tirelessly all over the farm. She was dead by the time my years of perfect seeing ended.

It was probably a good thing that Ganges was gone by the time the Epoch of Walking ended, since what came after that were my own years of masturbation, which began shortly in advance of my love affair with Marietta Streetfield and continued, as if there were doubt, after our affair had come to an end and Marietta was gone.

However powerful the forces were that impelled me in those initial post-Epoch years, I think that Ganges's presence might nevertheless have brought embarrassment or self-consciousness, possibly enough to render me unwilling—or unable—to perform the acts that I later understood to have been my first efforts, unsuccessful or not, to hold things together by engaging myself literally in the universe of space and time.

Lying down in one of my many hiding places outdoors, however, and opening up my pants—or, as it happened, removing them altogether, along with shoes, underwear, shirt, and socks—in order, from one position or another, to send four or five thin white sudden-appearing tendrils of my semen onto earth, grass, or stone—I might well have been hindered in doing these things, no matter how much I loved her, by the presence of Ganges, who would have been sitting on her haunches, watching me with her head cocked to one side in the same pose she invariably struck to ask for food, her ears perked up, her tongue lolling out to the side from a mouth that seemed always smiling in expression of the same innocence that made her invariably happy and always incapable of malice.

•

Ganges was semi-long haired, black except for two white anklets, a white swath from her forehead down the middle of her nose, and a patch of brown around her left eye. She was a friendly, good-tempered, and easily shameable dog. With a single harsh word from my father, she could be reduced to a humiliated grovel. By saying just one thing— "Bad dog," for example—my father could cause her to go down on her belly, press her chin to the ground, turn her eyes up imploringly, and sweep her tail through the dust in hopelessness and shame. With me, on the other hand, she leaped and bounded in the highest of spirits, running with an energy that seemed endlessly renewable.

•

In the mornings after I untied her, when all the others were still asleep, we would run off in any of several directions. One of my favorites was down the Y-shaped west leg of the driveway, west along the road to the Rock Island tracks, then north either on the ties and rails or inside our own fence up to the north boundary of our land, then east again to the lone cherry tree on the fence-line between Thom and Evelyn Ridley's farm and our own. Around the base of the old cherry was thick, fallen-over grass to lie down on, or I could sit instead, if I chose, with my back against the trunk. From that point, the view extended miles off to the south and west, although much of the time, of course, field corn stood like a high wall on both sides of the line. At those times, the little grassy space around the base of the tree became a nest with perfect, absolute, unbroken privacy.

•

When we first moved there, the farm was plentiful with the fruits and ornaments of the past, although even then many of these—as with the ruined trellises in the wood shed, for example—had gone untended and had fallen into dereliction.

Along the road going down the hill east from our house was a row of high lilac bushes, the ones where Ganges ran. Inside from the lilacs and parallel to them was a row of apple trees that gave way, as you went down the hill, to plum trees and then finally, at the bottom end, to currant bushes. Between the lilacs and the row of fruit trees, in the shadowy tunnel formed by their mingled foliage, Ganges had worn her smooth dirt path by running there again and again in her races with eastbound cars.

Sometimes in the mornings she and I would set out along that path, running down to the bottom of the garden past the currant bushes and then either out to the oak-stand in the center of the Ridley's east field or north along our own fence line to the stand of tall pines east of our barnyard, where once again there was long, soft, fallen-over grass to lie on.

There, too, stood yet another row of apple trees, though these were much older and entirely neglected, making me think that they dated from the earliest years of the farm. Now they bore only small, tart, green, misshapen apples that I sometimes nibbled at one after another while lying on the cushion of grass and old needles under the pines.

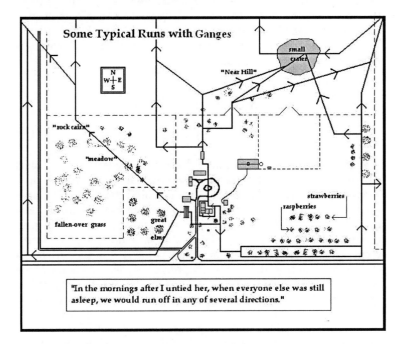

Some Typical Runs with Ganges

N
W+E
S

"Near Hill"

small crater

"rock cairn"

"meadow"

strawberries

raspberries

fallen-over grass

great

elm

"In the mornings after I untied her, when everyone else was still asleep, we would run off in any of several directions."

If Ganges and I went straight north from the yard, we always made a dodge in order to run through the wagon-way of the old corncrib, the wood of its south arch darkened by the spattered blood of the Sunday-dinner chickens my father would hang there from their feet and then behead. After the corncrib, we would continue straight north to the pasture, I climbing over the fence and Ganges squirming under it. Once in the pasture, we would veer east for fifty yards before making a hairpin turn back west, making it possible this way to run down into each one of the meteorite craters there (I learned later they were places where gravel had been taken) and up its other side. After the two craters, we would go pell-mell, almost falling forward, down the steep north slope of First Hill and into the valley bottom where there were the hummocks to jump across like stepping stones and where the sun hadn't yet reached, so that air down in the bottom still felt cooler than up higher. From the valley-bottom, we ran up the gentler—but longer—slope of Second Hill, and then, in the sunshine just below the crest, we would fling ourselves to the warming earth as if we had been shot by arrows.

The cows would often be there too, especially in early summer, drawn by the same warmth of the sun that drew us. With no pause in the slow work of chewing their cuds, they would turn with their great dark eyes to gaze imperturbably at Ganges and me—I on my back, Ganges flopped on her side—as we gasped and panted for dear life, filling our up lungs again and again.

VIII
The Chair on the Lawn, Continued

1

At the beginning of each summer, the cows had to learn certain habits all over again, as if they had no memory of them from the year before.

In early May or so, when the weather was mild enough and the grass mature enough for them to stay out all night, they would linger in the barnyard after milking time, showing no inclination toward the pasture gate. With each passing night, however—and with each incremental rise of warmth in the air—they would stay in the barnyard a shorter time, until at the height of summer they would file out of the barn after milking and not even pause outside the barn door, but would make their slow, easy way, one at the tail of another, out through the gate and into the pasture.

It was the same thing in the mornings. Until the end of May or so—or even into June—Ganges and I would find the herd on Second Hill in the sun. Only later, with the gathering heat of summer, would they take it upon themselves by that time in the morning to have migrated down into the valley and up First Hill to the barnyard gate. Later still, they would go all the way into the barnyard, and, in the very peak of summer, they would enter the barn of their own accord and walk into their proper stalls ready for the morning milking.

•

Before that, though, my father would have to come out through the barnyard gate to the edge of the pasture and call them in. He would stand just outside the gate and cup his hands to his mouth and call out across the valley, "Come, boss, come, boss," collapsing the first syllable and drawing out the second so it sounded like "C'm bahhhhhhhhhhss, C'm bahhhhhhhhhhss."

If Ganges and I were over on Second Hill at that time, I would of course hear my father, and see him also, under the trees on the other side of the valley. Ganges's ears would perk up and she would look first one way and then another, so that I doubt she was able to see him. He looked very small at that distance. I would raise an arm over my head, and my father would raise an arm in the same way before turning away and disappearing under the trees on his way back to the barn.

Ganges and I would run here and there among the cows, and I would talk to them, and slap two or three on the haunches to help them start moving. I did this especially with Donna, who was in fact the boss and would begin moving first, followed then by the others, who would straggle gradually into a group. When they had walked far enough across the pasture to come upon one of their meandering paths, they would fall into single file and make their slow swaying way up toward the barnyard gate.

Walking along beside their great heavy bodies, with the sun steadily warmer and Ganges off to the side snapping at the white moths that fluttered up out of the grass, I would feel as though I had already been up and awake and outdoors for hours and hours, the day already grown old.

I was accustomed to this rhythm, and to the delicious, unfettered privacy of getting up long before the others, and of being entirely alone—which is partly why I was so shocked the morning I came down and went outside to discover that my father was already there, out on the lawn, sitting in the chair, facing south.

2

I knew it was him, as I've said, when I saw the posture of his right hand and the way his fingers held the cigarette. Seeing that, I leaped over my mother's pansies and zinnias and phlox, bounded the few yards out to the middle of the lawn, and stopped alongside the arm of the white wooden chair.

Reclining there, my father said nothing. He made no move of any kind, stayed entirely still, showed no sign of unease or discomfiture whatsoever.

I, on the other hand, seeing his nakedness, realized instantly that I was caught in an impossible trap and found myself scalded by embarrassment, awkwardness, and shame—and by a curiosity that confounded and overrode all of these.

My father had on not a stitch of clothing. Because I was standing, and therefore higher up than he was, I found myself staring down at his narrow, slim, reclining body and being struck by its odd variegation of colors—the head, neck, and forearms browned deeply by the sun, the rest a frog-belly white except for the narrow, long-toed feet, which had the addition of long veins of blue and green. And then, of course, there were the genitals, completely unlike my own for possessing a thick patch of black hair that thinned and disappeared only after having crept some distance up my father's white belly. And then there was the penis itself, thick, long, and huge, in color the red-brown of a brick, and in posture flopped, like the snout of an exhausted dog resting on its paws, flaccidly outward across a tundra of white thigh. The testicles, meanwhile, pimpled like chicken-skin, bulged up tightly from the pressure created by the way my father was reclining, his legs crossed at the knee, one foot planted on the grass, the other hanging down in air.

When my father said, in a voice at once hushed and intense, "Just look at this," I thought, for the thousandth part of a second, as any boy my age would, that he meant I should look at his penis. At the same time, of course, it was impossible: he couldn't mean that.

I bolted. Motionless one instant, speeding away the next, I ran to the front edge of the lawn. There I stopped, and there I stood, looking earnestly to the south, out through the blue morning haze, my back determinedly toward my father. And I did as he'd told me. I looked.

•

I looked out across Harve Shuha's receding field of high green corn, past Corrigan's Woods off to the left, and toward West Tree.

Of course I was still unbearably conscious of my father behind me; I felt him there, like heat from a stove. I understood clearly what my error had been: the slightest circular gesture of the right hand, the one raised up, with the cigarette, showed that my father hadn't meant his penis at all but instead the entirety of the morning itself, the width of it, the breadth and depth of it, the perfection and wonder of it. But understanding wasn't enough. There were still the burning questions of embarrassment, humiliation, discomfiture, uncertainty. And of what to do. I had seen, I had looked, I had stared, and now my father was still behind me, waiting, not having moved, and I was confronted with the insoluble problem of where to go, how to behave, what on earth to do next.

I couldn't stand at the edge of the lawn looking south forever, since it would only seem proof all the more that I was afraid to move. It was equally impossible for me to turn around and speak casually with my father, pretending, as he seemed to have pretended, that he wasn't really naked, or that I hadn't noticed.

It was insoluble, and, unable to think of any way of escape, I was frozen there, welded to my spot at the front of the lawn. It was a moment, as I've said before, of almost limitless complexity. And it was to stay with me for the rest of my life.

•

Luckily, I remembered Ganges. I pivoted to my right, keeping my glance from roaming anywhere near the direction of my father's chair.

As naturally as I could through a strangled throat, already moving toward the driveway, I said, "Untie Ganges." And then, with a pipeline vision that let me look only straight ahead, blinding me on either side, keeping my father out of existence, I sprinted up the driveway, around the woodshed, into the back yard, and bent down to untie Ganges, who, in silence, leapt up as if her life depended on it, trying to lick my face.

PART II

I
The World After My Father on the Lawn

1
There, really, is the end of things.

•

Later, although I don't know exactly when, it began to grow clear to me that the morning of my father on the lawn had been a marking point of life-altering importance. On a single morning, I had received my last glimpse of a world in which space and time were still coherent, the Epoch of Walking still existed, West Tree had not begun to disappear, and my father himself had not yet—that I could perceive—begun the slow downward spiral into alcohol, grief, and despair that was to transform him—although he was never any the less loved whatsoever—into a feared and tyrannizing figure who in the end would, as though inevitably, abandon me altogether.

2
My growing up was made difficult not simply by the things that happened in it, but by the much more important fact of its having occurred in reverse.

The key to the meaning of my life, that is, was given to me before I had achieved the ability to make use of it or even to understand its function. It was impossible, as a consequence, for me even to begin grasping the true enormity of my early life's meaning until I had first became able to understand two other essential and basic things.

These were:

1) The fact that what I'd seen on the morning of my father on the lawn was in actuality an image of wholeness, harmony, and radiance—an end-glimpse, that is to say, of a world in which time, space, and therefore also history still existed, for the moment, coherently with one another;

2) and that what I began to see from that point on were images, increasing rapidly both in intensity and in number, not of wholeness, harmony, and radiance, but of what it is that's left after the disappearance of those things.

•

The incident of my father in the chair was a benchmark, and during the brief time of the incident's taking place, I was myself witness to nothing less than the last few earthly moments of the Epoch of Walking.

3

(A summer afternoon, once again on our front lawn. Marie and Lutie, in a small gesture of return for our having visited their house for a summer dinner, had been invited for "tea." My father had driven in to West Tree to pick them up and bring them back, since by now the Epoch of Walking was gone entirely.

Marie and Lutie, though aging rapidly, were nevertheless troubled about not having made their way on foot. In their customary way, they were modestly self-deprecating and at the same time intensely eager to remain polite, it being out of the question that they would ever in even the very slightest way hope to seem presumptuous, ungrateful, or rude, whether in reference to themselves or to others.

They were drinking glasses of sherry offered by my father, and they tended to giggle in the conversation, in effect acknowledging the enormity of the subject by the need to seem to treat it lightly.

"It's a terrible thing," Marie said, "how old we've gotten." She tried to smile politely. "Many a time we walked much, much farther than this for a visit."

Lutie nodded, following the cue of her sister and smiling also. The movement of her head forward when she spoke made her seem to me birdlike again. "Yes," she said. Although her voice quavered, as did Marie's, her tone remained determinedly light, uncomplaining, attempting even to seem amused. "There were many times when we walked much, much farther."

•

(Marie sat in the white chair that my father had sat in, and Lutie on the only other lawn chair we had, a folding one with a canvas back and seat. The rest of us, my mother and father and Hannah and Ingie and I, sat on straight chairs from the kitchen and dining room. The ground was dry and hard, and the legs didn't press down into the lawn.

I remember five or six visits of Marie and Lutie to the farm, all between 1949 and 1952. Half were in summer, on the lawn, and half in winter, not long after Christmas.

This certainly wasn't their first summer visit, nor could it have been their last, which was quite large and included my grandmother in her wheelchair, and my aunt Signe, and also my aunt Hannah with her two children, Eldon and Charlotte.

That very last visit took place three years before my grandmother left West Tree for good, but less than a year before Marie and Lutie died.

•

My memory of the earlier visit, when Marie sat in the white wooden lawn chair, is an unhappy one, melancholy and uncomfortable. It was almost certainly in August, but in any case a dry time. The lawn was rock hard, and large areas of grass had turned brown. Many of the elms were burned so that their leaves were brown and crisp around the edges.

A wind came directly from the south rather than from the southwest or west-southwest, or even, as it sometimes did in the truly clear summer weather that came after storms, from the northwest.

This wind was different—hot, unpleasant, and dry. It wasn't quite strong enough to pick up dust, but it moved the topmost branches of trees, and the sound of it going through the dry leaves was melancholy and hollow.

Marie and Lutie, with their brown shoes and long dresses, and with their haircuts from the 1920's, seemed to me terribly out of place on the farm. It would have been natural for them to be in their own garden or on their own lawn, or walking on the sidewalks of West Tree from one place to another.

But they shouldn't have been on our lawn, or on our farm, with cattle in the barn nearby, or making their way in from the pasture for evening milking. Instead, Marie and Lutie should have been on their own side porch, at a small table there, having iced tea, or perhaps moving slowly through their garden, collecting flowers and vegetables, with baskets on their arms.

•

And yet even so, I would give anything now to have them there again, even on the dry burned lawn, even amid the homely circle of unmatched chairs from the dining room and kitchen, even in the dry, hot, sad wind, even with the cattle coming in for evening milking, since I know now something I didn't know then. I didn't know then what my great-aunts' absence would mean, but I know now that it is permanent, irreversible, profound, desolating, calamitous.

4

My father, like any father, remained a mystery for me. He remained a thousand mysteries for me.

•

(The morning I discovered him on the lawn was the first time I had seen him entirely naked, although not the last. I had, it was true, seen his penis before, but only peripherally, standing next to him at men's room urinals, for example, during family car trips, when I could tell only that it was brown and large. I had never seen it, however, or his testicles, or the full expanse of his naked body, from close up before, and never would again.

He was so naked that he didn't have even his wrist watch on, but only the band of belly-white skin where it usually went. He had with him nothing but a pack of Pall Malls and his zippo lighter, both of these resting on the flat wooden arm of the lawn chair.

•

Over the next few years, before the farm collapsed, there would be times in the hot summer months when my father, after a day of field-work, would come out of the shower with nothing on, stroll to the front screen door and stand a few moments to let the breeze cool his body.

I happened to be in the dining room once or twice when he came through this way, and although of course I made an effort not to look, I wasn't always able to avoid a glimpse before he turned his back to me at the door, which, because of his height, he seemed to fill entirely. These unavoidable glimpses were shocking to me when I saw how low my father's testicles hung between his legs, slung in their loose, skinny sac like elongated weather balloons when they're ready for release from the ground and the helium hasn't yet expanded.

This was the time in my life—at eleven or twelve—when I went through my period of being terrified by death. The fear included the vivid certainty that death could come from any direction, horizontally, for example, as in the case of something chasing me, or vertically, as in lightning or bombs or explosives bearing down on me from the sky.

In any such cases, it would be absolutely essential to trust my natural fleetness of foot as the only means of escaping death. Consequently, I kept my shoes on as much as I possibly could. I wore ankle-high leather boots, as I've said, and it was perfectly clear to me that without their protection I would never be able, when necessity arose, to run full speed across, say, fields of stubble, or along stony gravel roads, or through thistles or nettles, or any significant distance at all, certainly, through snow or broken ice.

In the evenings, when the rest of the family went upstairs to change into pajamas or bathrobes before coming back down to read or look through magazines, or—in Hannah's case—practice piano, or much more rarely play cards or table games—at these times, certain that at any moment I might be required to flee from death, I broke from the others' example by remaining dressed and, even more important, keeping on my shoes.

Obviously I couldn't go to bed wearing them, however, which was a part of the reason why going to bed was so often, during this period, a frightening time for me. In bed, shoeless, unable to run, I was defenseless. Formations of high-altitude bombers droning from low on the horizons, intruders with poised knives creeping up the stairs, flames from the furnace licking the insides of the walls, unsettled nights in the heat of summer with the sudden tossing of trees, the certainty that tornadoes were about to descend from the lightning-licked underbellies of angry clouds, gyrating their way toward the old, dry, easily splintered house where I lay in my bed, cowering in vain for protection under my blankets, sweating miserably.

How could I possibly escape death from any of these causes, in short, if I didn't have my boots on? How could I tear down the stairs, leap from the window, run for my life cross-country the way I had run when Ganges was alive, to escape from the bombers, the tornadoes, or the heavily-breathing pursuer with his razors and knives?

Thank god I wasn't my father, the sight of whose scrotum had been so upsetting to me: his testicles like pheasants' eggs hanging down in the bottom of their low, loose, wrinkled, narrow sac of skin—there was no conceivable way that my father, no matter how long his legs might be, could jump from bed and run for his life, boots or not, without his testicles flying out like chestnuts on strings and being flung up and down against his thighs, belly, legs, until the crippling pain (which I also knew, and also feared) that these twin parts of the body are subject to would bring him down in a cowering heap, curl him on the ground in a knot of agony and impotence while lightning, bomb, earthquake, villain, tornado, or inferno made its way toward him, closing in upon him relentlessly and unstoppably.

During my the years of perfect seeing, when I was free to run with Ganges over the width and breadth of the farm, I gave no thought to my testicles whatsoever, tucked up tightly as they were, little walnuts scarcely even bulging out against the tightly-drawn skin holding them. A slip of my foot once when I was climbing over the top plank of the barnyard fence taught me the agony that even a small but well aimed blow was able to bring about; but even so, I could continue to run like the wind, Ganges racing beside me, uphill and down, the two of us leap-frogging over hummocks, rolling down hills, without even a thought of my testicles, let alone any fear of their flying about untethered and bringing me to a stop, paralyzed and curled up with pain.

That, however, was already some time back. By now, I had passed my eighth year, and ninth, and was moving through my tenth toward my eleventh, even twelfth. My years of perfect seeing were over. Ganges was dead. The Epoch of Walking had come to an end. The farm was beginning its collapse, I had come upon my father naked on the lawn, and, along with all this, I had begun to notice that my own testicles were descending, my scrotum loosening, the skin of it becoming more wrinkled, the whole loosening apparatus falling down farther, dreadfully, between my legs.

I tried to deny it, hide it from myself, pretend it wasn't so. But it was. And, once having begun, it was a process destined only to go on. For the first time in my life, I sensed that my body was no longer intact, integrated, whole, made up sturdily of nothing but itself, but that my very flesh, like the world around me, was now for the first time failing to cohere, revealing itself to be composed not only of identifiably discrete and separable pieces, but of discrete and separable pieces that were in fact now beginning to come apart from one another. And if this was so, as it seemed clearly to be, it was every bit equally as clear that the end result of such a process, at one point or another, would necessarily be the disappearance not only of one's own body but also of the external world that previously had been wrapped, like a blanket, around it.

II
What I Really Saw on the Morning
of My Father on the Lawn

1

It was 1950, the morning of my father on the lawn, the month of August, or conceivably late July—to judge, at least, by the quality of the early-morning air, warm and soft and yet at the same time cool, all three at once, and by the particular gray-blue haze in the air, and by the sounds of things, and by the angle of the sun-streaks that lay low across Harve Shuha's field of cut oats, touching the tops of the hills but letting the shadows lie sleeping in the darkness between them.

I loved that morning, to a degree far beyond any ability I have to say, just as I loved all such glorious mornings in my years of perfect seeing. Yet I didn't know it at the time. A terrible, terrible thing it was, the fact that my growing up had taken place backwards: the fact of things happening to me before I had the key to their meaning.

•

If my father hadn't been naked, it would never have happened, or in any case not in the same way—it wouldn't have happened: the moment that I understood later to have been the most important single turning point in the history of my entire intellectual life.

•

If he hadn't been naked, I wouldn't have run from the side of the chair. Not having seen what I did see, I would have had no reason to escape.

•

And yet at the same time, although without knowing it, I was in fact being obedient, doing exactly as he instructed me to do.

If he had been fully clothed and had said to me, "Just look at this," what would have happened? Would I have fled? And what about the circular movement of his hand, his cigarette between its fingers, the small movement that nevertheless meant "everything around us, everything in sight"? If he had been clothed, would I even have noticed it, wondered about it, pondered its meaning? Would I have looked?

No, this is what would have happened: If he hadn't been naked, I would have remained by the chair, looked southward for a moment, found the sight only half interesting, and then gone to untie Ganges.

•

Everything about it, clearly, had to be just exactly so—the nakedness, the misapprehended command, the gesture of the hand understood only after the flight.

In the absence of just this combination, I wouldn't have run; I wouldn't have stood as I did, looking south; and my father wouldn't have been directly behind me, with the result, in effect, that I was looking out not through my own eyes but through his.

2

I saw the gravel road. Across it, I saw Harve Shuha's rolling field with the sunlight touching its hilltops. A distance away to the left stood the shadowy darkness of Corrigan's Woods. And a mile and a half straight ahead I could see, as always, the top of the chapel tower of New College, diminished by distance and scarcely visible above the low green density of treetops. Nearer and to the southwest, I saw more woods—the ones along the back edge of Oliver and Roswitha Piken's long narrow fields—and then, straight to the southwest, I saw Old College Hill rising slightly up, and on it the roof and bell tower of First Hall, and then, a few degrees farther west, distant and tiny, the wooden structure of the Nordic ski jump.

Most of West Tree, though, lying in the river valley as it did, between the two colleges, was hidden from my sight.

•

(I imagine my father pushing himself up out of the white chair and walking back to the house. Because he is naked, he bends forward slightly, almost as a person would do if walking on tiptoes, or barefoot on stones or hot sand. As he moves, his skin looks absurd, ghostly white against the surrounding greenery and dark foliage. In his left hand he carries his cigarettes and lighter. Behind him, from down in the grass beside the chair, a tiny tendril of smoke rises up where he stripped the paper from his last cigarette and left the tobacco to burn itself away.

My father does this, crosses the lawn, disappears again into the front door of the house, while I am in the back yard untying Ganges.

•

Here is something interesting: not until many years later, after my father had been for some time dead and gone, did it ever occur to me to think of him getting up from the chair and going back into the house.

•

I did, although once again only later, imagine him remaining in the chair for a very, very great time, until the disappearance of everything. I imagined him sitting there after the collapse of the farm, after he had become a faculty member at New College, even after he had died.

I imagined watching the chair from somewhere to the east of the lawn, sixty or seventy feet away, where I rested comfortably twelve or fifteen feet up in the air, over the place where once—in 1947, when we first came to the farm—the raspberry bushes had grown, and the broad patch of strawberries had spread out along their north side.

From my place in the air above what had once been the garden, I watched the chair in the middle of the lawn, with my father in it, as the grass around it grew tall, topped out in seeds, then gradually became mingled with taller kinds of growth. I watched my father remain there as the house deteriorated, bricks falling from the chimney, shingles

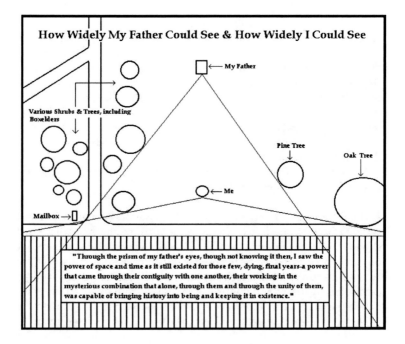

How Widely My Father Could See & How Widely I Could See

← My Father

Various Shrubs & Trees, including Boxelders

Pine Tree

Oak Tree

← Me

Mailbox →

"Through the prism of my father's eyes, though not knowing it then, I saw the power of space and time as it still existed for those few, dying, final years-a power that came through their contiguity with one another, their working in the mysterious combination that alone, through them and through the unity of them, was capable of bringing history into being and keeping it in existence."

blowing up in the wind, windows breaking, doors standing open for a time, then falling from their hinges, first the top, then the bottom, until they lay flat and the wind, the dust, the rain and snow were given free entrance, were extended an invitation to stay as long as they chose. At last the house began to crumble in on itself, a process taking a very great, long, slow time. The white chair remained where it always was, though obscured now by overgrowth and weeds, and with the difference that my father no longer sat in it, but lay scattered, a piece of bone here, another there, in among the roots of weeds and tall grass. After an even greater, longer, and slower time, the chair was gone as well, as was the house itself, leaving only a low mound, a scar, a swelling on the earth, where it had stood.

3

(My angle of vision was wider than my father's, since I stood twenty feet in front of him, at the lawn's edge, and my view was therefore less obscured by trees. The symbolism was not diminished by this fact but increased.

Because of the way I stood, in front of him, I was looking through his eyes. I was my father's eyes. But at the same time I was seeing more widely than he.

•

I understood later, of course, that he was also speaking of things beyond merely sight. He meant, as well, the feeling of the air, the softness of it, the paradox of its cool warmth, and the scent of it, perfumed and delicate and complex, made up of all the growing and blossoming things that it had ever touched as it moved over the surface of the earth, and of all the varied scents of the earth itself.

4

(At the very last gathering, in August of 1953, the weather was different, better, fine. Deep green was everywhere, there having been steady moisture throughout the season. The elms rose up in their stately way and were lost to view in the luxury of their own foliage.

None of the chairs in our house matched except for the three oak ones that normally stood at the dining room table. But all the chairs we had were out on the lawn anyhow, regardless of being mismatched, chipped, of different colors. There were even the two stools from the kitchen that no one had ever gotten around to painting. Blankets were spread out on the grass for those—meaning the "children"—who might sit cross-legged or lean sideways on an elbow while they ate. The kitchen table stood in the center of things, laden with pans, bowls, casserole dishes, and pitchers of things to drink. The table itself was covered with its usual piece of oil-cloth, patterned with red and white checks, hanging down over the sides. But that oil cloth, instead of making the table look familiar, somehow made the sight of it out on the lawn, with grass underneath it and trees around it, seem all the more anomalous, unusual, and out of place.

There were many more people this time. Both my aunt Signe and aunt Hannah had come to stay with my grandmother in West Tree for a time, so they were at the gathering (this was the summer I vomited out the car window on our the way to the Mississippi river). So my cousins Eldon and Charlotte were at the gathering as well. Charlotte was now thirteen and Eldon fifteen, a year older than my sister Hannah, just as Charlotte was a year ahead of Ingie.

Marie and Lutie were also there, for the very last time, and so were their second-youngest brother, my great-uncle Edgar, and his wife Klara. Like Marie and Lutie, Klara wore a long dress of a dark color, while Edgar wore a suit and vest. He had hung the jacket from a low branch across the driveway. Hanging there, near our gathering, it looked like something left behind from an Impressionist painting.

Edgar seemed to prefer standing, doing so most of the time behind Klara's chair, although he also moved and stood behind Marie or Lutie's chair, or even behind my grandmother in her wheelchair. He was a big man, tall, with a very high, rounded forehead, traits that I knew had been shared by my dead grandfather. He had a deep voice and an always-ready sense of humor. He was especially fond of making declamations in Latin, which no one understood except Marie and, most of the time, my father. Each time, Marie would lean over and whisper in Lutie's ear the meaning of what Edgar had said.

•

The table, chairs, and blankets were all placed in the shade about a third of the way toward the road from the front door. Farther toward the front of the lawn, in the sun, Eldon and my sister Hannah had begun a game of croquet. When it was over, Ingie and Charlotte, who had been pushing one another on the swing, went over and joined them for another.

Whenever a car went by on the road, the people inside it would stare at us as they went by. I knew that I would have done the same thing if I had been going by. Many times, when riding with my family and passing gatherings like ours at other farms, I had stared as we went by. Often the groups I saw were even larger than ours, filling the whole yard and making it festive, with chairs everywhere, and tables, and colors, and children running in one direction and another, even climbing in the trees.

•

My grandmother asked Signe to pull her wheelchair backwards a bit and turn it so she could watch the croquet game. My grandmother's fingers and hands, by this time, were so misshapen that she couldn't grip the silver rims fixed to the wheels in order to turn them.

After Signe moved the wheelchair, there came one of those moments when conversation stops. In this case, it was partly because everyone else also turned for a moment to watch the game. The lawn was bumpy, with a rise in it going up toward the oak tree, and the balls didn't always go as intended. What I liked best was the brief wooden click of the balls when they hit one another. In the silence when everyone was watching, my sister Ingie's voice rose up clearly, "Ooooh, that's not fair," but from her tone you could tell she didn't mean it.

•

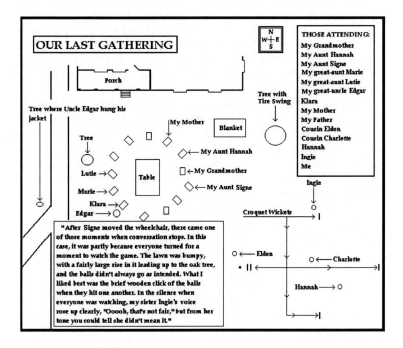

"Isn't it wonderful seeing the young ones play," my grandmother said. Then she added, but as a statement to my father, not a question, "Harold, remember how much you loved playing croquet in the back yard, with Rolf and Signe and Hannah. Of course you remember. Who could ever forget."

•

She tried to turn her head in the direction of my mother, who sat on her right. My grandmother, apparently, thought that my father was also there, standing near my mother's chair. Her neck, however, had stiffened up too completely for her to turn to see him as she spoke to him. And furthermore he wasn't there any longer. He had gotten up and gone in through the front door.

•

My mother reached out and drew me toward her by tugging at the rolled-up part of my shirt sleeve. Still pulling on it gently, to make me come even closer, then to make me lean down so she could whisper in my ear: "Run in and see what your father is doing."

•

Three years later, my grandmother left West Tree forever.

After Labor Day in 1956, Signe drove her to Baltimore, where for the next seven years the two of them lived together in Signe's bungalow there. Near the end of those years, she had the help of nurses. By the time she died in 1963, my grandmother had had eight operations, lost both legs above the knee and one arm up to the elbow.

Marie and Lutie lived nowhere near so long, both of them dying quite suddenly, in Marie's case not even a year after the picnic, since she died in March, Lutie in October.

My sister Hannah was next, dying eight years later, in 1960, when in a near-collision she was thrown from her open car onto the highway.

Six years after Hannah's death, my father died in the West Tree Hospital, at age 58, failed by his liver, lungs, and heart.

I never saw Edgar or Klara again in my life, even though Edgar lived until 1969. By then he was 81. Klara died three years before him. I don't know her age.

My aunt Hannah died in 1973, at age 62. At the time of her death, like my grandmother, she was living with Signe in her house in Baltimore.

My mother died a year after that, at the age of 66.

Having cared for my grandmother, and then for Hannah, Signe herself died in Baltimore in 1983, age 70.

My sister Ingie died in 1996. She was 56.

Charlotte died in 2002, aged 63.

Eldon—whom I still remember folding up one side of the wing-like black hood of his mother's car and showing me that the twelve head-bolts were capped in chromium, died in 2006, at age 69.

•

(With everyone else outdoors on the lawn, there was an unnatural silence inside the house, as if it had been suddenly emptied out years before. Except for the kitchen table and most of the chairs, however, everything was in its place, although the missing pieces left enormous empty spaces. I glanced into the living room but saw no sign of my father. The bathroom door was standing open, so I knew he wasn't there. The kitchen was empty and still. I peered out the back door, then went outside and ran hard for a few minutes, going out behind the corncrib, then looping back through its arch, then once around the turn-around of the driveway, and after that a few times around the three cars that were parked side by side. I slipped open the door of the pump house and looked inside, even though there was no conceivable reason why my father would be in there. It was stuffy inside and warm. The windows were closed, and there were cobwebs over them.

•

Back in the kitchen, I went to the sink, turned on the cold tap as fast as it would go and held a glass under the stream until it grew icy, the way the farm water did. Obliquely, through the open doorway to the pantry, a movement caught my eye. I turned off the faucet, set down the glass, and went in through the door. There was my father, in the pantry, not even looking out the window, but facing the closed cabinets on the north wall. On the counter were a liquor bottle and a jelly glass, and he was holding the glass but not lifting it up.

In the narrow pantry, he looked even taller than usual. He towered. He filled the tiny room. I stood frozen there.

He showed no surprise at all, and his voice revealed none either. Very slowly, he turned his head and looked down at me. Then he said, in a voice that had no question mark at the end, and in a tone expressionless and flat and bored and dead and without energy: "And just exactly what in the name of fucking christ almighty do you think you're doing?"

5

(I came later to the conviction, and held to it firmly, that my father fell into his depths of bitter depression in exact proportion to his certainty that the Epoch of Walking was coming to an end.

•

The Epoch of Walking, after all, had constituted the entirety of my father's past. What I came to understand only later is that he relied upon it also to constitute the entirety of his future.

•

Therefore, when the Epoch of Walking ended, my father's future ended with it.

6

How else explain his plunges into despair, or his brief but equally familiar swings—on the slender vines of hope—upward into bliss?

•

The pivotal morning two years earlier, for example, on the front lawn: what powerful impulse could it have been that tore him suddenly from bed, away from my mother's side, and propelled him outdoors if it wasn't an otherwise inexpressible certainty and conviction of promise, futurity, happiness, coherence, entirety, and wholeness?

•

Or his nakedness that same summer morning: what could it have been if not a way of responding naturally to an overwhelming sense of oneness and harmony, of the absence of divisions between one thing and another: between time and space, past and present, here and there, self and other?

•

And therefore of course the absence of these same blessings, and their being replaced by the equally powerful certainties of stasis, absence, nothingness, death—it was this absence that would have made him kick the pail in the barn, or slip away to drink gin in the pantry, staring at the cabinet doors inches from his face, as he was doing when I peered around the door, rigid with terror at what might be there—before he slowly turned, looked down, and asked, but with no question mark and altogether tonelessly except for the insurmountable scorn piled on the meager, crushable pronoun: "Just what in the name of fucking christ almighty do you think you're doing?"

•

(And when I became an adult, I grew to know also, with perfect understanding, how small a thing it can be, how small a catalyst is needed, to change everything for you, to drop you free-falling over the edge into a cavernous valley of despair: one pathetically simple thing or another—the sound of croquet balls, for example, hitting one another on the grass; Marie leaning over to translate a phrase of Latin into Lutie's ear; the sound of a voice on the still air, Ingie's, for example, calling out "Ooooh, that's not fair," though the tone let you know she didn't mean it—but just the sound of it, the human sound of it coming to you over the still air, in the warm afternoon, joining one place, one thing, one person, with another.

7

(It was as though I were looking through a kind of prism, you might say, my looking out through my father's eyes—the important thing being, again, that until years later I didn't know what it was I had seen.

This was true even of the soft-shadowed morning haze between me and Corrigan's Woods, or between me and the wooded horizon where the descent began down into the Wagon River valley, or between me and the woods at the back edge of the Pikens' fields.

I saw the haze, but at the time I saw it, it was only that, just haze, nothing more.

The same was true of the beams of sunlight laying themselves down on the rounded hilltops but not reaching into the valleys, and it was true of the way the darkest shadow was the one that clung under the west edge of Corrigan's Woods.

It was true of the way the sun touched only the highest points: the corners of the Gothic tower on the New College chapel; the rooftop and bell-tower of First Hall at Old College; and, far away, the gray wood and curved slope of the Nordic ski jump.

It was true of all things everywhere, that at the time I saw them, they were nothing more than themselves: the way the rows of Harve Shuha's fields, for example, seemed to curve as they disappeared into valleys and then reappeared farther on, growing closer together as they diminished into the distance.

And it was the same for all those things not seen at all, but heard, or felt, or smelled: the rising and untuned chorus of birdsong; the breeze that had risen but would soon die down again, and the way it moved against your skin, in countless invisible tongue-flicks and eddies; and the indescribable scent that came with it of a moist, earthy sweetness, flowered, clover-nectared, perfumed.

•

Just look at this, my father had said. He was in one of his moments of ecstasy, one of the moments when he desired all things. The tone in his voice; the half-pained look on his face, suggesting a pleasure too great to bear; the small, circular, all-inclusive motion of the hand—these revealed the truth of what he was really saying: all of this is glorious, all of this is one, I am going to die, we are going to die, all that we see and know will come to an end and be gone.

•

Because of his nakedness, I didn't dare turn to look back, although I could easily imagine what he looked like behind me, as I can still do even now—reclined low in the white wooden chair, one arm raised from the resting point of its elbow, the cigarette held between two fingers, the long white legs crossed at the knees, one foot planted in the grass, the toes of the other suspended two or three inches above it.

•

He drank and drank and drank, smoked and smoked and smoked. Without respite, he wished and wanted and desired. Then he died once and was gone forever.

•

Through the prism of my father's eyes, not knowing it then, what I saw were the power of space and time as they still existed—for those last, few, dying years—in contiguity with one another, working in the mysterious and then still-existent combination that alone, through them and through the unity of them, was capable of bringing history into being and keeping it in existence.

•

I saw, in other words, all of time at once; I saw how time was bonded to its own being by space; and in this way I saw how wholeness and oneness were brought into being.

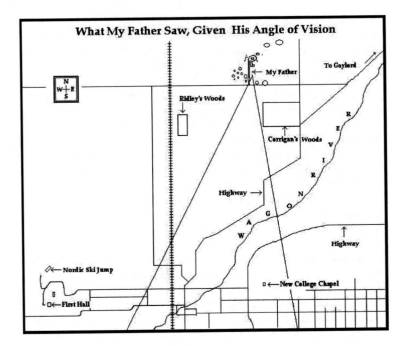

What My Father Saw, Given His Angle of Vision

To Gaylord

← My Father

Ridley's Woods

Corrigan's Woods

R
E
V
I
R

Highway →

N
O
G
A
W

Highway

↗← Nordic Ski Jump

New College Chapel

First Hall

•

This brief moment of seeing would later reveal itself, as can easily be imagined, to have been the most important and pivotal moment in the entire evolution of my intellectual life, coloring the way I was to look at the past and the way I was to look—during what remained of it—at the future.

8

(That morning, at the front of the lawn, looking south, my father naked behind me, I saw everything that had formed my life up until that moment; and, because of what those things had been, and the implication of what influence they would have, I saw everything also that was to occur in my life afterward.

•

Through the agencies of space and time, not yet estranged from one another, I saw everything with an almost perfect simultaneity: I saw moments in time, locations in space, and, through the nurturing combination of these, glimpses of events that even at that moment were still continuing to exist inside of history.

•

I saw, for example, my paternal grandfather, on a day in October of 1922, dressed in his loose black suit, walking past a stone wall with his briefcase hanging from one hand.

At the same time, I saw him in a hospital bed in Cleveland, Ohio, on January 19th, 1923. His eyes were closed, his chest not moving. My grandmother sat on a chair pulled up close to the bed beside him, her head bowed forward. Her reddish-brown hair was rich, thick, and long, piled abundantly on her head and pinned there.

I saw my father, at exactly that same moment, in the family's house in Brooklyn, looking out an upstairs window. I myself seemed to be looking in through the window as my father was looking out of it. On one of the walls of the room behind him hung a Boy Scout canteen with a fitted canvas jacket and chained metal cap. Near it was a painting of a Roman temple, half in ruins, viewed from low in the foreground, seen against a purple sunset.

•

My father disappeared from the window. The family disappeared from the house. And then, in the next instant, I saw a great number of images at once:

1) My father on a passenger train, in early evening, standing between two of the cars and leaning out into the rushing air;

2) another train pulling into the station in West Tree, in June 1925; five people stepping down onto the red-brick platform in the sunlight; these being my grandmother and her four children, ages 16, 14, 12, and 10;

3) and then, in the same place but not the same time, in 1910 instead of 1925, my great-aunt Marie stepping down from a train onto the same red-brick platform into another flood of mid-afternoon sunlight, though as I see her she is wearing a wide-brimmed hat that keeps her face, with its high forehead and long jaw, obscured in shadow.

•

I saw, in glimpses that were scattered everywhere throughout (I know now) the morning light and everywhere on the scarcely-moving morning breeze:

4) My great-grandfather, on a dirt road in a woods in central Wisconsin, riding on a one-horse wagon, in 1856;

5) Marie and Lutie, walking side by side on a dirt road over low hills outside of Archer, Nebraska, in the summer of 1899; there being no trees or houses visible in any direction;

6) Marie, sometime in 1897, in Columbia, Missouri, in a room with a single tall window, reading, wearing a long dress with high collar; her hair, voluminous and so dark a brown as to seem almost black, twisted

loosely into a bun and worn low at the back of her neck;

7) Marie and Lutie, one morning in November of 1916, coming out of a house on Old College hill and going down the steps together;

8) my great-grandmother, in the winter of 1924, in the first-floor room in the northwest corner of Marie and Lutie's new house, lying in her bed, breathing heavily, then not breathing at all;

9) myself, in the summer of 1949, in the heart of my years of perfect seeing, looking in through the doorway of that same room, then stepping all the way inside and staring at the summer light as, falling across Marie's desk and chair, it was filtered, cooled, and made a shadowy green by the vines that covered the window;

10) Marie and Lutie in their garden—when? in 1925, 1928, 1932, 1937—each wearing a broad-brimmed hat, each bent forward at the waist, each with a basket hanging from the crook of her left arm.

•

(And then, even more rapidly, more relentlessly, all pressed into a single extended moment, there showered down upon me, before me, and around me, with an awesomeness and beauty that—as I understood later, in the same way that I understood everything later—were undeniable and at the same time overwhelming, images of:

11) My great-aunts Marie and Lutie behind the porch-railing of 917 Woodland Avenue one afternoon in June 1925, looking down toward the curb as a taxi pulled up and stopped, and then as

12) five faces looked up at them in turn from the windows of the cab;

13) the back yard of 917 Woodland Avenue, my aunts Hannah and Signe swinging, the two of them on the swing at once, one on the lap of the other, facing one another, pumping higher and higher;

14) an August afternoon in 1934, gathered for a picnic lunch in the same back yard, my great-aunts Marie and Lutie, my towering great-uncles Edgar and Marcus, their wives Klara and Nora, my great-uncle Albert, the oldest of everyone, and his wife Karen, along with my grandmother, and my own mother and father, married a year, and my aunts Signe and Hannah and my uncle Rolf, nineteen and a junior at Old College, his death to be in 1997, when he was eighty-two;

15) the absence of myself at the picnic in 1934, or of my sisters Hannah and Ingie, or of our cousins Eldon and Charlotte; the grandeur of the tall elms reaching overhead, the blue sky above them, the dappled sunlight coming through and splashing onto the grass below; the clothing of the group, my great-aunts' long dresses with sleeves tightly buttoned at the wrists, my great-uncles' vests with watch chains hanging across the fronts, their loose-armed white shirts, their generously-cut trousers, their jackets hanging from nearby trees; my own parents'

clothing, my mother in a short-sleeved dress of thin material with a flower pattern, my father in a white linen suit and in white shoes of woven leather mesh, his jacket not hanging from a tree but being worn by him (his shirt open at the neck, his hands resting casually in his pockets) as he stands talking (slim and elegant, as tall as they are) with my great-uncles about

16) (the Icelandic Eddas, the economic history of ancient Greece, Thucydides, Herodotus, the Peloponnesian War, the Germanic and Scandinavian roots of the English language as they date from the Saxon era, the remnants of the inflection system in dialects of late Middle English, and varieties of other things, often, furthermore, in languages, that

17) I can't understand, however hard I listen, or try to, watching their lips, their confident and self-assured faces, their stances and their clothing, seeing them laugh from time to time, and me

18) envying them, envying them, envying them their knowledge, appearance, accomplishment, until I felt I could no longer possibly

•

But nothing stopped. My father, behind me, naked, smoking his cigarette, having said to me, with the small circular gesture of his hand, "Look at this," having caused me to remain rooted to my spot at the front edge of the lawn, looking up, and out, and around (although not back, not back, not back), into the soft, cool, blue morning haze and seeing, in a great, colorful, singular simultaneity,

18) my father, alone, cross-country skiing south of West Tree, along the Wagon River, in 1927;

19) my father, in 1926, camping in Vreeland Woods with his high school classmates Karl Halbrunn and Haken Swenson, on a hot day, sitting in front of a canvas tent, all three drinking from Boy Scout canteens with fitted canvas jackets;

20) my father, in the summer of 1928, standing up on a high wagon-load of grain sheaves, pitch-forking them down onto the loader of an old-fashioned threshing machine;

21) my father, in early October of 1925, in the middle of the Third Street bridge over the Wagon River in downtown West Tree, leaning back against the railing of the bridge while he talks with my mother, who looks up into his face;

22) my father, in the summer of 1927, at the wheel of the family's long black car, in the Rocky Mountains;

23) my father, talking on the telephone to my mother, in the upstairs hallway of the house at 917 Woodland Avenue;

24) my father going down the Nordic ski jump, wearing goggles and a reindeer-pattern sweater, leaning forward, and then, at the lip, sailing off high into the air;

25) my father at the rail of a ship at sea, in the South Pacific, the wind flipping up his tie and the points of his shirt-collar;

26) my father in a field of high grass in 1946, bending toward his tripod, a thick black cloth over his head, as he takes a picture;

27) my father at the dining room table at Marie and Lutie's house, in 1949, when I see him from above, and when I see my own chair at the table, empty;

28) my father kicking the pail of milk in the barn;

29) my father on the front lawn, early in the morning, naked, in the white chair, smoking his cigarette behind me

30) so that I knew I mustn't, no matter what, turn around, since then not only would I see him again but in every likelihood it would appear as if I wanted to see him again, his being naked, with the result that at any cost I must keep on facing south, looking out at the fine mist of images that still fell down upon and before and around me, including

•

31) myself, in my winter coat, sitting on the top step of the Emerson School, losing control of my bowels, and being raised up by that force from underneath me, for just a moment, as if to the height of my tall great-uncles,

•

and including also me

a) watching the fish in Mr. Leitch's goldfish pond as they moved, then hovered, then moved again below the shadowy surface of the water;

•

b) walking with my grandmother on Woodland Avenue to Mrs. Peterson's store, in August of 1945;

•

c) riding in the back of Harry Bauchman's white convertible, over low hills, as darkness gathered and then deepened;

•

d) watching a blimp overhead, floating northeast against a blue sky before it disappeared through green foliage;

•

e) seeing Harve Shuha plowing with his two work horses in late autumn of 1947;

•

f) asking my mother, as she pinned white sheets to the clothes lines, why the Wagon River had the name it did;

•

g) an old grain-wagon abandoned along the river, its spoked wheels immersed to their hubs in moving water;

•

h) sitting on the toilet in the upstairs bathroom in Marie and Lutie's house, seeing the white curtain move, then fall back;

•

i) from my bed, in the deepest part of night, hearing a train whistle across town;

•

j) waking up, in my first memory, and hearing Hannah and Ingie and my mother talking under the window;

•

k) being with my sisters, in 1944, in the sprinkler behind the hospital, the mist coming down with rainbows in it, while, on a bench nearby, Marie and Lutie sat in their long dresses and brown shoes;

•

l) standing by the iron hitching post and seeing Marie and Lutie for the first time: seeing them walk toward me out of the 19th century, and then, as I remained unmoving, seeing them walk away from me toward the corner, going back into the end of the 19th century.

9

(From where I stood, and in the relatively short time I stood there, I saw all of these things, as well as countless others unmentioned, although I didn't yet know, and would realize only later, that I in fact was seeing them or in fact had seen them.

•

I also knew, and in exactly this same way, that through the interacting agencies of time and space I was looking into a world that for the moment was still integrated and coherent, and was therefore capable, for however brief a time, of sustaining both itself and the existence of its history within itself.

•

I knew also that the pressure upon me created by this knowledge, to whatever degree conscious or not conscious, was enormous.

•

And I was aware, finally, that this pressure and its attendant discomfiture were made known to me by my entrapment at the front of the lawn, where I was imprisoned on the one hand by my father's command that I look out into the morning and on the other by the extent of my shock at my father's nakedness, the latter of which kept me from turning around, since, although of course I did in fact want to see his nakedness again, I would prefer death itself to my actually being seen wanting to see it again.

For a time, therefore, I was free neither to flee nor to turn around. When my feeling of paralysis and imprisonment, however, became

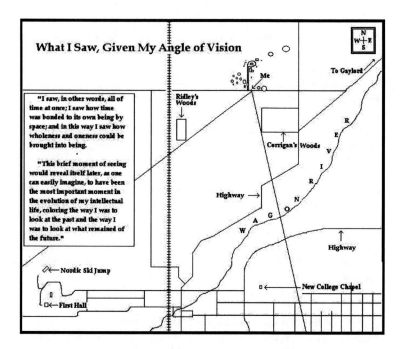

What I Saw, Given My Angle of Vision

"I saw, in other words, all of time at once; I saw how time was bonded to its own being by space; and in this way I saw how wholeness and oneness could be brought into being.

"This brief moment of seeing would reveal itself later, as one can easily imagine, to have been the most important moment in the evolution of my intellectual life, coloring the way I was to look at the past and the way I was to look at what remained of the future."

Ridley's Woods

Me

To Gaylord

Corrigan's Woods

RIVE

Highway →

RANGO

WA

Highway

✐← Nordic Ski Jump

☐

☐← First Hall

☐← New College Chapel

too great to bear—however great an amount of knowledge may have been flowing simultaneously and unbeknownst into me—I remembered Ganges, as I've said, waiting to be untied. And so, with no further thought, I turned, rigorously avoiding even the slightest glance toward my father, and trotted with a carefully controlled appearance of unhaste up the driveway—then in a full, gravel-spitting sprint the minute I was out of sight—around back to Ganges, who, though she too would soon enough meet death, leapt up so high in trying to lick my face that her back feet lifted up again and again off the ground.

III
I Reach Puberty

1

I loved Marietta Streetfield from the moment I saw her, even though at that time I had only the most chaste feelings for her.

•

I became aware of her in the fall of 1952, when I entered seventh grade and found that she was a "new person" in the class. Only three years later, she and her parents moved out of town. I don't know what became of her.

She was thin, and I think that she must have grown very rapidly in the time just before I knew her, because she never stood up quite straight but slumped forward in a slightly self-conscious way, as if trying to hide or go unnoticed. To me, however, as my love for her secretly grew, the self-effacing way she held herself made her only more desirable, since it suggested her sensitivity and shyness and drew attention also to the length and thinness of her neck. Her hair was very light, almost the color of rain-bleached straw, and, cut short, it tightened into curls that followed the shape of her skull and left bare the valley in the nape of her neck. That part of her body, doubly exposed because of her way of carrying her head bowed slightly forward, was inexpressibly desirable to me and made me wish, as I wished also of Marietta herself, to be near it and able to touch it whenever I wanted.

My desire at this time went little farther than that, but it hardly made any difference—what I felt—anyhow, since the extremity of my own shyness made me far too hesitant to make my feelings known.

Instead, I recited her name to myself, repeatedly, gazed at her from across the room in the one class she had with me, and at other times of the day, between hours, went by a long and indirect route through the school corridors, risking a late-penalty in my own next class, because I knew there was a strong chance of my seeing her at her open locker.

I was infatuated with her, and during long solitary hours at home thought of her constantly. I visualized her, imagined her, saw her in my mind's eye, wrote her name on pieces of paper. I wished, amid a sense of hopelessness and impossibility, that I could have her with me, for no other reason than to know the feeling of her body against mine, the warmth of her flesh, the smoothness of her skin, the scent of her hair.

2

By this time the Epoch of Walking had ended once and for all, the farm had entered its mid-stage of collapse and first stage of disappearance, and my father's voyage into despair was rapidly growing more firmly established and, day by day, more easily observable.

In regard to myself, as it happened, this period of acceleratingly swift decline in the history of the farm, of West Tree, and of my father coincided with that period in my own life when, quite suddenly, I at last became aware of the full range of potential uses that resided in my penis.

•

Obviously, I had for some time been aware of my penis as more than a means for urination. My father's desire for experience of the world in the greatest possible degree of wholeness, in addition to his tolerant attitude (or his desire for such an attitude) toward nudity, had together and for some time given me glimpses, as I've said, of mature male genitals—and a considerable anxiety regarding them when I became afraid that if my own scrotum were to become lengthened even half as much as my father's, I would never again be able to run with the speed and abandon that I had so much treasured when Ganges was still alive, in my years of perfect seeing.

Nor had I remained unaware, even in my innocent years of perfect seeing, that more was involved with the penis than only urination, especially in consideration of the organ's inexplicable way of stiffening (a trait that my own penis had had for as long as I could remember).

Living on the farm, too, even if only during the last few scenes of its existence, gave me an education not readily available to all. I saw cats and chickens mounting one another in the barn, yard, and chicken coop, and I even saw—on farms where they were kept: at the Pikens', for example—the larger-scale mountings of hogs and sheep.

In my own family's case, early in my years of perfect seeing—in the spring and summer of 1948—an arrangement was made between my father and Tom Ridley whereby the Ridleys' bull would be made available to service our cows when they came into heat. I remember Tom Ridley and my father coming across the top of Second Hill with the bull—his name was Max—walking between them, Tom Ridley holding Max off to the side with a long pole attached to a ring in the bull's nose.

I sat on the top rail of the barnyard fence, and, once everything was finally arranged, watched Max mount and enter one of our cows, an experience leaving me no longer in doubt as to one function of the penis—an organ that in Max's case, once it came out of its sheath, was as thick as my forearm though longer, and in color the bright glistening red of Christmas candy after it has been sucked on.

Even after seeing the event, however, I was still ignorant as to precisely why Max had been impelled to put his penis where he had, what his motive in doing so could have been. I was still ignorant, that is, of precisely what physical feeling may have been involved, just as I was ignorant of the exact purpose of Max's enormous, heavy, and low-hanging testicles—lower even than my father's, and. for that matter, not wrinkly, but smooth—and I was still ignorant as well—though this was to prove unquestionably the most important aspect of all—of the relation of any of it to the mysteries of space and time.

3

(I was on my bed one summer night reading a comic book, no one else at home, when the feeling first happened to me. Or when I first made it happen, I should say, since admittedly I had been playing with my penis as I lay reading, having by that time begun to hear things in school, from one boy or another, or one group or another, directly or by hint, boasting about the variety of things he or they knew, or had already done, or claimed to have done.

In my own case, nothing seemed to be happening—except for the wooden-stick feeling, of course, which was so commonplace as to mark no achievement—and a very faint sense of pleasure—until without warning came a short, sharp, searing pain, and at the same time something—little of it, whatever it was—a thin liquid, just a few drops, came out in a very quick spurt or two, my first thought being that I would have to get to the doctor immediately because certainly I must have torn a part of myself somewhere inside.

The pain and discomfort—and the discomfiture—of the experience kept me away from it for a considerable time, until unexpectedly—a year later? a year and a half?—the same thing began to take place by itself, as I slept, with no help from me at all except that I happened most often, at least after the first several times, to be in the midst of a dream about Marietta Streetfield. These occurrences, producing considerably greater volume of liquid than the original drop or two, resulted each morning in stiffened pancakes of dried starch on my sheets, these preferable to the original patches of sticky wetness, which grew quickly chill and kept me, in avoiding contact with them, balanced precariously for hours on one far edge of the mattress or the other.

But now that I had been given a clear idea indeed of the pleasure that could be associated with them, my efforts to achieve more emissions of this kind—while I was awake, not sleeping—resumed again soon. And the result, it is necessary for me to say, was of an importance far—infinitely—greater than I could ever have imagined in even the remotest corner of my mind.

For it was only now, when I had reached this stage in my education, that I began to develop a conscious understanding of the enormity of what I had discovered, along with an emerging idea, too, of the equivalent enormity of what I was to be faced with in the unfolding course of my life.

In, during, and through orgasm, I had felt, learned, and seen such things as I had never seen, felt, or known before. And, coming as they did at this particular moment in my life—when I was in love with Marietta Streetfield, when the farm was nearing its last collapse, when I had so recently been introduced to the cloud chamber—these things had a cumulative effect that was, I believe, so remarkably profound and far-reaching for the very reason that they brought fully into my consciousness for the first time in my life what I had known before only through image, echo, innuendo, feeling, and hint—namely, that it would be essential, necessary, in fact imperative, if I hoped to achieve not the impossible wish of bringing it back once it was gone, but to achieve simply the keeping alive in memory of some infinitesimally small part or token of the lost, nurturing, harmonious world whose last few breaths I had had the enormous good fortune to have been witness to and a part of—if I could accomplish even this small harboring achievement with the expenditure of my life, it would of course be essential, toward that end, that I give over willingly every fiber of my being and every ounce of my energies to the unflagging and rigorous study of space and time.

IV

The Epoch Over

(The world around us had deteriorated sufficiently by this time to create in my father a degree of misery that revealed the outlines of what his later, full-blown despair would be like.

This was the period in my own life when I formed the habit of avoiding him as much as possible, in great part because my presence—for reasons I didn't yet fully understand—served to exacerbate his misery, converting it, usually, into either sullenness or rage.

Most of our out-buildings, including the barn, had fallen into disuse by this time; my years of perfect seeing had long ago come to a close; and with the end also, at last, of the Epoch of Walking, there had been no hope for the survival of the farm. After our cattle had been sold— this happened quite early, even before the death of Ganges—my father made a brief attempt to raise steers, the notion being that they could be grown solely for their beef, living to maturity in a lean-to shed off the north side of the barn and never being let to pasture. The gloom of this sordid arrangement was enormous and deep, leaving its additional mark on my father, while even the economics of it, given the passing of the Epoch, were at first only narrowly profitable and bitterly competitive, and in the end utterly futile.

After the failure—that is, the large financial loss—brought about by a second crop of steers, an idea was hit upon that would once again enable my mother to lend her own efforts more meaningfully to our well-being. She had clearly made such efforts also long ago, during my years of perfect seeing, in numerous ways, among them by feeding and caring for the laying hens and their eggs, tending the garden and fruit trees, and canning vegetables and fruits in enormous and recurrent quantities (the shelves of the pantry where my father stood in 1952 had only a brief time before that groaned under the weight of my mother's harvest).

What followed the steers, then, were more chickens, but chickens, this time, that were raised to be eaten, not for their eggs. The venerable old barn, redolent once of the smells of cattle, leather, clover, hay, and silage, was converted now into a three-floor poultry factory filled only with the dry, acrid, thin, dusty stench of chicken body-heat, dander, and feces. Three times a year, two thousand yellow chicks arrived, grew into a half-feathered and gawky adolescence, then finally achieved young adulthood and were loaded into crates and put onto open trucks, twelve chickens per crate, eighty-four crates per truck, and driven away to slaughter.

The results were both miserable and unprofitable, the chickens living in dust, filth, airlessness, and squalor; the effort to maintain them being relentless, exhausting, and vile; and the price fetched at market being insufficient, for so small a crop as this, to cover the costs of purchase, transport, and feed.

•

(The period that followed stays with me in memories, equally vivid and equally unhappy, that come from both summer and winter.

It was a period, among other things, of my mother's being mainly absent, through her having taken a job as clerk in a slowly failing music and art store in West Tree. The same was true of Hannah, who worked at the local newspaper after school and on weekends, studying with double diligence meanwhile in order to finish high school a year early and move away from West Tree. As for Ingie, it was a period, for the most part, of her closing herself up in her room.

For my father, it was a time of sitting for whole days at the desk he'd moved down from the drafty bedroom upstairs, placing it in the southwest corner of the dining room, facing the wall, so that when he sat at it, his back would be turned to anyone else who might be present.

As for me, it was a period primarily of hiding.

•

(From the closet, I could see through the open door into my father's darkroom, which, having by this time been abandoned for purposes of photography, was packed so tightly with filing cabinets, cartons, and storage boxes that you couldn't enter it.

In winter, I often stayed in the closet for the better part of the afternoon, paging through my father's photographic annuals. In some, there were female nudes, one image even showing pubic hair, making it a photo I stared at more than others. Several of the volumes consisted entirely of photos of the war. For a time—during my death period— I terrified myself by studying them in detail, riveted and horrified in equal measure. At night, especially in winter, it seemed a certainty that death would come down in flames from the sky. Insofar as possible, I never removed my shoes.

•

From inside the closet, sounds from outdoors were distant, small, and far away, muffled by the coats, suits, uniforms, and dresses that hung from the rod along the east wall, and by the linens piled on the shelves.

•

Some distance into the heart of the summers, after the humidity and heat had had a chance to build up, there would develop the unmistakable scent of mildew in the house. This was true especially in the living room, the room least used, especially in summer. Because of trees standing close to the windows, it always seemed shadowy there. The air was always still, even with the bottom halves of the windows propped open by sticks of wood. The scent of mildew, which I always found secretly pleasant, was in the carpet and chairs, and in the rows of books standing undisturbed on their floor-to-ceiling shelves.

•

(Assume a Saturday afternoon not in the heat of summer but in the empty core of winter. Assume the 18th of February in the year 1953.

At such a time, my mother and Hannah would be in West Tree at work, Ingie in her room, my father at his desk facing the wall. If the day had stretched into afternoon, and if the time were past two, he would have begun drinking. As for me, I would be in the closet, or perhaps, by that time and that year, I would have begun going up to hide in the low attic over the kitchen.

•

(Within two months after that winter afternoon, my great-aunt Marie would be dead. In slightly under five months more, so would Lutie. Seven years and six months after the same afternoon, my sister Hannah would die, on the highway, at twenty-two, thrown from her car. Ten years and four months later, my grandmother, missing two legs and an arm, would stop breathing, one Monday morning, in Baltimore, Maryland. Thirteen years after the same winter afternoon, my father would be failed by his liver, lungs, and heart. My aunt Hannah, who threw her head back in song as she drove Signe's car on the way to Barn Bluff, would die twenty years later, my mother twenty-one later, and, thirty years after the winter afternoon, my aunt Signe. Forty-three years after the same afternoon, my sister Ingie would die. Forty-nine years after, my cousin Charlotte. And fifty-four years after it, in 2006, Eldon would follow. Eldon has now, therefore, been dead for four years, and the August afternoon when he opened the hood of his mother's car to show me the chromium head-bolts under it was over half a century ago.

•

Things change. As I look back, it seems to me that they have changed utterly.

V
I Begin Trying to Hold Things Together

1

(There is very little left. In a despairing repetition of history; in an undertaking that could lead only to doom as time and space grew further separated; my father followed the ghosts of my great-aunts and -uncles by becoming a member of the faculty, if only part time, at Old College.

That is why I happened to be sitting in our car outside First Hall on the June afternoon in 1949 when a student dropped his cigarette from a second-floor window.

I learned that day that time can stop, proven by the fact that now, at this moment, as I write these words, sixty-one years later, the cigarette is still dropping from the window, is still suspended in the air, still hasn't reached the ground.

•

Interesting at first, then fascinating, this fact in the end became terrifying. Through dedicating my life to the study of it and its corollaries, I came to see not only the impenetrability of the subject but also the ruin destined to come from its study.

•

And this without even the additional complication of space, since the inclusion of space into the equation resulted in even greater terror, complicating the subject exponentially.

2

(An increasing disparity between the inside and the outside of my father began to grow evident. When he went up onto Old College Hill, he dressed in ways that suggested sunny, dry, crisp autumn weather. His tweed jackets contained mixtures of light brown, rust, or ochre. He wore ties of similar colors along with shirts either widely striped or of solid pink, blue, or even gray, these along with freshly pressed slacks of gray or brown, while on his feet were brown polished oxfords, wing tips, suede desert boots, or sometimes cordovans the color of dried blood and buffed to a deep shine.

I often watched him leave the house, sometimes simply by happening to be in the kitchen or dining room as he went out, but more often by spying from the square window in the gable of the attic above the kitchen, or from any other of my customary vantage points—the narrow passage, for example, between the caved-in chicken coop and the car shed, or from inside one of the bins of the granary, whose ancient walls offered plentiful cracks and peepholes, or even for a time from inside the cupola on top of the barn, which I found a way to climb up into, although admittedly staying there for extended periods was not a habit I continued for long.

•

The importance of my father's gradual but sure transformation during this period of my life was that he became even more confusing to me than he had been before. This meant, among other things, that I was less and less able, through him, to find evidence of logical continuity in the history around me. What I found instead, through study of him, were indications only of disjunction, fragmentation, uncertainty, and collapse.

•

An increased difficulty in my attempt to internalize the principle of continuity had been created, for example, simply by my practice of hiding in the closet where my father's naval uniforms and my mother's old dresses hung—as well as other articles, such as the voluminous and belted coat my father wore on December 7th, 1941. Other than in the photograph taken that day, never had I seen this coat so much as removed from its hanger, let alone worn by my father.

And what could such a thing possibly mean, after all, if not that the coat had significance in 1941 but had none now? Or that my had father placed significance in it then but placed none now? And, by an association both material and symbolic, how could the answers to these questions not lead logically to the corollary assertion that the day of my homecoming had held significance once but held it, now, no longer?

•

It became increasingly clear to me that the past had meaning, the present did not.

•

Earlier difficulties of discontinuity had been created for me, as I've said, by my family's move from West Tree to the farm in the first place.

Fundamentally, the only convincing or understandable motive I could ever imagine for my father's having made so radical a move was his belief that on the farm he could work more effectively to delay—or conceivably even prevent—the end of the Epoch of Walking.

But could this possibly have been true? And if it were true, why then hadn't my father addressed his task in a more practical, immediate, and direct way? Why hadn't he immersed himself wholly in farming as a means of nurturing, protecting, and preserving the continuity of history—instead of living, as he did, among the accumulations of one disparate hint, image, action, or object after another—his glasses, his lighter, his eagle, his belt, his anchor, his bare head, his khaki pants and shirts, his darkroom, his kicking of the milk bucket, his drinking in the pantry, his sitting with his back to the room—all of these suggesting the discontent, yearning, and discontinuity that was everywhere around and within him: hints, images, actions, and objects pointing as if in one small step after another to his later sullenness, misery, loss, sorrow, and despair?

•

My confusion was in no way lessened when my father, at Old College, adopted his tweed jackets, colored shirts, pleated pants, and stylish shoes. The day the cigarette fell—the day the cigarette is falling—I saw him disappear through the door of First Hall, tall, elegant, long-legged. But that was only an image of his surface, for at home later in the day I would see him in work boots and khaki pants, slumped miserably at his desk in the corner, the curve of his back to the room, his sullenness and despair taking over the house as his cruel wordlessness seemed to fill the rooms behind him—no movement or alteration in or of the scene occurring throughout entire days other than the movement of his right hand across sheets of paper and the curling of smoke from his left, against which he leaned his head, using his left thumb as resting place for his left temple, the first two fingers of the same hand serving to hold his cigarette. Other than these, his only movements were those required by trips to the kitchen for coffee and, later in the day, trips to the pantry for gin. Gradually the trips to the pantry began earlier and earlier, while those to the stove came to an end sooner and sooner.

•

As for other aspects of our lives, little changed, at least not outwardly, and certainly not rapidly. In 1955, my father left Old College and moved to New College. On balance, this was probably a good thing, since New College, less old-fashioned, was a place where my father's vari-colored clothing was more customary and therefore less conspicuous.

•

The change of colleges, however, had nothing to do with the despairing and history-grieving elements inside my father. Nor did his being either at Old College or at New College make any difference whatsoever in the steady changing of the world around us.

•

The truth was that by this point my father had given up, had accepted despair as a way of life. The consequence of this exhaustion and collapse for both his epistemology and his metaphysics—the legacy that in turn came down to me—was that he no longer believed in history as either existent or as living within time.

•

The Epoch of Walking, then, had at last ended absolutely, entirely, and completely. Therefore, although I didn't yet know this clearly, everything else was destined also to begin disappearing soon, along with it.

3

(By this point I had begun in a conscious and intellectual way to understand the drawing apart of space and time and to be increasingly aware of the dislocation and despair that would inevitably be caused by their breach. This pernicious and fearful separating, I grew more and more certain, would at some point inevitably occur on a broad and perhaps even universal scale. I had, after all, already seen it starting to happen in my father, on our farm, and in my family.

Perhaps because of my youth, however, or because of a certain native idealism (inherited, I feel certain, primarily through my mother), I wasn't yet ready to accept the full measure of the catastrophe or to abandon my desire to struggle against it by whatever means I could.

My age (I was now somewhere near fourteen), my doomed love for Marietta Streetfield, my affection for our dying farm, my treasured memories of Ganges from my years of perfect seeing, all of these—along with the influence, unexpectedly, of Dr. F. K. Kampfer—converged to help me in this effort, all serving to bring about, in the little time remaining of my early life, one of the most obviously significant and important episodes—failure though it may have been—in my intellectual education.

•

My dreams of Marietta Streetfield, as I mentioned, led to things happening while I was asleep that, while not themselves especially pleasurable, led me to experiment with bringing about the same end in a waking rather than sleeping state. These experiments, to my initial surprise, succeeded with a wild excess and extraordinary ease, bringing me to understand quickly one of the fundamental elements that had been missing in my knowledge and understanding of my—or of any—penis, namely the great pleasure that emissions of the sort I had at first feared but now frequently and voluntarily achieved can bring with them.

In my own case, however, more than merely pleasure proved to be involved in the matter. In orgasm and through orgasm, I found myself swept also toward—and then lodged within—a simultaneous intellectual experience of extraordinary complexity, resulting from convergent forces of the kind I've mentioned, none new but all major—the collapse of the farm, my love for Marietta Streetfield, and, of a towering importance, the absence of a relation between the inside and the outside of my father, this last prefiguring a corollary breakdown between past and present, a collapse in turn indicating, inescapably, the disappearance of time.

•

There was more.

It can come as a surprise to none that, having discovered the pleasure accompanying them, I began to bring about with frequency these emissions from my penis. Somewhat more surprising, however, may be that the most remarkable characteristic of them might never have been recognized had it not been for my earlier association with Dr. F. K. Kampfer.

For the fact was that the liquid product of my emissions, which, before (being asleep), I'd never before actually seen during my moments of rapture, was reminiscent of nothing so much as the thin, ductile, gray-white lines in Dr. Kampfer's cloud chamber in Lilledahl Hall. My emissions, too, were ductile, thread-like, and thin, in color closer to white than gray. Of most obvious importance, however, was that, precisely like the threads in the cloud chamber, these also came into being suddenly, unexpectedly, and out of absolute nothingness.

Coming into their sudden existence, my threads, too, remained poised, seeming to hang in the air for a split second, exactly like the trails of fog in the chamber. In my case, of course, the substance was liquid and not mist, and yet in its whiteness, in the way it hung in the air before falling, in the way it came from a prior nothingness, and in the way it cast itself, threadlike, outward—it was a parallel, truly, to those rays themselves, revealed to me by Dr. Kampfer, rays that traversed the very world, the universe, the entirety of the cosmos itself. Nor could I escape another association, this from the clear resemblance that my own ejaculations had, also, with the ductile arcs of milk that, from nothing, leapt up out of the bucket kicked by my father, then stayed in mid-air for the briefest of instants before falling to the floor of the barn.

And so through milk, through Dr. Kampfer, through the cloud chamber in the empty room in Lilledahl Hall, I saw that I too, with these new tendrils of my own, could hope to believe also in my own potential talent for bringing about connectedness—a talent that, once I'd seen and felt the possibility of its existence, I naturally made every waking effort to harness and exploit, my salient desire being, if it were in any way possible, to reconjoin all that so clearly was broken already, not only in my own life but in the world as I saw it steadily beginning to uncohere around me.

4

(Without question, what followed was a period of the most intense intellectual rigor I had experienced so far in my life, as I embarked upon making the most strenuous effort I was capable of to disarm or neutralize the forces of divisiveness, dissolution, and loss that were everywhere around me.

I was still strongly attached to the memory of Ganges, although I had no idea to what an extent of awareness and understanding that attachment was now about to lead. Almost all of the new understanding of this period came to me during the summer between my ninth and tenth grades, when, unsurprisingly, I spent almost all of my days alone. By this time, my father's condition had worsened—he no longer made any trips at all to the kitchen stove, and he had, besides, stopped acknowledging the presence of anyone, or in fact speaking words of any kind.

Other than for him, the house was—or seemed to be—empty. Late that spring, Hannah had moved to St. Paul to work as a journalist. My mother was still a fixture behind the worn counter at Berman's. And even Ingie had taken a job—as night-shift telephone operator—with the result that she slept the days away in her room upstairs.

As a result, the entire farm was all my own, a laboratory of learning, which I made use of to the utmost.

•

Just like long before, in my years of perfect seeing, I got out of bed early—before my mother was awake, before my father was at his desk, and before my sister had gotten back from work—and left the house, although now I was careful to take food with me sufficient for the day—chunks of bread and cheese, anything left in the refrigerator—chicken legs, for example—that was nourishing, portable, and quick to seize. I grouped these supplies at the center of an oversized bandanna, drew the four corners together, and with one quick knot secured them.

Carrying this bundle in front of me much as football runners sometimes carry the ball, I stepped cautiously to the back—no longer the front—door, stepped outside, closed the door quietly behind me, and then—the great difference being the enormous absence of Ganges—ran for my life.

My scrotum, as I feared, had now proven itself to be one of the few physical traits handed down to me from my father. As for tallness, I stood at five feet six and a quarter inches, the height that was to be my lifetime measure. My scrotum, however, hung down exactly like my father's—a long, low, swinging, wrinkled sac that descended alarmingly far between my legs, with exactly the inhibiting effect I had so greatly feared—except, as I quickly enough learned, at three specific times, these being when I was cold, when I was on the brink of tipping over into ejaculation, or when the time was still very early in the morning.

Which is why, just as in my years of perfect seeing, I was now able to run with complete freedom again, making my way along all the same routes I had followed with Ganges years before.

Besides the absence of Ganges, however, there were other significant differences: I was, now, in continual search of places to hide my supply of food, and of places also where I could subsequently hide myself for various parts of the day, since, unlike in the old times with Ganges, I would seldom return to the house until evening, for the end-of-the-day meal, though, as time went on, less and less often even then.

This meant that if only for the sake of distance it made good sense to run as far as I could while my scrotum was still well tucked up, namely in the earliest segments of the morning. Later in the day I could always, Indian-fashion, make my way about the farm stealthily and at will, those being the times, as in the still, silent, dead of the afternoon, when my scrotum was low, and when running fast was therefore all but out of the question. It was in the later parts of the day, as well—my father with his back to the room, Ingie asleep, my mother and Hannah both gone—when I had the richest plenitude of time to devote to plans, considerations of new ideas, and slow, stealthy movements of whatever kind I chose.

Stealth was essential for other reasons as well, not only because at frequent intervals (depending on how hot the day was) I needed to return to the old stock tank for water, but also because I spent a good part, sometimes all, of each day naked. Once I was initially out of sight of the house, I would often stop just long enough to strip myself, quickly roll my clothing into my bundle—except for the shoes—then run again until I reached whatever spot I had chosen for that particular day to deposit both clothing and food. By then, too—in keeping with what was the central purpose and characteristic of this period in my life—my penis would of its own accord have changed from its retracted, early-morning nub into its typical state of readiness for one of the emissions that had already proven more philosophically revelatory to me than anything in my life had before—so that it stood out from my groin at a forty-five degree angle, holding its position so stiffly that even as I ran full speed, it hardly bobbed up and down at all but seemed all but a rigidly fixed part of my body.

Haste was no issue, since the entire day was mine. Even if my penis were to stiffen and stand three or four times—five or six sometimes happened—my sixteen hours away from the house gave me citadels, palaces, estates of time to live in at leisure, going from place to place as I chose. Candor would have me admit that first thing in the morning I might feel greater haste in arriving at the pleasure of sending out my tendrils than I might feel later in the day. But the true purpose of the undertaking, overwhelming and complex as it was, remained the same and was therefore equally observed whether first thing in the morning or last at night—this purpose being, namely, to observe the unaccountable phenomenon of something coming from nothing; and, further, to experience the equally unaccountable but far more overwhelming fact that during the moment of this coming of something from nothing, all things, far and near, large and small, cosmic and local, self and other, then and now, was and is—all of these, if only for the passing few instants of rapture, were unified and made into one.

And this meant, most important of all, that space and time were unified as well: resulting, this recombinance of the two essential and mysterious forces, in the resurrecting of history once again to something that lived not only within time, but within me.

5

(It's possible, though I didn't know it then, that I may have gotten my faint awareness of unity long before, in my years of perfect seeing, when Ganges and I would fall panting and exhausted on the ground under the crest of Second Hill, I on my stomach, she on her side—when I would be aware of the enormity of the earth under me, the massiveness of it, the sense of its supporting me, when in turn, as I lay there, I would allow myself to be pulled against it, then curl my fingers into it and cling, like moss or lichen, as if trying to pull myself into it. Then, through embracing it, would come a more intimate feeling, a faint and faraway understanding, a knowing that one oneself, somehow, long ago, in one form or another, indisputably, had emerged, physically, from the earth, had once been a part of it.

•

(In these later days, therefore, when I started out near dawn by running as hard as I could and then, as the day wore slowly on, made my way by cunning and stealth to all those same places Ganges and I had visited years before, my main purpose, the chief activity that compelled and drove me, proved in fact to constitute the last, doomed, most dedicated and sustained attempt I had ever made in my life to draw space and time back together, to give new strength to the failing connections between all things, to keep history from dying, and to save the farm.

•

(If by chance I did come out the front door instead of the back, I could quickly make myself invisible simply by speeding across to the far corner of the lawn and disappearing into Ganges's old pathway behind the lilacs. Then I could follow her old tunnel to the bottom of the garden—now only weeds and tall grass—remaining unseen from any direction (assuming, that is, that the corn was tall in the Ridley's field to the east) as I went north along the bottom of the garden, then in under the tall pines below the barnyard. At any of these spots I could stop if I chose, and might well come back to do so later in the day, but more often I kept going out along the crest of First Hill, protected from view on my left by the trees and shrubbery of our own farmstead, and by Second Hill off to my right, until at the wooded corner of our farmstead I would enter into the rows of high corn—these being the last two or three years when the field crops would still be grown by my father's

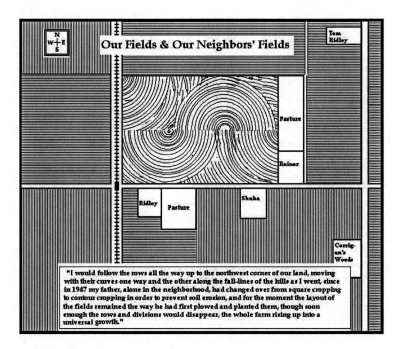

Our Fields & Our Neighbors' Fields

Tom Ridley

Pasture

Reiner

Ridley   Pasture

Shuha

Corrig-an's Woods

"I would follow the rows all the way up to the northwest corner of our land, moving with their curves one way and the other along the fall-lines of the hills as I went, since in 1947 my father, alone in the neighborhood, had changed over from square cropping to contour cropping in order to prevent soil erosion, and for the moment the layout of the fields remained the way he had first plowed and planted them, though soon enough the rows and divisions would disappear, the whole farm rising up into a universal growth."

rental farmer. I would follow the rows all the way up to the northwest corner of our land, moving with their curves one way and then the other along the fall-lines of the hills as I went, since in 1947 my father, alone in the neighborhood, had changed our fields over from points-of-the-compass planting to contour planting in order to cut back soil erosion, and for the moment the layout of the fields remained the way he had first plowed and planted them, although soon enough the rows and divisions would disappear as the entire farm gradually disappeared under universal growth.

From the northwest corner, the highest point on our land, I could simply stand up, if I chose, and still be able to see out over the tops of the corn, since the plants there were low and stunted by the thinness of the hilltop soil. From that spot I could see much farther than I had ever been able to see from the front edge of our lawn, and with a field of vision far wider as well. It would be at this spot, as likely as not, as I stood with only my shoulders and head above the corn, looking out across the southeast and south and southwest, that—especially if I were naked already—I would send out the first crop of tendrils of the day, struggling valiantly to keep my eyes open even at the moment of most intense oneness, the paroxysm of unity-bliss, my frequent inability to keep them open, nevertheless, making me all the more able to see without sight the real truth of my many-connectedness, since, with my eyes clamped shut, I didn't see with them and therefore felt with my entire being instead the tendrils shooting out not just their usual four or five feet, where they hung in the air a fleeting instant before falling to dirt-clods and corn-stems, but I felt them—I knew them—to be extending down and outward and across to every point between me and the road below, to every point between me and West Tree, every point in West Tree, and every point between me and all the horizons that lay beyond.

•

(I had often failed to return home for dinner, and now, in the heat of the summer, I brought blankets from inside, making an effort to keep them dry, and sought out a variety of places to spend the night. My father, I knew, at any time past late afternoon, would no longer notice whether I was in or out. Hannah was away, Ingie had other concerns, and although my mother might have worried about my absence, she, too, by this point in the rapidly accelerating dissolution, had begun to join my father each evening in his hapless drinking, and besides, she would, by nightfall, have expended her entire capacity for worry on him, leaving no extra that I might need be concerned by.

I was as free, therefore, as I would ever be again to press my effort to the utmost, to weave a web that would once again connect all things everywhere with all things everywhere.

•

(I returned to each of the locations Ganges and I, years before, had made regular visits to, and I searched out new locations as well, managing, at some point during the summer, to send out tendrils countless times from every one of them, the old and the new.

There was a secret spot in the west grove, a meadow of tall grass amid the trees, where the sun came in only during the middle of the day. In cool weather, Ganges and I had gone there during the hours when the sun poured in, and on hot days we had reversed the pattern, visiting only when the meadow had grown shadowy again in the late afternoon. Half buried in the long grass was a cow skull, bleached white by rain and sun, that I had discovered in the fall of 1947 on my first exploration of the grove. How long it had lain there before that, I had no idea.

In that meadow, with my clothes, food, and blanket nearby, I lay for a long time on the grass, gazing up past the green leaves of the trees and into the blue sky beyond, until I turned on my side and sent long thin milky tendrils over the grass to the skull, where they fell like threads across the bone. I did the same—in the cool of early morning, or at midday, or in the stillness and heat of the afternoon, or even in the depth of night—on the tops of First and Second Hills, in each of the meteorite

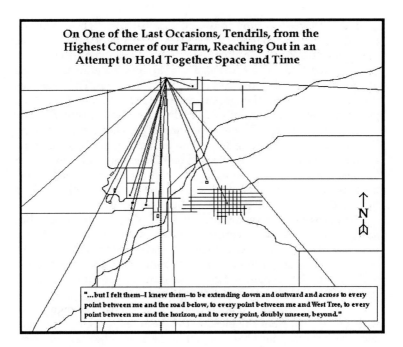

On One of the Last Occasions, Tendrils, from the Highest Corner of our Farm, Reaching Out in an Attempt to Hold Together Space and Time

N

"...but I felt them—I knew them—to be extending down and outward and across to every point between me and the road below, to every point between me and West Tree, to every point between me and the horizon, and to every point, doubly unseen, beyond."

craters (where I spent the night several times), in the rock-cairn just northwest of the skull meadow, at the high-point at the northwest corner of the farm, under the lone cherry tree along the north boundary, in Ganges's tunnel between the lilacs and the dead fruit trees, on the soft beds of needles under the high old pines and antique apple trees below the barnyard, even under the copse of oaks in the middle of the Ridleys' big field to the east, in the direction of the highway and river.

In none of these places was I ever detected. In my stealth, I remained unseen even when, naked then too, I climbed up through trapdoors, ascended the ladder and crossed the rafters to the cupola on the peak of the barn roof in order to send out tendrils, or stole my way into the old granary to do the same, doing so as I peered out into the yard through the ancient nail holes, knots, and cracks between the dry, weathered boards.

For water, three or four times a day, I stole through the barnyard, entering it from the north. The stout board fence that had once kept the cattle penned in was long gone, the yard itself near-impenetrable with ragweed, thistle, milkweed, quack grass, and nettle. The silo stood abandoned and empty, its iron doors fallen in a rusted heap at the bottom of its ladder. So, too, with the barn: its three doors all stood open, two of them half-fallen from their hinges, the third flat on the ground, with weeds sprung up around it and between its boards. Inside the barn, there was no longer any trace of the smells of cattle or hay or silage or lime, but only the lingering, dry, fetid, dusty stink of chickens.

On the south edge of the barnyard, the old stock-watering tank, made of poured cement, had lost the better part of two sides. The jagged remains of the structure, though, still managed to hold water. A half-inch pipe ran from inside the barn out to the tank, and the shutoff valve, which I remembered well, was still just inside the southeast corner door. When I opened it very slightly, a slow trickle of water began flowing again into the dusty, rubble-filled old tank. I spent half an hour tossing out pieces of broken concrete as the water gradually came in and settled the dust. Over the next few days, a semblance of the old tank—which I had loved as much as anything on the farm—began to return.

Back in the summers of my years of perfect seeing, on especially hot days, the cattle would make their way back in through the north gate from the pasture in mid-afternoon, long before milking time, just to get water from the shadowy, cool, brimming tank before meandering back again to the sunlight and grass—or sometimes to lie down under the low shade trees on the top of First Hill.

The tank, during the summer, would be left all day and night to fill with a slow feed from the pipe, so that between drinkings it would come back up to brimming, and a thin, perfectly clear skin of water would sometimes flow over the thick curved edges and down the sides of the tank. After their drinking, though, the cattle would have very nearly emptied it, and the thick green moss that grew at the bottom and halfway up the sides would be flat and exposed, starting to float softly again only as the tank gradually filled.

There was nothing whatsoever that I loved more, in those days, than being there on a summer afternoon when the cattle came up to drink. I would lean against the far side of the tank and reach my hand out to pat the cows' big, firm, rocky foreheads as they lowered their heads to put their noses into the cold water, and I would sense their contentment through my hand, listen to their wonderful guzzling sounds, see them close their enormous long-lashed eyes, hear them pause now and again to sigh, and watch the water level go down as one group finally moved away and another came up.

6

(It didn't work, none of it worked, although I lived on hope and faith and belief, knowing nothing else, not having yet experienced despair.

•

Because the tank was jagged and broken on two sides, there was no lovely skin of water to glide like moving glass over its smooth edges, but a small narrow pencil-stream flowed out instead, like water from the lip of a tiny pitcher, at the lowest point of the breakage, and the tank would fill to only a third or so of its old capacity. When I came up to drink, keeping to the paths I'd made through the barnyard, I invariably paused before I emerged from the edge of the weed-forest, since coming out to the tank put me in sight from the house. My father, presumably, if he happened to be on his way to the pantry for more gin, could see me through the kitchen window or door, or the same if he happened to look out the bathroom window. But never once did I see the least sign of movement. In the still, dead heat of each afternoon, the house would stand impassive and silent, saying nothing, sending me no message. The lawns around it were unkempt and high. The perimeter of high weeds, where no mowing was done, moved steadily inward.

At the tank, I would go onto my knees at the lower of the broken sides, put my face down to the water, and drink my fill. It was as cold, sweet, clear and quenching as it had ever been even in the very first years of perfect seeing. After slaking my thirst, I would carefully slip away again into the weeds, and from there steal out to the farthest perimeter of the farm.

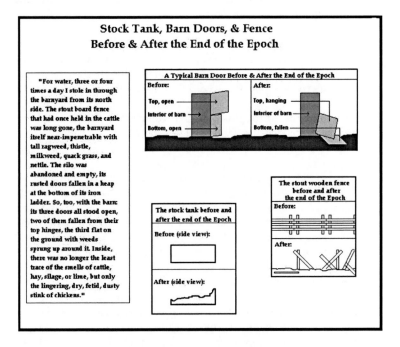

Stock Tank, Barn Doors, & Fence
Before & After the End of the Epoch

"For water, three or four times a day I stole in through the barnyard from its north side. The stout board fence that had once held in the cattle was long gone, the barnyard itself near-impenetrable with tall ragweed, thistle, milkweed, quack grass, and nettle. The silo was abandoned and empty, its rusted doors fallen in a heap at the bottom of its iron ladder. So, too, with the barn: its three doors all stood open, two of them fallen from their top hinges, the third flat on the ground with weeds sprung up around it. Inside, there was no longer the least trace of the smells of cattle, hay, silage, or lime, but only the lingering, dry, fetid, dusty stink of chickens."

A Typical Barn Door Before & After the End of the Epoch

Before:
Top, open
Interior of barn
Bottom, open

After:
Top, hanging
Interior of barn
Bottom, fallen

The stock tank before and after the end of the Epoch

Before (side view):

After (side view):

The stout wooden fence before and after the end of the Epoch

Before:

After:

Before summer came to an end, moss had begun to grow again under the water, just as it had years before, turning slowly into long waving hair. But that was the only thing that changed in such a way as to hint back, even slightly, to the way life had once been. Nothing else changed, nothing else whatsoever, not in the house, in the outlying buildings, on the land itself, nowhere around me for as far as I could see from one horizon to another.

7

(And then suddenly events began moving faster. Exactly how it came about doesn't matter, but I began to see Marietta Streetfield, doing so for the first and unquestionably the most important time on a day near the end of August. Before the end of October in the same year, her parents were to move away from West Tree, taking Marietta with them, and, just that quickly, she disappeared from my life.

•

Perhaps it could never have gone any further, I'll never know. But I know that I loved her past measure, found her desirable beyond words, believed her to be more lovely and sweet than imagination could conceive. She marked my life forever. I still allow myself to believe that she loved me equally, at least for a time.

•

When I knew I was going to see her, I knew also that if I told her the things that were of truest importance to me—my studies of space and time, the way I had spent my summer undertaking them—she would have considered me mad. But if I didn't tell her, then I would go mad.

•

By the time these thoughts had made themselves clear to me, I was riding into West Tree on my bicycle to meet her.

8

I'd stolen into the farmhouse at midday, crept silently behind my father's back, and climbed the stairs to my old room even more quietly than I had ever come down them in the lost, long-ago summer dawns of my years of perfect seeing. From the house I stole soap, a towel, and fresh clothing, all of which—I was relieved to be back outdoors—I laid on the long grass in the smaller meteorite crater. After letting a few hours pass just for safety's sake, I stripped, took the soap and towel as I went through the barnyard weeds, checked to make sure that the house showed no sign of life, and climbed into the cold water of the stock tank—careful not to slip on the moss—and washed myself thoroughly before getting out. I slipped back through the weeds and lay in the sun on the north slope of the crater until I was dry and completely warm again. Then, for the first time since the beginning of summer, I put on fresh clothes.

I had to sneak back into the farmyard one more time, to get my bicycle—the old one with balloon tires that I had learned on, Ganges running along beside me—from the lean-to shed behind the kitchen. The safest route back, once I had gotten the bicycle out of the shed without making any noise, was to wheel it behind the granary and from there behind the car shed, chicken coop, and corn crib, back out to First Hill. From that point I followed the north edge of the grove to the rock-cairn at the corner, then pushed the bike through the cornrows until I got to the Rock Island track. I followed the tracks to the place where they crossed the back road to West Tree, where I finally got on and began riding.

It was still an hour or so before dark when I knocked at Marietta Streetfield's house, which was small, one story high, its front wall covered by tarpaper tacked down with strips of lath. The house was near the river in the low part of south central West Tree that was called Hungry Hollow. A boat sat in the driveway on a trailer. When Marietta opened the front door her father was standing behind her, barefoot and wearing an undershirt with no sleeves. He looked me over but said nothing to either of us, not even to Marietta when she said goodbye.

•

Oh, Marietta! Marietta! Marietta! Marietta!

•

She rode side-saddle on the crossbar of my bicycle, her hands pressed together side by side on the narrowest part of the handlebar. I had never been so close to her before. Her arms and long legs were bare, as was much of her back, and she was tanned from a summer outdoors. When I leaned forward to pedal at the uphill places, I breathed in the simple, fresh, clean, outdoor smells of her skin and her hair, dizzying to me in ecstasy and disbelief.

We rode down Front Street to the town square and went over the Wagon River on the Third Street bridge, which crossed just forty feet or so downstream from the mill dam. Once we were on the west side, we rode to the bottom of Woodland Avenue and started uphill, past the railroad station, past the empty block on its hill where the Emerson School had stood, beyond that past Mrs. Peterson's store and then my grandmother's house at number 917, where a for sale sign stood on the narrow front lawn, leaning backward as if holding its face to the sun. We turned north on Poplar Street, went by Professor F. K. Kampfer's house, and then on West Third turned right in order to pass by the front of the hospital. On the next cross street we turned left to Christiania Avenue, then turned north past the old wading pool. It was dry now and filled with broken glass, its bottom heaved up into jagged pieces from frost. Behind it, where the esplanade had been, was a parking lot for the hospital. Farther up Christiania Avenue was Marie and Lutie's house, its windows blinded with pieces of plywood. Past that point, going up Old College Hill, the incline got very steep and I leaned forward, breathing in the scent of Marietta's hair and skin all the way up, sometimes even holding my cheek against her back as I leaned into the pedals, around the first curve, past the huge wide lawn in front of First Hall, then around the second curve, where the hill was steeper and the road curled around it on a ledge cut into its side. We came out at the top by Lilledahl Hall, went around the library, then around the chapel, where I turned away from the middle of the empty campus, past the machine shop and boiler plant, and out onto the northeast shoulder of the hill into the small clearing under the looming, shadowy form of the Nordic ski jump.

(Marietta Streetfield got off, and then I did, propping the bike against one of the huge, inward-leaning timbers that formed the legs of the jump. Darkness was gathering fast now, making it less and less likely that anyone would notice us, and soon we would be swallowed up in night. I made a stirrup of my hands so Marietta could put her foot in it and I could lift her up high enough so that she could get started on the first rungs of the wooden ladder, since a number of the bottom rungs were missing. Marietta's foot was small, and I felt the living weight and movement of her as she pressed down against my hands and reached up for the rungs. When she had gotten on safely, I jumped as high as I could three or four times until at last I got a hanging grip on a crossbeam. Then I swung myself back and forth until I was able to clasp my feet around the beam and pull myself up. Once I was on the crosspiece, I stood up and walked over to the bottom of the ladder and started up after Marietta.

Her shorts were white, and she had on low white tennis shoes without socks. Whenever I looked up, there she was. I could see her feet and thin ankles and long legs and white shorts as she kept on climbing above me.

(The ladder seemed endless, and I forced myself not to look behind or down. The most frightening part was at the top, when we had to get up off the ladder, with nothing behind us, and somehow crawl up onto the platform itself. I stayed right below Marietta and pressed up with one hand against the back of her thigh to help as she went over. Then I followed.

(On the platform, there were railings at the sides but none at the back or front. From the last light that hung near the western horizon, I could look down the great wooden pathway that fell away in front of us, so steeply at first as to seem almost a straight drop and then, far below, curving gracefully back out onto the level before abruptly ending very far away, and very far below, where my sight failed—the last daylight drained from the sky—so that from where Marietta and I were sitting, with our legs over the front edge of the platform, there seemed to be nothing below us at all.

What I Saw from the Top of the Nordic Ski Jump

CHAPTER 6

THE DISAPPEARANCE OF EVERYTHING
(1857–2010)

I

My Studies

1

(Over the years, I made a number of return visits to West Tree, most
often, although not always, on the occasions of deaths. Each time I
came back, more of West Tree had disappeared.

•

As chance would have it, I was at home when Hannah died. This
was in 1960, in the summer. I was staying in the farmhouse during a
time when Ingie and my parents were all away. The news of Hannah's
death came by telephone.

•

I undertook, earlier that same summer, two projects that were of importance to me.

One of these was a retracing of the steps I had made four years earlier,
during the period of my sexual awakening, when, through the agency
of myself, I had tried to preserve the existence of the past by holding
space and time together and thereby uniting all things and all places.

The locations where I'd undertaken this effort were, as I've said,
locations I first came to know in the late 1940's, in my years of perfect seeing. So, at the time when my sister Hannah died, in 1960, and
opened the doorway to the future, I was involved in an attempt to go

back the other way, to the lost years of 1947, 1948, and 1949.

•

It became increasingly clear to me that time was narrowing in the entire region of West Tree. Hannah's death helped show that there were no rooms opening into the future, while at the same time it was growing steadily more difficult to locate, let alone go back into, the years of my own perfect seeing. The future, then, was moving closer to the present, and the past, as it diminished more and more rapidly, was in effect retreating forward. Soon, as time continued narrowing in this way, the present would be squeezed into nothingness. Then, eventually, time would stop.

2

It was impossible not to notice, in the summer of Hannah's death, the extent to which the farm and house had already been altered by this narrowing.

The fields were no longer being cropped, and only faint traces of my father's contour plowing were still visible among the grasses, tall weeds, and scrubby patches of volunteer corn. The pasture was largely unchanged except that the grass was tall and punctuated by a general scattering of purple-blossomed thistle. In the lower field near the grove, alfalfa still grew. It was tall, dry, and scraggly, but it had reseeded itself plentifully enough so far to hold off most other growth.

•

The barnyard, on the other hand, was so thick by now with weeds as to be impenetrable. The stock tank no longer held water, since only one of its four sides remained even partially upright. The roof of the barn had fallen in on the east end, toward the silo, and the cupola with its weather vane was missing, only a square hole in the down-slanting roof-peak where it had been. The roofs of the chicken coop and granary had collapsed entirely, both of them lying now on the floors. The end-walls of the chicken coop leaned inward, drawn by the weight of the collapsed roof. As for the granary, only two adjacent walls stood, at a right angle, while the other two had fallen outward and lay flat.

Three upstairs windows of the house had broken out and were covered with plywood, the rooms inside left dark. The mowed area outdoors was much smaller than it had been even four years previously. Weeds and underbrush were creeping inward in a slowly strangulating movement, having come up already as far as the milk house from the east and as far as the turn-around from the north.

The front lawn was a different case insofar as it seemed to have remained weedless. The fine-textured grass there had just continued growing even as the yard grew more deeply shaded by trees closing in overhead.

The lawn chair where my father had sat on that long-ago morning when I looked out through his eyes remained where it had been in the middle of the lawn, although it, too, was falling more deeply into shadow. Grass was growing up through the slats of its seat.

3

(In the years after my trips with Marietta Streetfield to the top of the Nordic ski jump, my studies of West Tree intensified both in pace and depth. Soon enough, however, by necessity, they waned and grew sporadic, since only three years later I left West Tree for good. Insofar as possible, I made use of my return visits to keep up the work.

The summer of 1960, for example, in the weeks preceding my sister's death, I set out to visit again and re-evaluate the roads leading into West Tree. As I knew, there were eight entranceways (not counting railroad or river), and I hoped to discover which of these—if any—continued even at that late a date to exist inside of history.

I wanted to know, that is, on which of the roads time and space still remained sufficiently unified so that those roads would not be threatened with immediate disappearance by reason of no longer containing a past, and therefore, inevitably, being deprived also of a future.

•

And I found, to my pleasant surprise, that six of the eight roads at that time still existed inside of history, and that history, therefore, still existed also inside of them.

In two of the six, however, this characteristic was true only to a seriously compromised degree. Of the four that remained, on the other hand, it was true to so remarkable an extent that the effect upon me was doubly intense though also contradictory:

1) I was overjoyed and renewed—as I visited these entranceways— by the experience of dwelling again, for however short a time, simultaneously in the present and in the past, where, around me, space and time remained united;

2) but I was plunged also into grief by this great pleasure, since its presence reminded me of the coming inevitability of its absence, and of the already-destined loss of what had brought it into being.

•

The two entrances containing no past and therefore no present were the highway entrances from the north and south. Approaching town, these entrances were bare, widened, and treeless, going past sunburned areas where gravel and dead grass were home to abandoned automobiles and broken farm equipment. Further on, the roads went past boarded-over food stands and single-story office and executive buildings made of brick or stone but having no windows, suggesting that what took place inside were experiments in torture through isolation or deprivation of sunlight.

Once they had entered West Tree, these highways, as if they were ravenous eaters of the town itself, cut diagonally over wide areas where once had stood houses, stores, and buildings on a grid of streets—all now leveled, buried, gone, non-existent.

•

(From the west, and again from the northeast, came highways that were in fact smaller, narrower, and less heavily traveled than the time-dead roads from the north and south. On the highway approaching from the west, the traveler was given a view of the back side of Old College from many miles away. The old hilltop buildings gradually drew closer as the traveler approached, and then they disappeared from sight as the road curved in tightly around the southern base of Old College Hill. Then, however, when it should have entered in among the shade-trees of West Tree itself, leading into Woodland Avenue, the road diverged southeastward instead, swelling into five lanes that were as wide, vacuous, unshaded, and grass-burned as the big north-south highway was—and in fact then merged with that highway at a wide and pitiably characterless intersection that had neither sidewalks nor trees, but only acres of sunburned grass and weed.

The entranceway approaching from the northeast was similar except that it afforded a view not of Old College but of New College, a view that differed further in not being visible from miles away, but in coming upon the traveler all at once, from quite close up, as the road rounded a bend curving to the southwest and leading at the same moment sharply downhill to the Wagon River.

The great disadvantage to this entranceway was that it gave a close view of the extreme degree of separation that had already occurred between space and time at New College, with the result that history there—far more so than at Old College—was absent entirely and the present already halfway so. Buildings in some cases had shrunk to half their original size. Others reflected sunlight so intensely that they grew invisible the more closely you studied them. Still others—the least unappealing, perhaps, but most lamentable as well—were sinking gradually into the very ground they stood on, some remaining upright although entombed to their eyebrows, others disappearing into the earth at odd angles, some corner first, others on end, and one turned entirely upside down and sunk now so that only its foundation showed.

The four remaining entranceways were all much smaller, far less traveled, and infinitely more significant to anyone, like me, trying to find traces of authenticity remaining from the unified world of the past.

•

(Of the four entranceways that still existed simultaneously in the present and the past, and within which the present and past simultaneously existed, two were on the east side of town and two on the west. Each was remarkable in its own way, but with no question the greenest of the four was the entrance called Old Cemetery Road.

The name was no less picturesque than the actual cemetery that gave rise to it, an old burial place located along the road about three and a half miles east of West Tree. It always felt to me, whenever I passed by, that the road had a certain delicately respectful manner of seeming to have forgotten altogether about the existence of the old graveyard alongside it, a kind of passing-by that only added to the peacefulness, austerity, and handsomeness of the place. The land east of town—for as far as fifteen or twenty miles—was flatter than the rolling hills to the west and southwest. But even so, whoever had established the cemetery, and whenever they'd done it—one stone was dated 1833—had chosen a hilltop so subtle that it gave you no sense of climbing or rising at all until you were already at the top—perhaps even inside the spidery iron fence, perhaps taking a rest on the long grass among the weathered stones and gazing out at the surrounding countryside, unbroken and beautiful all the way to the horizon.

The cemetery was small, sheltered only by a poor clergy of four or five oaks. By every conceivable measure, the height of summer was the best time to visit—on a warm day when the breeze was soft and carried the scent of earth, drying grasses, and ripening grain, and when the huge bowl of sky itself seemed too lazy and good-natured to chase off the few white cumulus wandering across it—and the nodding grass around the iron fence whispered words to put you to sleep if you lay down for even the shortest time and listened to it carefully.

•

An aspect of central importance in all of the entrances that were still living was this: not that they brought travelers into town abruptly (although there was always an element of suddenness), but that they did so with a certain kind of handsome, natural, singular purposefulness. In this way, they served to keep the distinction between one place and another—the inside and the outside of town—perfectly clear, thereby doing a dignity to each.

The best way to imagine this quality is to imagine walking for miles in the unabated sun on the hottest of days and then, after simply rounding a bend, or climbing a hill, or crossing a bridge, finding yourself suddenly in the pleasant, cool, leaf-dappled shade of maples, elms, and oaks that lined the street, joining their arms high overhead to form a green canopy above.

This would be an experience, in other words, of finding yourself elsewhere than where you were; not any longer where you were, but in a place distinct in and to itself; in a place, that is, furthermore, that couldn't exist if it weren't for the place you'd just come from, just as that place couldn't exist if it weren't for the one you'd just entered.

•

If two places become alike, both disappear.

•

Without question the greenest entrance was also this same one, the Old Cemetery Road as it entered from the east-northeast. In broad sunlight, with wide and near-level fields on both sides, the road all of a sudden took you unexpectedly downward, across a narrow stream, then steeply uphill as it made a right-hand curve—and you found yourself in a pleasantly darkened cathedral of foliage.

Here, along the southeast edge of the New College campus, grand two, three, and even three-and-a-half-story houses stood quietly at the backs of their deep lawns, just as they had done from a time dating even before the earliest years of the Epoch of Walking,.

•

(The other East Side entrance made its way into West Tree from the same high farmland as the Old Cemetery Road did, but from the southeast rather than the northeast. It, too, dipped down unexpectedly to cross—farther upstream—the same creek, although here the descent was more shallow, as was the rise that brought you up and then into town—along streets where the houses were smaller than those near the Cemetery Road entrance, sometimes only a single story high, and, standing on much smaller lots, were constructed of wood rather than of brick or stone.

These houses, although more humble than the others, were just as old, and in some cases even older, dating from as early as the 1860s, when there had been a town grid but as yet no sidewalks, sewers, or curbstones. This meant that they dated from a time before even the earliest conception of the Epoch of Walking, let alone its later periods of significant maturity.

•

(Riding my bicycle, I passed Professor F. K. Kampfer twice at these entrances, both times as he was entering town and I was going out. As usual, he glanced up at me almost furtively, revealing no hint of recognition.

By then, in 1956 or 1957, Professor Kampfer was the last human vestige of the Epoch of Walking in all of West Tree. As such, no matter how eccentric or even alarming he may have seemed—with his baggy shorts, popping eyes, and twitching face—he was unique, irreplaceable, and therefore of a vital, inestimable, unknowable significance.

•

(One of the two West Side entrances that still contained history in a degree of near-completeness was the one that approached from the southwest. This entry was the terminus of an unpaved road that connected West Tree with a little crossroads town known as Damville, four and a half miles away.

For most of the distance from Damville, the road followed the Wagon River, passing through farmland and in and out of small groves. Delightfully, it brought you into West Tree under the shade of a copse of trees. On the left, rising uphill, was the back lawn of the orphanage, which had its entry on Woodland Avenue near where my grandmother's house once was. On the right was a grain- and cereal-processing mill with trees leaning over its loading ramps. At the east

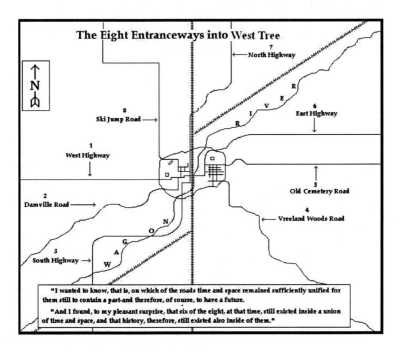

KEY TO THE EIGHT ENTRANCEWAYS
1. Highway from west
2. Road from southwest
3. Highway from south
4. Road from southeast
5. Old Cemetery Road
6. Highway from east
7. Highway from north
8. Ski Jump Road

end of the mill, a spur of the Damville, West Tree, and Minneapolis railroad had its terminus. A railroad turntable stood there that I remember from the time when my father took me to watch a steam locomotive drive onto it and stop as the turntable operator then slowly turned the locomotive around a hundred and eighty degrees, allowing it to drive off in the same direction it had come from.

•

(The last of the entranceways still inside history was Ski Jump Road. This route came in from the rolling countryside to the northwest, then, curving, passed under an avenue of trees that hugged the base of Old College Hill. The trees, at one point, opened up briefly to offer a perfect view, from below, of the looming face of the Nordic ski jump high above. The road then curved to the right, approached a stop sign, and found itself transformed at that point into a plain city street, intersecting with the upper end of Christiania Avenue just a block and a half from the house my great-aunts Marie and Lutie built in 1921.

II
The End

1

(When I returned for my father's funeral six years later, in 1967, over forty years ago now, the farm was already far less recognizable than it had been at the time of Hannah's death. The unattended fields had gone to weed, the old contours no longer visible at all. Of the outbuildings, the chicken coop and granary had become little more than low piles of gray wood with weeds coming up through them. The barn roof had fallen through entirely. All of the upstairs windows of the house were covered with plywood, and the chimney had fallen, scattering bricks across the north slope of the roof, with a considerable number of them lying also outside the kitchen door.

Weeds grew up against the foundations of the house everywhere except in the front, where for some reason the grass remained, though high and unkempt. It grew up higher than ever around the legs and through the slats of the white wooden chair, itself decayed and half collapsed but still in its place in the middle of the yard.

•

After another eight years, when my mother died, the barn walls had fallen in on themselves, leaving only another pile of wood inside the old stone foundations. The farmhouse was by this time uninhabited. The doors stood open. The plywood covers had fallen away from the upstairs windows, and those downstairs were also broken. The wind, as it chose, was free to blow in through the front and make its way out the back.

•

My mother died in West Tree, in a room of the orphanage, which toward the end had been converted into an old people's home. A year after her death, that building also was torn down.

•

Of the eight roads into West Tree, only one by this time—Old Cemetery Road—continued to exist inside of history and to hold history inside of it.

On my next visit to West Tree, that was no longer true of the Old Cemetery Road either.

2

(For many years I stayed away, there being no occasions to return. By the time my sister Ingie died, in 1996, she had lived in western Wisconsin for almost fifteen years, so that was where I went for the funeral. Afterward I passed through West Tree, even so, to have a look at it and see our farm. Both were very much altered. The farmhouse by this time had itself begun to collapse. The roof over the kitchen had fallen in, and the same was true where Hannah and Ingie's old room had been. Even the front lawn, by then, had been overtaken by weeds and the beginning of underbrush. The white chair, though fallen over onto one side, remained. It was sufficiently obscured by now, however, as to be unnoticeable except to someone who knew it was there.

•

I studied elsewhere, traveled, married. My wife and I had two children.

•

Throughout, I studied West Tree continually. I studied history, memory, and the relationship between the future and the past.

As expected, that is, I took up the study of space and time.

And inevitably, as a student of those mysterious forces, I became a student of the extraordinary, insurmountable loss that occurs when they draw apart.

•

(I made my last visit to West Tree slightly more than four years ago, not long after my cousin Eldon's death. On that occasion I discovered that West Tree had disappeared entirely.

The Wagon River was gone as well. The Rock Island Railroad tracks were no longer there, nor were those of the Damville, West Tree, and Minneapolis line. Every hint, trace, or vestige of the town or its environs was absolutely and entirely gone.

Only the landscape remained. In most cases it was unchanged, while at certain spots it was scarred in curious ways. In small disparate areas it was mounded, slightly built up, almost as though, in these places, it had become welted or callused, much as healed flesh can become thickened in healing from a large wound.

•

(Roads and streets were gone. I conducted the whole of my visit on foot.

3

(Our farm, and the land that had been the Shuhas,' Pikens,' and Ridleys'—all of it had become weedless, grown up now in tall, sturdy, aromatic prairie grasses that swayed in the hot wind, sometimes forming deep moving waves like those at sea. During my visit, which was in early summer, these grasses were intermixed throughout with tiny blossoming yellow and blue flowers.

•

First Hill and Second Hill were where they had always been, and so too were the meteorite craters. But of things that people had built, nothing was left. The house had left no trace other than a faint depression under the grass. The granary, corn crib, chicken coop, and milk house had vanished without a trace. Of the barn, nothing was left but half or so of the stones of the west foundation, resting unmoved just as they had ever since someone had fitted them carefully on top of one another in the summer of 1877, before the wooden beams were laid down to support the wall posts.

Any trace of my family, of my mother or father, of Hannah, of Ingie—or of me—was gone perfectly, utterly, absolutely.

4

(I admit that I felt sorrow in the enormity of this absence. It was less powerful, though, than what I felt as a result of my trip into West Tree itself.

There, I walked from one end of town to the other, from east to west, then again from north to south. The Wagon River, as I have said, was gone, though Old College Hill and New College Hill remained. As for buildings, houses, bridges, mills, railroads, or any kind or variety of artifice whatsoever, there was nowhere the least trace.

I walked to the place our house had stood at Fourth and Maple—where I had had my first memory, had heard the train whistle, had held two red pennies, had seen the blimp, had looked down into Mr. Leitch's goldfish pond.

Not a trace of it remained. The streets themselves, the great trees that had lined them, the curbs, sidewalks, and boulevards dating from the earliest years of the Epoch of Walking—none remained, while in their places stood the same tall, blossoming, aromatic grass that also grew now outside of town, where the farm had been, bending over as the wind rose, then straightening up again as it died.

•

The great shade tree outside Sherry Nichols' side of the house was gone.

The iron hitching post where I saw my great-aunts Marie and Lutie walk out of the nineteenth century and then back into it again was vanished and gone.

•

It seemed to me possible, as a result, that everything was gone.

5

(I walked to the vacant place where New College had stood, then across to Old College. I went to where my grandmother's house had stood on Woodland Avenue, and lingered for a time on that spot—where, in the cellar, had been the broken croquet set; in the upstairs hallway the old-fashioned telephone; in the attic the old tennis rackets. I remained there for some time. Here, after all, was the place from which my father had set out on his skiing and camping trips in 1926 and 1927. Here was where he had gone upstairs to change into tennis clothes or to read at his desk. Here is where he had waxed his skis before going down the Nordic ski jump again, and again, and again.

6

(Where Marie and Lutie's house had stood were only two or three low mounds in the earth, and a faint slope downward toward where the garden had been in back of the house.

(The garden was gone, of course, the shed was gone, the driveway was gone, the house, the dining table, the crèche, the three water pipes going up the kitchen wall, the two beds upstairs, the bathroom, the curtains that had blown outward for a moment, the white chair with a folded towel over its back—all was gone, even the pillows that had lain at the head of each bed, and the blankets that had been folded neatly at the foot.

7

(There was this possibility to be considered, quite clearly: that if nothing was here, nothing had ever been here.

8

(I knew without any question, just by looking around me, that my early life was gone, that it had vanished along with any vestige it might conceivably have left behind.

(What I didn't know, however, and couldn't understand, was whether this meant also that my grandfather had never walked past a stone wall in his black suit, carrying a black briefcase.

View of West Tree from My Final Visit There

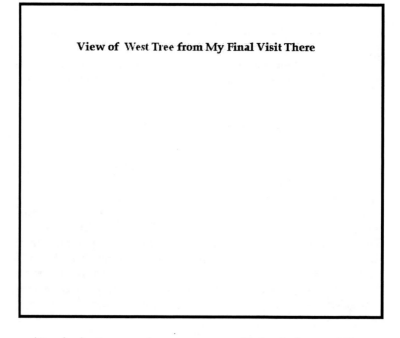

(Or whether it meant that my great-grandfather had never ridden on a wagon in the woods of Wisconsin in 1853.

(Or that my great-aunt Marie had never bowed her head forward, reading a book in a room with a single window, in Columbia, Missouri, in 1898.

(Or that my great-aunt Marie never did come to West Tree by train one summer afternoon in 1910; never did descend from the carriage and pause for a moment to gaze about herself, her chin raised slightly, her attitude neither timid nor disdainful as she looked once backward and once forward along the length of the train, on a day that was warm, still, and quiet, filled with the brilliant sunlight of midday.

9

(Nor do I have any way of knowing whether the continuing struggle with my studies will ever bring me answers to questions such as these. But having seen what I have seen, even so, I at least will always know (and this much, if nothing more, can never be taken from me), that more than can be said, spoken, known, or put into words has come already, without question, to an end))))))))))))))))))))))))))))))))).

CPSIA information can be obtained at www.ICGtesting.com
Printed in the USA
LVOW101253010313

322218LV00003B/305/P